THE EYE OF ODIN

ANDREW LINKE

LINKE|MEDIA

The Eye of Odin

Version 1.4

Copyright © 2015 by Andrew Linke

Cover Art © Nga Nguyen & Michele Altenkirch.

Visit and connect with Andrew Linke online for more novels, short stories, and blog updates.

Website   www.andrewlinke.com

Twitter   @alinke

Facebook Facebook.com/andrewlinke

Patreon   www.patreon.com/andrewlinke

Dedication

Thanks to the people who found my first novel, *The Staff of Moses*, read it, and sent me feedback. The writing of that first book was fueled by family support and hope that I could actually tell a story. This sequel was driven by the knowledge that people outside my immediate family actually enjoy my writing and maybe, just maybe, there is a chance that I can one day earn a living as an author.

So, a big thank you to Bruce, Kenken, Mike, Rita, and Torah.

CHAPTER ONE
CAVERN OF MIST

Oliver Lucas wiped the sheen of sweat off his forehead and blinked to clear the sting of salt from his eyes. The back and underarms of his khaki shirt were stained with sweat and clung to him uncomfortably. Up on the surface, the trade winds continually swept across the island, carrying away the worst of the humidity, but here, a quarter mile into the side of a volcanic mountain, the air was still, hot, and thick with moisture.

Ahead of Oliver the gray stone took a sharp dip downwards, concealing the source of the rushing, gurgling sound that he had been following for the last ten minutes. The passage was illuminated by a flickering blue light, which emanated from notches cut into the right side of the tunnel at intervals of about a dozen feet. In each notch a short gout of flame burst forth from a narrow metal nozzle with a soft hissing sound.

"I'd kill to know how they did that," Oliver muttered, pausing to examine the ancient gas lamp. The Chinese had used bamboo pipes to deliver naturally occurring gas to heat steam baths and forges for over a thousand years, but all of his research indicated that this tunnel had been cut into the side of the mountain by precursors of the Maori and other Pacific Island people, none of which had been known for their use of gas lighting.

Oliver shook his head in wonder and ran a hand through

his mop of short red hair, pushing it back from his face before turning from the gas lamp and carrying on down the tunnel. He moved in a slight crouch, the tunnel was just barely too short for his six foot frame, sweeping a powerful flashlight back and forth across the floor of the tunnel in front of him. The gas lighting was nothing short of amazing, but it was far from perfect. Oliver knew from long and bitter experience that many an ancient designer of tombs and temples had used subtle tricks of light and shadow to conceal deadly traps. He might wonder at the ancient gas lamps, but he would not depend on them for lighting.

As he moved cautiously down the tunnel, Oliver never allowed his right hand to stray far from the gun hidden in a concealed pocket just inside his photographer's vest. He hadn't seen anyone else in the hours since he had departed the beachside resort, but that did not mean that he was alone under the mountain. Other treasure hunters might have followed the same trail of ancient legends to this underground passage or, even if no other humans were nearby, there was always the risk of encountering a wild animal or some sort of supernatural guardian.

The sound of rushing water grew louder as Oliver crept nearer to the downward slope, which he could now see descended in a series of wide steps chiseled into the gray stone. Thick sponges of green moss, speckled with bright red fronds, grew in the corners and hollows of the stairs. Shining the beam of his flashlight down the steps, Oliver watched it pierce through a dancing haze of water vapor, which boiled upwards from the base of the steps.

Oliver paused at the top of the steps and surveyed the mossy stone steps for a moment, then fixed his flashlight on a spot where the green moss had been scuffed aside, revealing the stone beneath.

"Damn it," he breathed.

He slipped the gun from its hidden pocket and pulled the slide to chamber a round. "You'd better be a wild boar, or a monkey," he muttered, gripping the gun firmly in his right hand and pointing his flashlight down the steps. "If I came all this way only to be beat by a few hours..."

The passage angled down for about fifty feet before flattening out again. As Oliver descended the steps the roar of the water grew continually louder until he could hardly hear himself breathing. About half way down, squinting through the boiling mist, he spotted the lintel of a narrow doorway set into the stone wall just below the angle of the ceiling.

Oliver paused. He stepped sideways and pressed himself against the wall, then slowly slipped down into a crouch, watching the doorway over the sights of the gun as he moved. His flashlight beam played across the interlocking spirals of Koru engraved in the stone surrounding the doorway. The ornate triple lines and fractal curves twisted around and through smaller symbols which Oliver recognized as the storytelling glyphs employed by the Maori people who had dwelled on this island in the sixteenth century. As his flashlight beam moved away from the carvings the flickering light of the gas jets played across them in an eerie dance of shadows and blue light. Through the doorway Oliver could just make out a narrow ledge, beyond which the clouds of water vapor churned up like steam from a boiling pot.

He took a deep breath and sighed with relief. He didn't put his gun away, but lowered his hand and allowed himself to believe that he might be alone in this place.

Oliver turned his attention from the room beyond and looked to the steps as he picked his way down to the doorway, searching carefully above, to each side, and around the edge of the stair for any sign of a trap before setting his foot down. He reached the landing without incident and breathed a sigh of relief.

Beyond the carved stone frame of the doorway, clouds of mist continued to boil up from an unseen river, obscuring his vision. Oliver sidled up to the opening and darted his head out, then back again. Seeing no sign of other people, he stepped into the doorway and inspected the scene before him.

The noise of rushing water he had followed came from an underground waterfall, which spilled out of the shadows high above Oliver's head on the left side of the cavern. The water tumbled down in a cacophonous sheet, bursting out into showers of heavy mist where the falling water struck against outcropping rocks, and disappeared into a wide cleft that cut across that cavern floor.

Oliver put his gun away and got a grip on the ornately carved frame of the doorway, then leaned out into the cavern to get a better view. The ledge on the other side of the door was only five feet wide. A hundred feet below, the waterfall thundered into a roiling stream of water, only barely visible through rising clouds of mist, and rushed out of the cavern through an opening somewhere under the wall to Oliver's right. The entire scene was illuminated in a continually shifting flicker of refracted rainbows and moving shadows cast by the flickering gas lights set into the wall. The facing wall on the far side of the cavern, only about fifty feet away, was carved in a series of knotted shapes and twisting human figures surrounding a doorway, through which Oliver could see a solid wall of stone.

There was no sign of another person, living or otherwise.

"Alright. Let's see about getting past this," Oliver said.

Talking to himself while exploring ancient ruins was a habit left over from his first adventure into the jungles of South America. On that expedition he had been accompanied by his cousin Amber, who had continually pressed him to share his thoughts as they wound their way through the twisting mazes of a Mayan temple. These days Oliver tended to work alone, but he still felt the urge to talk through his discoveries. At times he would even share them with Amber, sending her encrypted e-mails or posting messages to a private Twitter stream so that she could both follow his adventures, and serve as an emergency backup if he disappeared while in the field.

Oliver ran the beam of his flashlight over the door frame, the floor, and the walls, searching for any sign of hidden triggers or tripwires. There were none. He slipped through the doorway into the cavern, eyes flicking to the dark corners of the open space, then turning upwards to search the darkness above for any sign of danger.

Again, nothing that he could see.

This was all feeling too simple. Sure, there was the matter of the forty foot wide hole in the floor, the bottom of which was certainly a swirling deathtrap, and the apparently blocked-up doorway, but such obstacles were little more than entertaining challenges to Oliver. He lived for solving puzzles like this, which was part of the reason he carried only a small charge of explosives tucked away in a hidden compartment of his vest, as a backup plan if he were trapped. Unlike some treasure hunters he had met online, Oliver didn't believe in blasting his way through hidden doors. The way he saw it, if he couldn't outwit the designers of this temple, then he didn't believe that he deserved the prize that lay within.

Oliver pulled a ruggedized digital camera body from one of the large pockets on the front of his vest, then reached into a padded pocket to retrieve a compact zoom lens. Working quickly to avoid getting too much mist into the camera body, Oliver unscrewed the protective caps on both the camera and lens, then slotted the two parts together and locked the lens into place. He flicked the camera on and crouched down against the wall, using his knees to stabilize the camera and flashlight as he searched the shadows on the far side of the cleft.

On the camera screen, the wall on the far side of the cavern leapt into focus. The carved lines of stone stood out in sharp relief in the bright light of his flashlight, glistening with droplets of condensed mist, deep shadows flickering through the hollows each time he moved his hand or shifted his legs. This was far from the optimal situation for taking salable photographs, with poor lighting further complicated by the constantly shifting haze of mist, which played havoc with his camera's image sensors, but the image was more than sufficient for him to pick out the threads of the story told in swirling lines, twisting bodies, and gaping faces.

Oliver sat on that ledge for nearly an hour, alternating between peering at the carvings though the camera lens and looking down to his phone, to consult the months of research notes that he had loaded into the phone before leaving his hotel room. He moved his lips, whispering the tale to himself in meandering fragments as the story of these people, progenitors of the Maori who had landed on this chain of islands east of New Zealand as a loosely knit band of fishermen and pirates, and two hundred years later emerged from it as the first recognizable members of a powerful people. It had taken him years to piece this together, working from scattered fragments of myth, obscure archaeological records, and more than a little guesswork. Even with all of his preparation, it took Oliver a long time to understand what he was looking at as he sat there, scanning the curving lines of Koru, attempting to first understand the meaning of the carvings, then place them in context of his research into the history and mythology of the Pacific Islanders.

Much of the difficulty stemmed from the fact that the symbols carved into the wall were not so much a language as a series of highly contextual icons representing characters, events, and emotions. They were not intended to represent spoken language in the way that the Roman alphabet did for European written languages. Instead, these symbols had been carved to serve as mnemonic aids for tribal elders and keepers of tales. Despite having a rich culture, this particular civilization had never developed a purely written language system. Rather, they had relied on a strong tradition of oral storytelling and songs, supplemented by ideographic totems carved into wood and stone, which served to remind the viewer of the sequence of events and characters in the story they depicted, but did not convey the full depth of the tale in themselves.

"Okay," he finally said aloud. "I think I've got it."

Oliver stood and stretched his back, then stepped through the doorway into the low passage to be away from the worst of the billowing mist as he removed the lens from his camera and stowed both away in his vest. After an hour sitting in the cavern his already damp clothes were now soaked through, but the waterproofing on the camera had kept it safe as he examined and photographed the carvings on the far wall of the cavern.

Oliver returned to the ledge and turned to face the wall. He searched the carved face of the wall to the left of the doorway until he found the symbol, vaguely human in shape but with a twisted, angry face, which represented the hero of the story he had just read on the far wall.

The story told of a boy named Māui who stole knowledge from the goddess Ro'e and delivered it to his tribe. Many of the symbols, and the names and concepts that they represented, were familiar to Oliver from the shared mythology of the Pacific Island peoples, but the specific details of this tale were new to him. That happened a lot when Oliver reached some hidden cavern or lost temple. Details that had been lost to time, or even intentionally erased from a tale, often awaited him at the heart of abandoned places.

Oliver touched a finger against the intricately carved stone and traced down from the carving that represented Māui about a foot until he found the depiction of Ro'e, here encircled with a knot of seven lizards, their tails and bodies braided together, which Oliver was reasonably certain represented her guardians. He felt bile rise up in his throat and his pulse quicken when he saw that the thin layer of moss covering the third lizard's back had been brushed away.

Someone else had definitely been here.

A scuffed up bit of moss on a step could be the work of an animal or someone who had stumbled into the cave accidentally, as unlikely as that seemed after it had remained undisturbed for over fifteen hundred years. Someone had clearly brushed the back of this stone lizard clean some time in the last few days, recently enough that the moss had not grown back. That could only mean one of two things: First, that another relic hunter had beat Oliver to this ancient place, or second, that there was still an active cult, guardian order, or tribal religion focused around this place.

"Oh, no. No, no. Please, don't be gone," Oliver groaned.

He pulled out his phone and consulted his notes again.

Then he smiled.

To the best of his understanding, this place had been used

exclusively for sacrifice and initiation rituals. It was unlikely that such elements of worship had survived over the centuries, and if they had, the people who came here for worship certainly would not have disturbed that particular glyph.

He pressed the third carved lizard.

The floor shook under Oliver's feet. A thrumming vibration that was accompanied by the sound of rumbling stones and gushing water. A tongue of volcanic stone, so pitted with holes that Oliver judged it to weigh less than a quarter of what one might expect for a stone of its size, emerged from the cliff face before the doorway, spanning the cleft from side to side with a bridge nearly three feet wide. Looking across the cleft, Oliver saw that the doorway on the side of the cavern opposite from him was now open.

Oliver waited, patiently listening to the roar of the waterfall as he watched the stone bridge and counted.

After about five minutes the floor shook again and a gout of water spurted out from the cliff face below the bridge. The stone trembled, then slowly retracted back across the cleft to disappear into the cliff. On the far side of the cavern a heavy stone slab slid down to block the doorway again, coming to rest with a thud that reverberated throughout the cavern.

Oliver lay down on the stone floor and peered over the edge of the cliff. Only two feet down he saw the hole into which the stone bridge had disappeared and, several feet below that, a round opening from which water still trickled.

"Hydraulics. Seriously impressive stuff for any culture this old," Oliver said. He nodded his head in appreciation and waited another minute to see if anything else would happen to the bridge.

Eventually, he arose and returned to the carving of Ro'e

and her encircling lizards. He inspected them again, consulted his notes, and muttered, "It's all about timing, isn't it?"

In the story, Ro'e would have willingly granted Māui the knowledge he sought if he had been patient and waited until she deemed him ready to understand it. The impatient youth labored three years in the service of Ro'e until the opportunity arose to steal knowledge from her. As he fled from her island in a boat, the stolen knowledge clasped to his chest, she had stood on the shore weeping, for she knew that he had stolen only the knowledge, but would not have possessed the wisdom to understand it for another four years.

The story did not say what had become of Māui, but Oliver thought he got the point of it.

Oliver brushed his fingers across the rough surface of the stone, causing bits of lichen and moss that had grown on it over the centuries to flake away, and counted silently to himself. When he reached the head of the seventh lizard he paused and glanced around. There was no sign of anyone in the cavern. Whoever had been here before him had either turned back here, or crossed over and disappeared into the doorway on the far side of the cleft. If they had ever returned from that journey, and managed to pass the sealed stone door, they would have found the bridge gone.

"I hope I understand this," he muttered, then pressed hard against the head of the seventh lizard.

The floor shook and the stone bridge eased out to span the gap once again.

Oliver stepped up to the ledge, knelt, and poked at the stone bridge. It felt solid enough. He sat on the ledge and pressed against the bridge with both feet, assuring himself that it was solid, then stood upright. The bridge held him without shifting. Oliver nodded, took a deep breath, and strode forward into the curtain of mist that wreathed the bridge. The black volcanic stone beneath his feet was so riddled with holes that the swirling mist did little to make it slick and Oliver had no difficulty keeping his balance as he crossed to the far side of the cleft.

Oliver couldn't be certain how long the bridge would stay in place. If his interpretation of the story was correct, it would remain extended until he returned and pressed the tail of the seventh lizard, but there was an inherent danger in trusting interpretations of ancient myths to provide guidance through tombs and temples, especially when one's understanding was assembled from a dozen different folktales passed down by tribal storytellers.

Though the stories drawn from oral traditions were often richer and more textured with human emotion, as far as Oliver was concerned, he had found that few things were more comforting in their accuracy that a coldly detailed and textually corroborated written account.

Stepping up onto the stone slab of the far side, Oliver pulled out his flashlight and gun, then slipped across the five feet of open cavern to press himself against the wall beside the doorway. He peeked one eye around the carved frame, not expecting to see anyone, but prepared to pull back and bring his gun up if any threat appeared in the dimly lit corridor.

The passageway was illuminated with flickering blue flames, just like the one which he had followed from the hidden entrance high on the mountainside, and tunneled into the rock only a dozen feet before taking a sharp turn to the left. Inspecting the door frame, Oliver found a groove carved into the inner sides of the frame, the stone within the groove polished to a slick sheen. Above, a wide slot was cut into the lintel, in which he could see the base of the wide gray stone that had blocked the doorway.

Oliver pulled back from the opening and leaned against the wall for a moment, breathing deeply, then swung around the corner and sprinted down the hall to the next corner, keeping his flashlight low and watching for the glint of a tripwire or any sign of trigger stone set into the otherwise solid floor of the passage. He reached the turn in the passage without incident and paused, back against the wall, to listen. The roar of the waterfall still echoed through the passage, but he was reasonably certain that he could not hear anyone around the corner. This was confirmed with a glance and Oliver rapidly covered the twenty feet to the next turn in the passage without incident. He continued moving in this manner for another five turns, twisting and turning through the heart of the mountain until the last turn revealed another doorway which opened into a vast dark space.

Oliver approached the doorway slowly, keeping his body pressed against the wall and his flashlight beam low. His entire journey thus far had been illuminated by the bluish glow of the gas lamps set into the wall, so his arrival at a place that was completely dark made him nervous. He slipped up to the corner of the doorway and glanced around, but the faint light of the tunnel lamps showed only a small patch of floor composed of tightly fitted blocks of stone. The remainder of the cavern was completely dark.

As long as there aren't any undead, Oliver thought. I've had enough of them for a while.

He turned and dropped to one knee in the doorway, shining his light into the cavernous space and following the beam with the glowing sights of his gun.

"Oh, god. Why did it have to be you?" said a voice from the darkness. The accent was vaguely Swedish, by way of British English. "I'd almost rather have starved to death down here."

CHAPTER TWO
Explosive Rivalry

Oliver swept his light across the cavern until it found the speaker.

He was a short man, with pale skin and short hair so blond it was nearly white. He was dressed in jungle camouflage and sat cross legged on a pillar that jutted up from the darkness, leaning his elbows on a large backpack that rested across his knees. Oliver pointed the light at his face, causing him to squint and hold up a hand to block the light.

"No cause for that, Oliver. I didn't mean it," the man shouted.

The face and voice were familiar to Oliver, but he knew the man couldn't be a friend. In his line of work you didn't exactly make a lot of friends who shared the same profession, except for the occasional retired relic hunter who enjoyed sharing stories, or less than scrupulous museum acquisitions directors who would be happy to share a drink and listen to stories that they would forever deny hearing.

No, this was a rival, someone who Oliver had met at least once before.

"Don't recognize my voice, Oliver?"

It clicked. "I recognize you. Leo, right? From Iceland."

"That's me," Leo replied, resting his arms on the backpack and grinning at Oliver.

"I don't have to tell you that I'm not happy to see you." Oliver called back. His memory was clear now. "I was hoping that you'd been murdered by your associates in Iceland. Those guides I hired from you were worse than useless."

"Now that was a fun little diversion, wasn't it?" Leo said, still grinning.

"They tried to kill me," Oliver said, keeping his gun aimed at Leo, even though he was clearly trapped on the stone pillar, which stood alone in the dark room at the center of a wide chasm.

"Yes. They did fail at that, didn't they. No matter. That's all in the past now and you seem quite healthy. Successful, even, to have arrived at this place so shortly after I did myself," Leo said.

"Only because I wounded one and left them both behind in the ice cave," Oliver replied, edging to the left so he could get a better look at Leo's hands. There seemed little chance of the man attacking him as, at the moment, Oliver was probably Leo's only hope for rescue before the traitorous bastard starved to death.

The cavern was nearly a hundred feet in diameter, with a ceiling that arched a hundred feet overhead and was spiked with dozens of long stalactites. The doorway through which Oliver had entered opened into the cavern about half way up the wall. A raised walkway of carved stone jutted out a dozen feet into the room before terminating in a sudden drop to the floor fifty or more feet below. Looking down over the edge of the platform, Oliver saw the vicious tips of a hundred stalagmites thrusting upwards. The rippling red mineral deposits were damp with dripping water and humidity that made them appear coated in a sheen of fresh blood. Across the floor of the cavern, the field of stalagmites was interrupted by rings of black stone, out of which jutted pillars of various heights. The pillar on which Leo stood was the highest of these and sprouted from the floor at the center of the cavern.

"Yeah, it's a nasty puzzle," Leo said.

Oliver flicked his flashlight back at the man and saw that he had risen and now stood, his backpack supported between his feet, a hungry glaze in his eyes. "I thought I'd solved it, but the pillars only stayed up until I reached the center, then they all dropped back into the floor again. Not that I had much warning, what with them rising and falling the whole time."

"Serves you right," Oliver snapped. He was inspecting the pattern of circles set into the floor, searching for the most likely path through the maze.

"Really, Oliver, you think anyone deserves to die alone in a cave?"

"It's what you paid those guides to do to me, as I recall. If I hadn't insisted on going into that cave myself they'd have killed me and brought the artifact to you." Oliver focused his flashlight beam directly into Leo's eyes and smiled as the man flinched and looked away. He didn't plan to kill Leo, but he certainly wasn't opposed to leaving him down here for a while longer, assuming that he could work out a way to bypass him and get to the far side of the cavern without becoming trapped himself.

"That was all, what, two years ago?" Leo said.

"More like fifteen months, but who's counting," Oliver replied. He turned his back on Leo and began searching the walls surrounding the doorway for any sign of Maori carvings or hidden levers set into the wall.

A bright light clicked on behind him, casting his shadow against the wall like a puppet in a play. "Come on, Oliver. All of that was in the past. We can help each other now." Oliver turned to see Leo holding a large flashlight and sitting, legs dangling, on the edge of the pillar. "Just let me out of here and I'll help you. You can even keep whatever we find."

Oliver chuckled and shook his head in amusement at that. "Nice, Leo, but no thanks. I think I should leave you here to rot and let your bones remain as a warning against other grave robbers."

"First of all, it's a temple, not a grave. And second, you're just as much a grave robber as I am."

"Quite true, but I've got a different proposition for you. Here it is: You give me something that's worth your life, and I let you out of here when I'm finished. Otherwise, I'll get past this puzzle all on my own and leave you behind." Oliver flashed Leo a wide grin and turned away from him again to inspect a section of wall that had caught his eye when Leo's light lit up the room.

A circular section of the stone wall had been carved into an inset panel, about the size of a generous medicine cabinet, with gently curving sides and a polished back. A variety of polished stone pegs protruded from holes drilled into the stone. They were carved from a variety of different stones, some solid in coloration, others displaying a cross section of variegated reds, whites, blacks, and greens. At the center of the collection, a single large rod of polished white stone stood out above all the others.

"That deal doesn't sound especially good to me," Leo called.

Oliver shrugged and continued inspecting the assembly of pegs. "Then enjoy watching your flashlight batteries die. There don't seem to be any of those little blue gas lights in this part of the cave, so you'll die here in the dark. Maybe I'll come back and 'discover' your body in a few years. It's not as if anyone would know that I just left you to die." Oliver slipped his gun back into the inner pocket of his vest and rested his flashlight on the floor at his feet, then pulled out his phone and swiped through several screens until he found the document he wanted. Without turning away from the puzzle set into the wall Oliver said, "I think I've got the solution to this little riddle all on my own, so you'll need to offer something more."

"Yeah, well, so did I," Leo spat.

Oliver gave a derisive laugh and shook his head in mock sympathy. He knew that Leo was smart. He was, in fact, something of a legend in their small and secretive community of relic hunters, but it was clear that in this situation Leo had overestimated his skills. "I suppose you thought that you had the stone bridge figured out also?"

"Obviously. You're welcome, by the way."

"For?"

"For solving that little puzzle. I don't mind telling you that it took me a good while to put that story in order and figure out how to extend the bridge." Despite his desperate situation, Oliver could hear an edge of pride slipping into Leo's voice.

Oliver grinned wickedly at the prospect of blunting the man's pride with some hard truth, then he felt guilty and swallowed the sarcastic response that had sprung to mind.

Then he chuckled and decided to say it anyway.

He called back over his shoulder, "Oh, so you think I walked right over the bridge that you left open for me?"

"Obviously," Leo said.

"Hate to tell you, buddy, but that bridge retracted about two minutes after you crossed it."

Oliver reached up and pulled a green peg, streaked with white, out of the wall, considered the array of holes for a moment, then slipped it into a new hole. He moved two more pegs, then paused and compared the arrangement of pegs to some notes on his phone. The key, he was certain, lay in understanding how each peg represented a particular tribe. If Oliver was correct, the correct holes indicated the positions of the various Pacific islands that the tribes would later colonize, relative to the position of the island on which he now stood. The whole point of the relic he sought here was that it seemed to have the power to unlock a capacity for intellect and forward-thinking in those who possessed it, so such an arrangement of pegs made sense.

Satisfied with his solution, Oliver put the phone away, picked up his flashlight, and turned back to face Leo, who was still sitting on the edge of the tall pillar, his face as hard as the stone around him.

"Like I said, I'm willing to help you," Oliver called out. "You just need to offer something that's worth your life."

"Like what?" Leo spat. He pulled himself to his feet and stood, arms spread, glaring at Oliver. "I'm stuck in the middle of a deathtrap with nothing but my exploring gear. You want a few more chemical lights? How about a new poncho? How about my backpack, I bet you could use a new backpack for hauling around all your fancy camera gear."

"Funny, Leo. You know what I want," Oliver said.

Leo glowered at him for a long moment, then hissed back, "Well you're not going to get it."

Oliver shrugged, doing his best to appear nonplussed, though inside he was seething with anticipation. What he truly hoped to get out of the deal was Leo's collection of research notes. His own collection was his most valuable asset, which was why all of his own full copies, whether on his phone, his home computer, or in one of his secure backup locations, were encrypted with 2048-bit ciphers. To the private relic hunter, a well organized and detailed set of research notes was second only to a solid client list in importance.

"Have it your way then," Oliver said.

He leaned heavily against the post in the center of the peg panel.

"No, wait!" Leo shouted.

The sound of rushing water came from deep in the stone walls. Oliver stepped quickly to the side to avoid the several jets of cold water that spurted out from the empty holes in the panel. The floor shook as the rumble of heavy stones shifting deep under their feet echoed through the cavern. Oliver shone his light out into the open space and saw Leo had dropped to his belly on the stone pillar and lay, legs splayed out, one arm gripping his backpack to him as the hand of the other grasped at the edge of the pillar. Below him, the pillar began to sink towards the cavern floor. All throughout the cavern, Oliver could see dozens of other pillars rising and sinking in a chaotic dance of impossibly shifting stone. Every few seconds a pillar would drop suddenly, followed by the echo of heavy stone slamming into other stones, sending out violent tremors that shook the floor, walls, and ceiling of the cavern. Several stalactites shook free of the cavern roof and came hurtling down to shatter in bursts of sharp stone fragments. Oliver threw himself into the doorway and rolled into a tight ball, forehead pressed to his knees and hands protecting his neck.

When the noise stopped Oliver stood, dusted himself off, and shone his flashlight into the cavern. The beam cut through a haze of dust to reveal a meandering line of pillars rising up from the floor of the cavern. None stood directly beside another, but many were now close enough that a daring person could hop from one to another with little difficulty, assuming that they had a good sense of balance. He shone the light towards the center of the room and saw

Leo still clinging to the top of the central pillar, which had now sunk to the point that the top rested only about twenty feet from the floor of the cavern.

Oliver smiled, strode to the ledge by the nearest pillar, and jumped. He landed atop the stone pillar, spotted the next one about three feet away, and hopped to it. After a few more hops he paused to survey his surroundings and rest his legs. He was now almost half way across the cavern. At the closest point, the meandering path he needed to follow would take him within ten feet of the central pillar before it swerved away towards the side walls of the cavern in a wide arc.

"Going to rethink your position, Leo?" Oliver called out.

Leo pushed himself upright and made an obscene gesture at Oliver. "You could have killed me," he growled.

"Unlikely," Oliver said, shrugging. "I didn't anticipate the movement being so violent, but you had a nice wide place to hold on to. Now, are you going to take my offer or not? A couple more jumps and I'll be at the best place for you to pass me your notes. After I pass that place, well, I guess you'll be glad of the reading material until all your lights burn out."

Leo glared at Oliver in the harsh light of their flashlights. His jaw worked with barely repressed anger and Oliver knew that the man would like little more in that moment than to kill him, but even if he was armed Oliver still represented his best hope at escape.

"Fine, it's yours," Leo snapped. He knelt and began rummaging through the contents of his backpack.

Feeling it prudent to be prepared for a desperate attack, Oliver dropped to one knee and pulled out his gun, aiming it at Leo while he searched for whatever he kept his research notes on.

Leo looked up, hands still in his bag, and froze at the sight of Oliver's gun. "How do I know you won't just shoot me when I give this to you?" he asked.

Oliver shrugged, keeping his gun pointed at Leo's chest. "You don't. But if you know enough about me to know my real name, and my business, then you should know enough to recognize that I'm no killer."

"You're threatening to kill me now."

"There's a difference between threatening and carrying through with a threat. If you pull a gun out of that bag, sure, I'll shoot you, but that would be to defend myself. I promise you, Leo, if you toss me your notes and wait calmly for me to finish my business here, I will help you escape."

Leo seemed to consider this for a long moment, then shook his head in resignation and stood, holding a large book wrapped in thin oiled leather and bound up with a leather strap. "This is years of my life, you bastard."

"You'll have many more years ahead of you to put your notes back in order. Besides, I highly doubt you're foolish enough to keep just one copy. Am I right?"

Leo shrugged noncommittally.

"That's what I figured," Oliver said. He put his gun away and hopped to the next pillar. "All you're doing is giving me a bit of a leg up on finding the next shard, or some lovely relics, assuming that I can even interpret your notes. You won't even be out of the game, just a bit behind me again." He jumped twice more and paused at the pillar closest to the one on which Leo stood. Oliver rested for a moment with his hands on his knees, trying to catch his breath. The last few jumps had taken more out of him than he had expected. After a minute he shook his head, looked up at Leo, and said, "Now, lets have it."

Leo took a deep breath and gazed lovingly at the notebook containing his research notes, then straightened and prepared to throw. He weighed the book with one hand, judging the appropriate force and angle of the throw, then tossed the book towards Oliver's waiting arms. Oliver caught the volume and clutched it to his chest, a smile breaking out across his face.

He quickly undid the leather ties and flipped through the journal, giving it a brief inspection to ascertain that it did indeed appear to be Leo's research notes. The book was nearly full of a tight scrawl, neat diagrams, and pasted-in photographs. Tattered sticky notes clung to several pages which, on a cursory inspection, appeared to bear notes about the Maori civilization. Oliver wrapped the volume and once more tied the straps, his grin growing wider as he thought about all the valuable clues he might find in the book.

"No need to gloat about it," Leo groused.

"Spare me. If the situation was reversed you probably would have killed me by now," Oliver replied. He pushed himself to his feet, then his head spun and he stumbled and nearly fell off the pillar. He dropped back to one knee and breathed in deeply, but he couldn't seem to catch his breath. He shot a look at Leo, immediately suspecting him of somehow poisoning him, perhaps with a skin-permeable toxin on the pages of the book, but Leo was looking back at him with a confused expression.

"Oliver! Are you alright?" Leo called out. "Don't fall now, I need you to get me out of here."

Oliver ignored Leo's cries and, moving sluggishly, pushed himself back to his feet. He felt his breath coming more easily then. Turning his back to Leo, Oliver leapt to the next pillar, which was positioned about three feet away and a foot higher than the one on which he had crouched to receive Leo's journal. He landed hard on his hands and knees, still clutching the journal in his left hand, then struggled to his feet. His breath came easier and Oliver began to feel his head clearing. His heart, which had been pounding against his chest, started to slow and ease back into a more normal pace.

This seemed a good time to rest, so Oliver paused long enough to shrug out of his backpack and drop the journal into it. As he rummaged through the bag he spotted his spare water bottle. He pulled it out and glanced back at Leo, who was sitting on the edge of his pillar, watching him.

"You have any water left?"

Leo shook his head.

Oliver held up the bottle. Leo held out his arms and Oliver tossed the bottle to him. He caught it, unscrewed the heavy plastic lid, and took a deep drink before looking at Oliver again.

"Thanks. I still hate you."

"Likewise," Oliver said. He turned away from Leo, took two more deep breaths and, convinced that he was not about to collapse, jumped to the next pillar.

He continued hopping from one pillar to the next until he reached the far side of the cavern. Once there, Oliver turned the beam of his light to survey the perimeter of the cavern. He saw the now familiar notches cut into the wall, where blue light should have flickered from the lead nozzle of a primitive, but ingenious, gas lamp. All of the lamps in this room had somehow been extinguished.

Oliver turned from the darkness of cavern, ignoring Leo's shouted urgings for him to hurry, to the dark doorway set into the wall. Shining his light into the passage, Oliver saw a set of wide stairs which climbed upwards for at least fifty feet before ending at another dark opening.

"Let's see if there are any more traps," he muttered, and began climbing up the steps, searching for any sign of traps as he went. Unlike the steps he had descended before entering the cavern containing the underground waterfall, these steps were almost completely bare, with only a thin layer of dust covering the polished black stone.

Ascending to the top of the stairs without incident, Oliver discovered the end of the passage through the heart of the mountain. He sank to one knee, chest heaving from the climb and a lingering sense of breathlessness, and gazed through an ornately carved doorway, the edges worked in carvings of beasts and heroes from the depths of Maori myth, which opened into a narrow chamber that glittered in black and refracted rainbows. This chamber had been carved out of a single massive block of black volcanic glass deep under the mountain. Oliver played his light across piles of desiccated vegetables, carved sculptures in stone and crumbling wood, chunks of uncut gems, and the stained bones of fish, birds, and men.

"Oh, yes," Oliver whispered, his face breaking into a wide smile.

He resisted the urge to bound forward and paused for a moment to consider the likelihood that the room was trapped. The place had a feel to it, an ancient and dark majesty that he had experienced before in secret chambers and long lost temples, which made Oliver believe that it would be safe to continue. In places like this the traps were more like challenges, which served to test those who would dare to enter and weed out the unworthy, those who lacked adequate knowledge or faith, before they could attain the inner sanctum. It was altogether different from the feeling that he got from tombs, which also had a different atmosphere from decrepit castles and their dungeons and treasure vaults. He approached the doorway and shone his light into the depths of the chamber, hoping that the prize he sought would still be there.

At the far end of the chamber, about thirty feet from the doorway, a shard of glittering silvery metal rested on a raised shelf above an altar of glittering black volcanic glass, which appeared to have been sculpted from the glass at time that the room itself was carved. Oliver felt his pulse quicken as he approached the altar and stood, gazing down on the shard. The air in the chamber was far cooler than that at the surface of the island, perhaps in the high fifties, which was to be expected so deep underground in a region where all volcanic activity had ceased several thousand years before, but it was certainly well above freezing. Despite this, a delicate tracery of ice coated the glass shelf on which the shard rested, condensed from the air and frozen by the chill that emanated from the shard. A puddle of meltwater had collected in the basin of the altar, and Oliver wondered whether the basin had been carved to collect the blood of sacrifices, or if the ancient people who had worshiped this shard had known that water would collect here.

Oliver extended a trembling hand towards the shard and paused just before he would have grasped it, fingers prickling with cold and anticipation. It was unlikely that any poison would have remained on the shard after so many years of it collecting and freezing atmospheric vapor, and he didn't see any way in which a trap could be concealed in the flawless, unbroken expanse of volcanic glass. But still... He glanced around nervously, searching the shadows at the corners of the room for any sign of supernatural guardians waiting to spring upon him.

You're starting to get superstitious, Oliver, he thought.

He shook his head to drive away the fear, then grasped the shard.

The moment Oliver's fingers touched the shard, he felt an

uncomfortable warmth rise inside his shirt, pressing into his chest with a heat and subtle vibration reminiscent of grasping the lid of a pot filled with boiling water. He gasped and dropped the shard, letting it clatter and splash into pooled water of the altar basin, then clutched at his chest. The heat faded away immediately, leaving a prickling sensation in his skin. Oliver set his flashlight on the altar and quickly unbuttoned his shirt, heart pounding, half expecting to find the pinprick of a poisoned dart in the center of his chest. Pulling his shirt apart, he saw nothing out of the ordinary. Just the skin of his tanned chest and, resting against it, the fragment of polished and smoothly curved heartwood that had fallen out of the staff of Moses when he had shattered it, a little over a year before. The wood was wrapped in a tight monkey's fist of oiled leather and hung around his neck on a loop of the same material.

"That was strange," Oliver said, shaking his head in bewilderment.

He reached down into the water pooled on the altar, which was already beginning to shiver with curls of ice spreading out in white fractal curls across the bottom of the basin, and plucked out the shard.

The instant his fingers touched the shard, the knot of glistening heartwood hanging around his neck pulsed hot against his skin. The surface shifted in luster, as if a surge of oil had pulsed to the surface of the wood, bearing with it the scent of olive wood and the heat of a glowing ember. The heated wood pressed against his chest like a brand, flushing his skin red and threatening to raise a blister. Oliver flinched and gritted his teeth, but did not drop the shard again. His hand darted to the bag at his side and he deposited the shard into it alongside the book he had taken from Leo. The heat faded as soon has he released the shard, but the skin of

Oliver's chest was now flushed red with a mild burn.

He pulled the leather strap over his head and inspected the heartwood. The heat had dissipated and he could see no sign of damage to the wood. He nearly put it back around his neck, where it had rested for much of the last year, but at the last moment he slipped it into a zippered pocket on the inside of his vest. The question of why the heartwood had burned him would have to wait for safer surroundings.

He pulled several battery powered lamps out of his backpack and positioned them throughout the chamber, hiding them behind the piles of offerings and clusters of carved wood and stone idols. The light spilled from the lamps in dramatic bursts, which reflected from the chipped walls of the chamber in glittering bursts of color and cast deep pools of shadow upon the path that led up the center of the room. He unpacked his camera and filled several memory cards with photos from a variety of angles. This adventure was already a massive success as far as he was concerned, what with his capture of the shard and the added bonus of Leo's journal, but that was no reason to neglect his cover story. These photos would sell well to any number of magazines and websites, and should be sufficient evidence for him to sell the directions to this temple to one of his more respectable, though not completely scrupulous, contacts within the archaeological community.

After about half an hour he packed up his equipment, added a particularly dazzling stone carving of a figure he believed to be Māui to his backpack, and set off back down the stairs to the cavern of pillars.

He reached the cavern and found Leo still sitting on the central pillar, a glum look on his face.

"You get what you wanted?" Leo called across the darkness as Oliver emerged from the staircase.

"More than you could imagine," Oliver said. It felt wrong to gloat, but his blood was still rushing with the hot glow of discovery and, at the moment, he didn't care.

"Good for you. Now, about getting me out of here," Leo raised his right arm, a small handgun gripped in his fist. Oliver noted that his gun arm was shaking rather badly. "Thought I was helpless, didn't you? I just didn't see much point in burning my only bridge, but since you decided to poison me..."

"Poison?" Oliver shouted.

"Yeah, that's right. Poison."

"Leo, I don't know what you're talking about, but I certainly didn't poison you," Oliver said.

"Explain this then!" Leo shouted, lurching to his feet and brandishing a half-empty water bottle in the hand that was not pointing a gun at Oliver. "I was feeling just fine until you showed up here. Then you come along, mess with the pillars, toss me this bottle, and now I can hardly breathe." Leo stopped shouting and coughed deeply, nearly tipping over the ledge of the pillar, then he caught his balance and fixed Oliver with a deadly gaze.

"Leo, I didn't..."

"Save it. You're going to get back over there and reconfigure the pillars to get me out of here. Make one wrong move, try to get away, reach for your gun, anything like that, and I'll shoot you dead."

Oliver wasn't sure he believed that Leo could reliably shoot in the right direction, let alone hit him in the dark room, but it wasn't worth the risk. "I'll do that. I was planning to all along. Can I move now?"

"Yes. Get over there now," Leo growled. He dropped to one knee and settled into a kneeling position, elbows resting on his backpack for support, and trained his flashlight and gun on Oliver. "I said go!"

Oliver moved cautiously to the edge of the platform, keeping one eye on Leo even as he approached the ledge. He paused to cinch his backpack straps, glanced at Leo again, then jumped to the first pillar. It didn't take Oliver long to navigate the twisting path of pillar hops path back across the cavern. As he approached the center, half way through his journey, he kept both hands well away from the pockets of his vest. Leo tracked him with the flashlight beam, though he directed it sluggishly, hardly keeping up with Oliver's pace across the cavern. It was clear that there truly was something wrong with Leo, but Oliver knew that he hadn't poisoned the man. A dull ache settled into Oliver's chest as he crossed the low pillars at the center of the room and he was soon panting for air again. Last time he had assumed that the exertion of jumping from pillar to pillar so rapidly was more strenuous than he had anticipated, but as he pushed onward through the pain and began ascending towards the exit, and felt the pain in his chest lessen, Oliver was struck with a terrible thought. He turned it over in his mind, inspecting all the elements and trying to find another explanation, but nothing else seemed to fit.

He arrived at the balcony of cut stone that thrust out from the cavern wall before the exit door and turned to face Leo. The man had risen to his feet again, having been unable to keep Oliver in his sights while remaining seated, now that the pillar had sunk towards the floor.

"Right. Now change the pillars so I can get out and we'll both walk out of here alive," Leo said.

"I'll do that, but first I really need you to put that gun away," Oliver replied.

"Like hell I'm putting my gun away. I just wish I'd had it out when you showed up, then I could have made you let me go long ago."

"Leo, I need you to understand, if you shoot that thing in here we're both..."

Leo's whole body jerked as he stiffened his gun arm, aiming somewhere above Oliver's head.

He opened his mouth to shout something and pulled the trigger.

Oliver saw the deadly glint in Leo's eye and knew that he was going to shoot even as he began to move his arm. He dove for the mouth of the passage back to the waterfall and was back on his feet running as fast as he could, even as the sound of the shot shattered the stillness of the cavern. The crack of the gunshot was instantly eclipsed by the roar of thousands of cubic feet of natural gas igniting in a hellish conflagration of blue fire.

CHAPTER THREE
THE SHARDS

"The blast threw me clear into the waterfall room. I skidded across the damp stone, scrabbling for a handhold, and plunged off the edge. Just as I thought I was going to fall into the underground river and drown, the fingers of my left hand snagged on an outcropping of rock and I jerked to a stop so hard that I nearly dislocated my shoulder."

"Hold on a minute," Hank said, setting his wineglass down with a harsh ring of glass stressed nearly to shattering. "I thought you said that the passage between the waterfall and the pillar trap zigzagged."

Oliver grimaced and pushed his stool back from the patchwork surface of the salvaged marble bar in his cluttered loft apartment. The fragments of marble were of all different colors and shapes, bonded together with strong food-grade stone epoxy. It looked a bit rough, but he liked things that way. As far as Oliver was concerned, too much of the world was sharp edges and clean lines, the sort his parents had been so enamored of during their seemingly endless remodeling projects in their northern Virginia plantation house. He turned away from Hank, took two steps, and buried his head in the refrigerator that rested opposite the bar, beside a wide sweep of countertop.

"Don't hide from me in there," Hank chided him, wagging a finger at Oliver as he used a finger and thumb of his other hand to tear off a chunk of bread from the loaf that had sat between them and dip it into the plastic tub of dressing. He crammed the sodden bread into his mouth and chewed contentedly for a moment, his eyes softening with pleasure at the taste of the freshly baked bread and perfectly seasoned dressing. He swallowed and said, "I've been listening to your stories since we were boys, Oliver, and I know when you're lying."

Oliver straightened and turned from the refrigerator with a bottle in each hand, kicking the refrigerator door shut with one slippered foot. "I'm not lying, Hank."

"You mean to tell me that the blast picked you up, bounced you back and forth down the tunnel like a ping-pong ball, and deposited you safe and sound beside the bridge?" Hank asked, laughter bubbling just under the surface of his voice.

Oliver proffered a chilled bottle of red wine to Hank, who pressed his large stomach against the bar and leaned forward to accept the bottle with a grin. "Don't think that this is a bribe to keep me from asking you again. I've listened to all your crazy stories over the years and believed most of them because you had evidence." He paused to grunt as he pulled the cork from the bottle with the characteristic squeaking pop of synthetic cork, sniffed at the red-stained rubber dubiously, then smiled to himself and tipped the bottle into his glass.

Oliver twisted the lid off of a bottle of cider and took a long drink, purposely keeping his eyes averted from Hank's face. The memory of the events in that passage, deep under the mountains of a remote Pacific island, still haunted his dreams. In the week since he had returned, Oliver had repeatedly dreamed of the wave of blue fire, rolling over him and slamming him to the rough-hewn floor of the passage, the heat prickling against his skin as he curled into a ball and screamed at the realization that this was how his life would finally end. He would awake tangled in the sheets, prickling flesh covered in a sheen of hot sweat that had soaked into the bedclothes.

Hank was talking again, pointing with his wine glass and a single immaculately manicured finger. Oliver realized that he had slipped back into the memory and lost track of the conversation. He took another swig from the bottle to cover his inattention and focused on Hank's words.

"...Together for years, you tracking down relics, me helping you smuggle them back into the country with my ingenious little devices. I think you can trust me with what really happened and not feed me some ridiculous story. Next you'll be saying you survived by hiding in a refrigerator and letting the blast throw you to safety."

Oliver exploded in laughter. Cider surged up his nose, choked him, and turned the laugh into a coughing fit. He stumbled to a stool, set his bottle on the bar, and pulled himself up onto the seat. He continued to cough and splutter foam from his nose for half a minute as Hank looked on disapprovingly over the steel rims of his glasses. Finally, Oliver managed to get a breath down his lungs without gagging. He sat up and wiped his face and eyes with the collar of his t-shirt, then pushed his red hair back on his head and gave Hank a wide grin. "Actually, I escaped the fireball by pulling out a bullwhip and using it to chase back the flames."

"Ah, I should have known." Hank's eyes narrowed and he set his glass down on the bar and began tapping the rim with a single dark, carefully manicured finger. "So, are you going to tell me about it? I can tell you're carrying a burden, Oliver. Allow me to help you with it."

"I think that wine is making you even more grandiose than

usual, but just on account of our long friendship, I will tell you. Just, please, don't ask me to explain it."

"You have my word of honor," Hank said, fumbling his wine glass over into his left hand, then holding up his right hand with three fingers extended. "One Star Scout to another."

Oliver smiled, took another sip of cider, and leaned forward to rest his elbows on the bar. He looked past Hank to the painted brick of living room wall, letting his gaze rest upon the heavy oak bookshelf that concealed the door of the large safe, in which he had placed the shard. The others, he had captured five in all now, were hidden in bank vaults throughout Virginia, along with paperwork for the various false identities that he had established to use when traveling through dangerous territory. This mystery had consumed almost his entire adult life and, after nearly fifteen years, he was no closer to understanding the origins of the shards. At least he thought that he knew their effect, if not their cause, and that was enough to make him keep searching.

He took a slow breath, turned to look at Hank, then said, "The gas ignited, just like I told you, and the whole cavern filled up with fire in an instant. I was blown down the passage and slammed into the wall at the first turn. All around me the world was on fire. Everything, Hank. I couldn't even see Leo through all the flames, but he must have been knocked from the pillar and burned to a cinder because after the flames were gone I went back into the cavern and I couldn't see any sign of him."

"Wait just a minute," Hank said, holding up a finger between them. He stabbed at the air as if nudging bit pieces of information into place on an invisible abacus, then fixed Oliver with a befuddled expression. "I'm slipping towards drunk here, but I'm not stupid. Did you just tell me that the whole cavern exploded, killing your rival and sending blasts of fire down the passages, and you walked out unscathed?"

"Not exactly unscathed, I did drop my flashlight when the blast hit me and when I found it the plastic lens had melted off and the LED was fused. I had to use my spare to get out of there."

Hank blinked twice and sat back in his chair. His mouth worked soundlessly, disturbing the neatly combed hairs of his black goatee as he tried to reconcile the story Oliver had just related with reality. Oliver waited, quietly sipping his cider and occasionally tearing off a bit of bread, dipping it in the dressing, and chewing it as quietly as he could. This was exactly why he had come up with the lie about being thrown into the waterfall room by the blast. Sure, that story was not especially believable, but it certainly beat claiming that he had survived a blast of fire hot enough to singe stone and melt plastic. He decided that it was a good thing he had not yet told the full story of this adventure to anyone besides Hank and, when the time came to tell his cousin Amber, he might just have to leave out the bit about the zig-zag passage.

Hank leaned forward again and set his wineglass on the bar delicately, then poked a finger at Oliver's face. "You're not lying to me again, are you?"

"No."

"And you're sure that you're still alive? I only ask because after all the tales you've told me I wouldn't discount talking to your ghost right now."

That made Oliver smile. "I assure you, I am alive, well, and sitting here in this room with you."

"I suspected as much," Hank sighed.

"I don't understand it any more than you, Hank."

"Could it have been one of the relics that protected you? You had the heartwood around your neck and the shard in your bag."

Oliver shook his head and sighed in frustration. "That's the only explanation I can think of, but I'm not eager to test it again."

"Obviously." Hank lifted a plastic lid from the countertop and snugged it down over the tub of dressing, then shifted his bulk off the barstool, snatched up the loaf of bread, and rounded the corner of the bar with an elegant pivot that belied his three hundred pounds. He set the bread in an antique wood and tin breadbox beside the stove, put the dressing away in the refrigerator door, and began rummaging through the refrigerator shelves. "What about the interaction of the shard and the heartwood. Have you experimented with that further?"

"Yes. It's really strange," Oliver said, turning in his seat to watch as Hank pulled a cutting board from the wall and began dicing sausages. "The shard doesn't appear to have any reaction to the heartwood. It remains still and cold no matter how close the heartwood comes to it. On the other hand, the heartwood reacts violently to the shard. If you move the shard towards it, the heartwood will slide away, as if it was being repelled by a magnetic field. If you force the heartwood towards the shard, it will begin pushing back. Keep pushing for too long and it will get hot."

"That's weird."

"It is. I wish that I knew the cause, but since I don't even know for sure that the shards are..." Oliver trailed off, eyes losing focus as he recalled the burning heat of the heartwood searing his chest when he lifted the shard from the altar. If only he knew the source of the shards, Oliver thought he might possibly be able to deduce the cause of the violent reaction between the two relics, but for all that he had devoted over a decade of his life to tracking down the shards, he still knew remarkably little about them.

Oliver had discovered the first shard among his uncle Peter's possessions in the attic of the family estate in northern Virginia. The shard had been hidden in a wooden puzzle box, which he had found at the bottom of a pile of papers in a battered footlocker while cleaning out his parents' attic over Christmas break. It was that box of documents, and the clues that he found while perusing them over the next few months, that had introduced Oliver to the mystery of the shards.

"I thought you believed the shards to be fragments of an ancient mechanism," Hank said, interrupting Oliver's reverie. He had finished cutting the meat and had a pan on the stove, butter already melting.

"Yes, that's true. Something like the Antikythera Mechanism, but perhaps with a more mysterious purpose, one that would cause, or require, the parts to be imbued with a supernatural power. The Antikythera Mechanism was essentially a hand-cranked computer, built by the Greeks for calculating astronomical positions fifteen hundred years before Europeans were even constructing mechanical clocks. I have no idea what purpose my mechanism might have served, but it was certainly important."

"So you've got a machine of unknown purpose and origin, created by persons unknown, at a time unknown, and you're still hellbent on finding all the parts, the number of which is still unknown, and putting them back together," Hank said. He turned from the stove and blinked at Oliver expectantly through the round lenses of his glasses. When Oliver didn't reply Hank sighed and turned to the cutting board to begin dicing potatoes. "I'll trust you that this machine, whatever it might be, is important, but I just wonder if there's a reason it was broken and scattered across the globe."

Oliver pondered Hank's words, considering the

implications as he watched Hank cook and finished his cider. It wasn't the first time he had confronted the mysterious origins of the shards and wondered if he ought to give up his quest to capture them all, but even as he wondered how he might go about reshaping his life if he abandoned the search that had been so central to his existence for fifteen years Oliver felt the unquenchable urge to know rise up within himself.

"I mean, think of this Oliver: You know where the heartwood came from, and I don't think there's any argument that it's a good thing, right?"

"Agreed."

"So if the heartwood, a fragment of perhaps the most unquestionably good relic you've ever found, shows a demonstrable dislike of the shards, perhaps that is a sign that they aren't the safest thing in the world to be collecting." Hank said, not looking up from the pan on the stove.

"You think I haven't wondered about that?" Oliver finished his cider and tossed the bottle into the recycle bin beside the refrigerator, where it clanked against the dozen or so bottles and empty soup cans. "I can't explain it, Hank, any more than I can explain why I'm still alive right now now. I just need to know the truth."

"I'm not going to try and stop you man, I'll even keep helping you smuggle the shards into the country, I just want you to think carefully before you assemble them, alright?"

"I'll do that."

"So what about that other thing you captured? Have you taken a look at the journals of the late and unlamented Leo whatever-his-name-was yet?" Hank asked, turning from the stove and leaning his large frame agains the counter. He held out a hand and Oliver passed him the wineglass that he had left on the bar.

"Oh, you bet I have. Hell, I was reading through that thing the whole flight back here. Some fascinating bits of information."

"Such as?"

Oliver leapt from his seat and strode into the open living room space, which was cluttered with book cases, boxes, and piles of artifacts. Along one wall stood a wide glass-topped desk, sitting opposite a worn leather sofa and beside a large television monitor and a rack of computers. In the center of the desk rested the leather bound book that Oliver had taken from Leo in the cavern of pillars, only an hour before the chamber had been shaken by a fireball that shattered several of the pillars, leaving them broken and scattered across the floor, and killed the previous owner of the book. Oliver grabbed the journal from the desk and carried it back to the bar, where he began flipping through pages.

"It's more than just a research journal. Leo kept all of his hardcopy notes in this book." Oliver flipped to a page covered in a tight scrawl of handwriting, then another on which Leo had pasted several folded photocopies of ancient texts. The space between each folded paper was occupied by dozens of notes in different colors of ink. "Here are his notes on the myth of Māui and Ro'e, the same story that led me to the island cave. He came at the problem from a different angle, but in the end we arrived at the same conclusion regarding the common origin of Maori legends."

"I'm still astounded that you were able to track down an artifact that had remained hidden for hundreds of years," Hank said.

"It wasn't easy, but the truth is that you just have to know what to look for. My Uncle Peter spent his entire career researching the origin of Mayan civilization and only stumbled onto the first shard by mistake. It took him over a decade to uncover the location of the second shard, and he never even managed to find it before his whole team was killed in the massacre. Well, everyone but Amber, that is. Since then I've become more adept than him at tracking down the shards, but only because I've developed something of a system."

"Care to share it?" Hank asked as he turned the hash over, unleashing a riot of mouth-watering scents and a sizzle that set Oliver's stomach rumbling. "Unless it's some deep dark secret. Maybe you sell a bit of your soul for each shard?"

"Nothing so dramatic, though the image of a crossroads at midnight is something we can work with. Picture it, then: A crossroads where weary travelers meet along two ancient roads that cut across the grasslands of some ancient land. As night settles, people mingle between camps, sharing stories, encountering long forgotten friends, meeting new friends. Before long they start sharing stories. A young storyteller wanders up the fire carrying an old scroll that he found wedged under a rock at the crossroads and tells everyone that the scroll contains a story he's never heard before. He reads them the story, we'll say it's about a dwarf named Doug who found an uncommonly fine gem and all the trouble it brought him, and everyone agrees that it is a fine tale. The young man returns the scroll to the nook in the rock where he found it and goes to bed. At daybreak the camps at the crossroads break up and all of the travelers depart to the four corners of the land, bearing with them the tale of Doug the Dwarf and his Diamond of Detriment."

"I'm not seeing how this relates to your little quest to find the shards of some ancient machine," Hank interrupted.

"You'll see it in a moment," Oliver promised. "My point is this: How do you find the source of the story after a couple hundred years have passed?"

Hank pondered that question for a few moments as he pulled plates from the cupboard and set them out on the patchwork marble of the bar. He pulled the cork from the bottle of wine and refreshed his glass, then stood in the center of Oliver's kitchen, swirling the wine in his glass and imbibing its aroma through his wide nostrils. Oliver did not hurry him. He had known Hank Thornton since childhood and, while their lives had taken significantly different paths during their college years, they had remained close friends. He knew that Hank preferred to quietly puzzle through a situation and arrive at a fully considered conclusion, an attitude that stood in contrast to Oliver's own habit of talking through almost everything.

After a time Hank stirred and began shoveling the hash from the frying pan onto the plates as he said, "I imagine that you might ask each person they encountered where they heard the story, then follow those clues back until you find a region in which everyone seems to know the tale."

"That would make sense if they still had the scroll, but remember that the young storyteller returned the scroll to its hiding place after reading it to the group gathered around the campfire."

Hank placed two plates of steaming hash on the bar and pushed one towards Oliver before hefting himself into a tall chair opposite. He stirred his plateful of hash with his fork a few times, then lifted a forkful and poked it towards Oliver saying, "So, if a concentration of stories doesn't indicate the origin point, how could you find the source?" He put the food into his mouth and chewed slowly, savoring the flavors as he waited for Oliver to respond.

"You need to find several different locations where there are concentrations of a particular legend, story, cult, whatever. Once you find those locations, you need to learn as much as you can about regional trade routes and historical migrations of peoples. With that information you can start looking for an empty place in the map, somewhere near the middle of everything that you've uncovered, where the people have drifted away and all the stories have dried up, such as in the ancestral homeland of a culture that has moved away and established a new capital somewhere far away."

Oliver stopped speaking and pulled his plate closer. He began enthusiastically shoveling food into his mouth. It had been months since he had enjoyed one of Hank's meals.

They ate in silence for a while, then Oliver set down his fork and went to the refrigerator to retrieve a fresh bottle of cider. He unscrewed the cap, took a swig, and returned to his seat saying, "Of course, that only works when the shard hasn't been found at any point in the past. People have been searching for these things for at least five thousand years, ever since the Creed scattered them. That's why the last one I found, the one in Iceland, was especially difficult to track down. The Creed had discovered it before me and moved it about the most remote location they could."

"You've mentioned them before," Hank interjected, "but I've never been able to pin down what you mean. What is this Creed thing?"

"I don't entirely know that, any more than I know where the shards come from. All I know is that at least five thousand years ago the shards began appearing all over the world. In places where the shards came to rest there was a brief explosion of culture and technology, which was soon followed by either a sudden decline or the people scattering outwards across the world, carrying their newly invigorated culture with them, but leaving the shards behind. This cycle repeats itself as the shards are captured, discovered, carried from place to place, until about a thousand years ago." Oliver paused to wet his mouth with another sip. His fingers drifted towards Leo's journal. He had rarely explained his theories in such depth.

Years ago he had given a single presentation to his doctoral advisory board, one semester after returning from the Amazon with a shard that had been lost to the collapsed wooden empires of the lost city of Z. That presentation, and his refusal to abandon the radically unorthodox theories of cultural and technological development which it had expressed, had been the genesis of Oliver's downfall from academia. Since then he had only opened himself up to his cousin Amber, who had accompanied him on the expedition to the Amazon, and Diana, a girlfriend with similarly mad theories. Both of those confidants were less than easily accessible these days, though, as Amber had married and settled down to a relatively calm life in northern Virginia, and Diana had managed to secure an additional year of funding for her research at the Louvre in Paris.

"You still haven't explained what the Creed is."

Oliver took a few bites, chewing them thoughtfully and staring at the pattern of patchwork marble in silence. It was one thing to say that he believed that the shards were somehow related to unexpected growth in culture around the world throughout the last few thousand years, to his mind that was no more unusual than claiming that cities tended to be built up around mines and wells, it was quite another to posit the existence of a global conspiracy that had spanned thousands of years. He finished his last bite of the hash, savoring the warm burn of spices in his mouth, then looked up at Hank. "I only have a few vague references to back this part up, and given what my former colleagues thought about my supposed evidence, calling this sketchy is probably the world's greatest understatement."

"I'm still here, Oliver. Just spill it."

"A few years back I was searching for evidence of shards in Europe. With all the developments that took place there in the last thousand years I thought that there couldn't help but be a shard there. Instead of finding anything like a solid clue, I ended up wasting six months collecting vague rumors that just ran me in circles. There were just too many things happening all in one place, everything overlapped and I couldn't find an origin point. What I did find, though, was indications of someone working against people like me. Whenever I thought that I was getting close to a solid clue, I would find that some key record had been burned, or a castle destroyed, or a pagan shrine gutted and refashioned into a church."

"That's not so unusual in Europe. The Catholic church alone had enough internal strife as the political structure of the church developed, and that's leaving out the inquisition, the reformation, the church of England, the crusades, and every bit of political intrigue that went on independent of the church."

"I'm aware of the complexities of European history, Hank. This was different. The holes in the historical record were so precise that you could almost use them to track the shards, which as it turns out is exactly what I did. I started looking for other people who had uncovered the secret of the shards, both throughout history and in the present day, and I realized that there have been dozens of us over the last couple centuries. Different searchers encountered different levels of success, but one thing is clear: assemble too much of the puzzle, and crow too loudly about it, and you'll end up dead."

"You're still alive," Hank said.

"I don't talk about the shards to many people. As far as my private clients know, I'm just a relic hunter, one of thousands throughout the world. As far as the world at large can tell, I'm just a travel photographer with a knack for getting into secluded historical sites before the archaeologists come and start digging holes everywhere."

"So you keep a low profile because you're paranoid that a shadowy conspiracy is going to kill you."

Oliver shot Hank a look. He would be the first to admit that his theories bordered on the paranoid, but it hurt to hear it from one of his few confidants.

"Hey, I'm just painting in broad strokes here. You're not giving me a lot to work with," Hank said, his tone walking a line between defensive and joking.

Oliver sighed and pushed his empty plate away. He was not doing a good job explaining the situation and he wasn't even sure how he could improve the picture for Hank. "Maybe I'm being too specific, too personal. You don't need to know how I know all of this, especially since a lot of it is vague to even me, you just want to know what I'm facing."

"Yes."

"I believe the Creed to be a loosely organized collection of individuals sworn to protect the shards and keep them from ever being reassembled into the original mechanism. I know for sure that they have existed since the middle-ages in Europe, working against Renaissance thinkers like Leibniz who attempted to collect the shards, and I strongly suspect them of infiltrating governments and religions throughout history to direct people away from finding the shards. I even have an account of a priest from medieval Belarus who was the sole survivor of a massacre, which I believe to have been caused by members of the Creed attempting to wipe out everyone who saw one of the shards."

Hank nodded thoughtfully, sipping at his wine as he contemplated Oliver's words. Oliver watched his face closely, waiting for a sign that Hank's apparent disbelief and uncertainty had slipped into distain. It was a familiar experience for Oliver, that appearance of scorn on the faces of people he respected.

Finally Hank shrugged and took another sip of his wine before saying, "I don't understand it, but I'm not going to call you crazy, Oliver. If you'd told me all of that a few years ago, I would probably have said that you're paranoid. That said, I've seen a shard or two myself and I can't deny that there is something strange about them."

Oliver pulled Leo's journal back in front of him and flipped it open to a page somewhere near the middle. He turned a few pages, scanning the tight scrawl of handwriting, searching for the beginning of a series of notes. "Here it is," he said, turning the notebook to face Hank. "Speaking of believing in something now that you would have called insane a few years ago, take a look at this."

Hank leaned forward, resting his elbows on the bar, and peered at the journal. His brown eyes flicked back and forth behind the glinting lenses of his eyeglasses as he scanned the notes. "May have found evidence that the eye is real," he muttered, reaching out to turn a page. Oliver waited, not wanting to taint Hank's opinion of the text any further. The index finger of Hank's left hand idly traced a sketch of a tree in the margins of the page as he read, "This ritual may open the gate to Yggdrasil itself." He drummed his fingers on the countertop, then turned another page in silence.

Oliver slipped wordlessly from his stool and crossed the room to his work table. Once there he pulled a battered old notebook from the small shelf beside the table, on which he kept notes and references that might prove useful to his current line of inquiry. This particular notebook was a collection of his own research notes from over five years ago, before he had begun keeping as much of his work as possible in electronic notebooks that could be easily encrypted and backed up in remote locations, or transferred to his phone for easy access in the field. Many of those old notes had been scanned and added to his digital library, those which he had deemed relevant to the ongoing quest to find the shards, or which had proven necessary to tracking down a more mundane relic for a client. This particular notebook, however, had never been so distinguished. In fact, Oliver had been more than a little surprised when he had managed to unearth it in a cardboard box of abandoned materials in the attic two days before.

He settled into a padded chair and thumbed the switch to turn on the desk lamp, then opened the notebook and began paging through it. Oliver had an exceptionally good memory, but it had been years since he even considered the theories described in this notebook. He continued to page through the book until he heard the creak of springs announce Hank lowering his bulk onto the sofa behind Oliver. Without looking around he said, "So, what do you think?"

"It's no more unlikely than anything else you've discovered," Hank said.

"What about that bit about Yggdrasil?"

"I don't know that I can take it literally, but how much more unlikely is it than the Creed, or the story you just told me about walking out of an explosion unscathed?"

Oliver smiled at that. He had to admit that his own stories were no more unbelievable than the clues he had uncovered in Leo's notebook. Sometimes, as he stood at the gates of some ancient temple, or when he had trouble sleeping at night, Oliver wondered at the direction his life had taken and tried to imagine how his childhood self would react to knowing what lay in store. He turned to face Hank and tapped the open page of the notebook he had been perusing. "I only ask because of this," he said. "Shortly after I got involved in the relic hunting game, I uncovered what I thought to be an ancient scroll from a monastery in Scotland."

Oliver pulled a photograph from his notebook and flipped it to Hank. Hank examined it, squinting at the photo and turning it to different angles as he attempted to read the faded lines of oddly squarish letters drawn on the ancient scroll in a precise hand. "That's old English, so don't worry about making out what the words mean," Oliver explained. "I spent a month translating that text, then another four months searching for corroborating texts and unusually precise legends that had already been translated into modern English."

"What is it?" Hank asked.

"An unusual version of the myth of how Odin lost his eye."

"How is it unusual?" Hank asked. "I'm familiar with the general story: Odin is a powerful god. He trades his eye for a drink from the well of wisdom. Now he is very wise and has a raven that flies around gathering information for him."

"Close, but not quite right," Oliver said. "Odin had two ravens. One was named Hugin, the other Munin. Each day the ravens fly out from Valhalla to survey the whole world, from the deepest roots of Yggdrasil, where dragons lurk in the shadows, to the farthest corners of Midgard. They return each evening to settle on Odin's shoulders and whisper news to him."

"I had it close enough for someone who isn't planning to use his knowledge of ancient myths to track down relics in ancient tombs," Hank said.

"True enough, but as you pointed out I'm a relic hunter who needs to get all the specifics right in order to work out the differences between reality and myth, especially when I'm trying to work out the aspects of the myth that are based on real events and relics. This text is unusual because it tells the myth of Odin surrendering his eye for a drink from the well of Mímir to gain wisdom, but it makes no mention of the ravens."

"But you just insisted that there were two ravens," Hank said.

"Precisely. Every account I've ever read of Odin's journey to the well of Mímir includes mention of his ravens. Children's tales in translation, old books in middle-English, ancient texts written in dead languages on the bleached skin of a goat, they all speak of Odin's ravens. Every account, that is, except this one, and this particular text not only lacks an element that is present in every other, but contains specific references to the location of the well of Mímir." Oliver leaned back in his swivel chair, crossed his legs, and pulled his old notebook from the desk to his lap. He began paging through it, reviewing his notes and thinking back to the weeks he had spent bent over ancient texts, searching for clues to support his theory that the absence of the ravens in this particular text indicated that the directions to the well were real. After while he looked up and saw Hank watching him.

"You think the well is real, don't you?" Hank said.

Oliver shrugged and flipped the notebook closed. The notes in Leo's journal had disturbed him, perhaps more than unexpectedly surviving the explosion in the underground temple. The evidence surrounding the well had been as strong as that which led him to the shards, but key parts were missing and he had been forced to abandon the search after nearly a year of fruitless inquiry.

"And if you do," Hank continued, "what are you going to do when you find it? Pluck out your own eye and toss it in?"

That was enough to make Oliver laugh.

"I'm serious. I don't want your next story to be about how you earned an eyepatch while trying to duplicate the efforts of a Norse god."

Oliver shook his head and, with considerable effort, hid his grin away behind a serious expression. "I promise, Hank, I'm not going to pluck out my own eye. I don't even know if I believe the well itself it real. What I suspect is that there may be a shard of the mechanism somehow linked to the origin of Odin, and that's where Leo's research journal comes in." He stood and walked over to the sofa, reaching a hand out towards Hank, who held up the leather bound book. Oliver took the journal and began turning pages until he reached the page that had renewed his interest in the myth of Odin's eye.

"This passage here, where Leo has translated a document that he stole from the collection of a neopagan priest in Germany. 'The unenlightened choose to believe in the trappings of myth, of magical hammers, ever-dripping serpent venom, and talking ravens, but the true servant of Odin knows the truth behind the accreted lies of the ages.'" Oliver read, turning the page so Hank could read the words scrawled out in Leo's precise handwriting. "That was written nearly five hundred years ago, if Leo's notes are correct."

"I saw that." Hank said, tapping the passage with his finger. "And I read on to the bit about, what was it, 'The path to true knowledge will carry the supplicant to the heart of Yggdrasil, and in the midst of its roots they will find the waters of wisdom." He looked at Oliver over the rims of his glasses, one dark eyebrow raised in skepticism. "You don't really believe this, do you? It's only been, what, a year since you returned from Egypt with a genuine biblical relic, how can you believe that the Norse gods were as real as that?"

"I didn't say that I do," Oliver said. "And for your information I don't believe that the Norse gods were actually gods, any more than I believe the world was formed from the body of a giant hung on the branches of an ash tree. What I do believe is that there are powers in this world that nobody truly understands, some of which are linked to the shards that I have been collecting, some to the Hebrew god, like the heartwood of the staff, and some to things that I can't even give a name to. I don't know the answers to everything, Hank, but I keep finding clues and that's why I keep searching for the shards of the mechanism."

He turned a page of the notebook in Hank's hands and pointed to a pasted-in photograph of an ancient parchment. "This look familiar?"

Hank pushed his glasses up on his nose and squinted down at the photo. He held out his left hand and snapped his fingers, then opened his hand to receive the notebook that Oliver placed in it. Oliver was actually rather surprised that it took him pointing out the connection before Hank spotted it. Hank's work repairing vintage cameras and, for a few select clients, engineering hidden compartments into everyday items, had developed in him a strong eye for spotting details in objects.

Hank glanced back and forth between the notebooks several times, then looked up at Oliver and said, "They're from the same parchment."

Oliver nodded. "I photographed that document in a museum in Berlin fifteen years ago. Leo stole his from the collection of an Aeser priest in Munich about two years ago, apparently while searching for clues that might lead him to a shard hidden somewhere in Germany."

"Aeser?" Hank asked. "I've never heard of that before."

"German neopagans. Started in the early twentieth century as part of a general surge in interest in European folk history," Oliver said.

"I see. So what does this tell you, Oliver? It's certainly interesting, both of you finding fragments of the same document hundreds of miles and many years apart, but it doesn't necessarily mean anything."

Oliver returned to his seat and settled deep into it, twisting around and swinging his legs up so his bare feet rested on the edge of the worktable. He steepled his fingers under his chin and tapped his pinkie fingers silently and he thought about Hank's question, trying to decide how he should respond. According to Leo's journal, the parchment Leo had stolen was only one of a dozen similar pieces, all related to Nordic culture. If he could arrange to inspect that collection he might find exactly the clue he needed to revitalize his search for the well of Mímir and Odin's eye.

After a long moment he sighed, slapped his palms against his thighs, and sat upright, swinging his feet back to the floor. "I think I'm going to Germany," he said. "I need to find the owner of this document and try to get a look at the remainder of their collection."

"That might prove difficult, seeing as you learned about the collection from a thief," Hank said.

"It's worth a shot."

Hank shook his head and gazed down at the notebooks on his lap, as if he didn't know whether to argue with Oliver or compliment his tenacity. He ran a finger down the page of Leo's journal and tapped on an entry, written below the translated text. "Your colleague noted the name of the man he stole this from. I've got a few contacts in Germany, collectors of antique cameras, who might be able to set up a more legitimate meeting for you, if you're interested."

Oliver nodded and grinned at Hank. "That would be perfect."

CHAPTER FOUR

Narrow Escape

Oliver zipped his leather jacket and pushed his hands into the pockets of his khakis as he turned left off Offenbachstraße and walked along Sibeliusstraße into a small community of houses set behind green gardens. The air of a September morning in Munich was chill, but it had not yet cooled enough to drive the lunchtime diners at the cafe down the street indoors. Half a dozen locals were gathered around a pair of tables that had been pulled together, sipping from dark bottles of beer and steaming cups of coffee as they carried on an animated discussion about the upcoming football match. Several tables away from the group sat a young woman with brown hair cut short over her ears, dressed in a tight red knit top and bleached bluejeans. She was bent over a sheaf of sheet music, idly tapping out a melody with her fingertips on the glass tabletop.

Oliver approached the woman and rapped on the tabletop with one knuckle to announce his presence. The woman started and looked up at Oliver in surprise, then smiled and made to stand, saying, "Herr Lucas?"

He gestured for her to remain seated and pulled a chair up to the table for himself. "Miss Evelyn Marby, I presume," Oliver said, speaking in German.

She nodded, then said, in a clear British accent, "Yes, I am she. And you would be Oliver Lucas."

"Yes. You speak English well," Oliver replied in English.

"Thank you. You speak German well enough, though clearly as an academic, not a native speaker."

Oliver raised an eyebrow as he cocked his head to the side, examining Evelyn Marby again. It was true that he spoke German with stiff formality and a strong Berlin accent, owing to his learning the language in college and primarily using it to translate ancient texts, rather than speaking it aloud in conversation. He had, however, not expected such forthrightness.

Evelyn laughed and extended a hand to him in greeting. "I have offended you. Sorry about that."

"No need to apologize," Oliver said, taking her hand and giving it a friendly squeeze. "You just caught me off guard. It's true though, my spoken German is terrible. I'm more of a scholar than a poet, you might say."

"There is no shame in that, Mr. Lucas. Far too many style themselves poets, to the suffering of our ears." Evelyn squared her sheet music and tucked it away into a heavy plastic folder that had been hidden away under the pile. "I am told that you wish to see what remains of my father's collection."

"That's correct. An associate put me in contact with your father's lawyer when he learned of Mr. Marby's death. Speaking of which, allow me to offer my condolences."

"No need, Mr. Lucas. You have never met me before and you did not know my father." She waved the sentiment away with a flick of her wrist and raised an arm to summon a waiter. "I will simply be pleased if the scraps that remain can be of use in your research."

Oliver nodded and glanced up as a waiter appeared. Evelyn switched back into rapid German, heavily accented with the tones of a native of the southern mountains, and requested her bill. While they waited for it to arrive Oliver said, "You mentioned that only part of the collection remains. May I ask what happened to the remaining pieces?"

"Certainly. My brother sold them."

"Ah," Oliver breathed, nodding solemnly and making no effort to conceal his disappointment. He had traveled far to see the collection that Evelyn had inherited from her father and it was frustrating to think that a crucial clue, one that had eluded him for a decade, might have been sold off.

Evelyn laughed and pulled a long, slim wallet of red leather from her back pocket. She began plucking Euro coins from a slit in the side of the wallet and laying them on the table as she said, "Do not worry, Mr. Lucas, we have not sold them to some private collector who will lock them away where academics like you can never get to them. If the information you seek is no longer present in the collection, I will gladly instruct my attorney to request that you are granted access by the new owners."

"That's good to hear, Ms. Marby," Oliver said. He stood, pushed his chair back under the table, and gestured for Evelyn to take the lead.

She rose, gathered her belongings, and guided Oliver through the thicket of tables to the wide sidewalk that ran along both sides of the street. As they reached the sidewalk and turned left down the narrow street she said, "What exactly do you study, Mr. Lucas?"

"The origins of myths. I am currently writing a book about the emergence of European folklore, specifically how the religious beliefs of ancient peoples transitioned into folk tales as traditional beliefs were subsumed and overridden by the burgeoning Christian religion."

Evelyn broke her stride and turned to face Oliver on the sidewalk, face contorted in near exasperation. "Please do not tell me you're here looking for more fuel for the fires of religious arguments, I really have had quite enough of that."

Oliver shook his head vigorously and waved his hands in denial. He had expected that the daughter of Dietrich Marby, collector of Germanic artifacts and noted promoter of a return to the ancient Nordic religion, would be more likely to trust him if he claimed to be working on a project compatible with her father's beliefs, but he seemed to have misestimated her own feelings on the issue. Fortunately, he seemed to have correctly judged her esteem for academics. "No, no. I assure you that is not my purpose. Honestly, Ms. Marby, this is entirely an academic work. I have no agenda." Oliver drooped his shoulders in shame and looked past Evelyn for a moment, then looked directly into her eyes with all the sadness and frustration a failed academic could muster and said, "Even if I had an agenda, this is going to be published by the university press. I doubt that many people will ever read it."

Her face remained hard for a moment as she held his gaze, then Evelyn gave him a conciliatory smile and laid a hand on his arm and gave it a slight squeeze. "No, I apologize. My father was man of great passion and his beliefs drove a deep cleft through our family."

Oliver nodded and gestured for them to continue walking. As they did, Evelyn explained, "I do not wish to explain everything, as it has no bearing on your research and some of the reasons are quite private, but suffice it to say that as my brother and I grew older we became disenchanted with our parents' belief that the ancient Norse religion was still relevant. Eventually, after we both had moved away, we each found our own paths." Evelyn's voice trailed off and they walked in silence for about a minute, paused at a corner, then crossed the street to stand at the gate of a small house that was mostly hidden from view by a thick growth of untrimmed shrubbery. A high wrought iron fence separated the garden from the road, broken only by a pair of whitewashed brick columns that supported an ornate garden gate and mailbox.

"I'm sorry to hear about your troubles," Oliver said, leaning against the column with the mailbox atop it.

"Do not concern yourself. I should not have allowed my private matters to interfere with our dealings," Evelyn said.

She sighed and rested the sheaf of sheet music on the other column, then extracted a brass key from her front pocket. She inserted the key into a large lock set into the gate, turned it clockwise, and frowned. She turned the key counterclockwise and the lock emitted a heavy "clank." She shook her head and tuned the ornately wrought handle, but the gate remained shut.

"Is something wrong?" Oliver asked.

Evelyn shook her head and turned the key again. The lock clanked and this time, when she turned the handle, the gate swung open silently on well oiled hinges. "Es ist nicht," she muttered. "The lock, it just seemed to have already been open. Perhaps my brother forgot to lock the gate after supervising the sale." She picked up her sheet music and stepped through the gate, then waved for Oliver to follow her.

Oliver did so, pausing only briefly at the gate to run his eyes over the lock. It was well oiled, but the metal was old and worn, making it impossible to tell whether the lock had been picked without a more thorough examination. *Don't worry so much,* he told himself as he hurried to catch up with Evelyn.

The garden path meandered around several overgrown holly bushes, skirted the edge of a garden bed bursting with herbs and flowers, their heads turning brown as the grip of autumn tightened around them, and ended at the whitewashed wall of the house. A door was set into the wall between two curtained windows, the wood of it painted bright red and the three angled window slits showing a dark room through thick panes of rippling glass.

When he reached the door she held out her sheet music to him and Oliver accepted the folder, holding it for her while she replaced the gate key in her pocket and extracted a smaller, more conventional house key. Evelyn smiled at Oliver and inserted the key into the lock. She turned it and frowned.

"Nicht gut," she growled, shoving the door open and continuing to mutter incomprehensibly to herself in German.

Oliver was about to suggest that they wait outside and call the police, or at least call her brother to verify that he could have forgotten to lock both the gate and the house door, but before he could say anything she strode into the house, still muttering. An uneasy feeling started gnawing at Oliver's gut. He followed Evelyn through the doorway into the dark entrance hall, wishing that he had been able to bring a gun with him. Unfortunately, he had not been able to acquire a German firearms permit and it had seemed unwise to risk smuggling a gun into the country on what he had anticipated to be a short and uneventful visit.

"The collection is in my father's study, just up here," Evelyn said, pressing a switch on the wall to turn on a ceiling fixture. The yellow light of a dim incandescent bulb oozed through decades of nicotine tar on the thick old glass of the ceiling fixture to illuminate a narrow hallway with wood paneled walls which led to a dark staircase at the far end. A stained oak bench sat against the right-hand wall under the wooden pegs of a coatrack. The air was dry and redolent of old tobacco smoke and dust.

Oliver closed the door and followed Evelyn towards the staircase. As they proceeded down the hall they passed closed doors on either side, each leading, Oliver presumed, to a different room of the house. He had seen this type of architecture before in old homes, especially in cold regions. The layout isolated each room from the others and from the draft of the door, allowing for more efficient heating of occupied rooms. Generally Oliver admired the ingenuity of the design, but at the moment, with the suspicion that someone might have broken into the house and could still be waiting for them, he would have paid to be walking through an open loft apartment. They reached the staircase and Evelyn pressed a second switch to illuminate the steps leading up to the second floor of the house.

"I am sorry for the condition of the house," she said, glancing over her shoulder as she reached the tight landing at the top of the steps. "My father lived here alone for nearly ten years after my mother died and he came to be as obsessed with pipe tobacco as with ancient religions. The housekeeper e-mailed me more than once to complain." She smiled wanly and turned to open the heavy oak door at the end of the landing.

The door swung inwards and Oliver caught a glimpse of a deeply shadowed room, the walls lined with wide shelves and the center of the floor occupied by a large desk or table. Then a dark figure exploded from the doorway.

A tattered black robe billowed from the figure as it slammed into Evelyn, knocking her back towards Oliver. She slammed into him and they both nearly tumbled down the staircase, but Oliver managed to grab the railing with a single outstretched arm. Sheets of paper burst into the air and fluttered down like leaves in a strong wind as the intruder whirled around and planted a sharp kick in the center of Evelyn's chest, knocking her away from Oliver and sending her careening down the steps. The figure froze for half a second and seemed to glare at Oliver from beneath the deep cowl of its cloak, then let loose an unintelligible scream of rage and threw itself at Oliver. Half fallen and unbalanced at the edge of the top step, Oliver was unable to evade the initial flurry of blows. Three solid blows hammered into his ribs and a brutal kick would have shattered his kneecap if the railing had not torn free of the wall at just that moment, dropping Oliver to the steep incline of the steps.

The missed kick threw the figure off balance. It thudded awkwardly against the wall of the landing, regained its footing, and leapt over Oliver's sprawled body to land on its heels halfway down the staircase. It skidded to the bottom of the steps and came to rest beside Evelyn, who was just tottering to her feet, her arms flailing loosely and her eyes unfocused.

The figure grabbed the front of her jacket just under the chin and slammed her against a wall. Its hooded face arched over her and Oliver heard the whisper of a rasping voice. The hand loosened on her throat just enough for her to whimper a response.

He rolled to his feet and launched himself down the steps, driven by an urge to go defend Evelyn from the cloaked figure. It wasn't until he was already half way down the steps that he saw the edge of the blade glinting beneath the tattered cloak. He acted on instinct, twisting as he fell so his feet slammed into the figure's legs, knocking it over and away from Evelyn. The blade scored a deep gouge into the floor as the figure toppled, righted itself, and raised the gleaming blade to thrust it down into Oliver's chest.

Oliver rolled out of the way just in time and the blade sliced through the leather of his jacket and across his right shoulder. Evelyn let out a choked scream and threw herself at the figure. She clawed at his face and kicked a knee into his groin.

The figure roared and swiped upward with its sword, the tattered sleeves of its cloak billowing like the wings of an angel of death. Oliver kicked upward before the blade had completed its path, slamming his booted foot into the depths of the figure's cloak. The figure gasped and stumbled backwards, its sword blow swing wild and cutting deep into Evelyn's hip, rather than slicing her in half. Before it could recover, Oliver rolled to his feet and slammed his right fist into the shadowed cowl. He felt his knuckles sink deep into a rough face that felt as if it were wrapped in bandages. The figure screamed in agony and dropped its sword as it stumbled backwards and collided with the paneled wall. Oliver struck out again, hammering it in the face with his left fist. It lurched to the side and Oliver's next punch cracked the wood paneling beside its head.

The cloaked intruder shoved Oliver away with a roar. Oliver landed heavily on his rear and slid across the varnished wood. As he came to rest he felt the warm leather of the sword hilt under his fingers. He leapt to his feet, brandishing the sword at the figure. It froze, chest heaving, hot breath rasping out in painful gusts as it regarded Oliver, then it spun about and launched itself towards the door at the end of the hall. It ripped the door open, turned, silhouetted by the bright daylight outside, and glared back at Oliver and Evelyn. It gave one last unintelligible roar and spat a gob of dark blood at the floor between them, then turned and ran out into the garden.

Oliver spun away from the doorway to see Evelyn laying

on the floor, groaning with the effort of repressing a scream. Her hands were clenched over a deep gash in her hip, but the blood still poured out between them to soak the fabric of her jeans and spill onto the floor in a widening pool.

Oliver turned away from her and shoved open the nearest door, revealing a sparsely furnished living room. That might help, but it was far from optimal. He turned away and strode to the next door, pulling his cell phone from a pocket as he went. A glance assured him that it had not been destroyed in the fight. He kicked the next door open as he thumbed 112 and pressed the call button to summon the local emergency services. He held the phone up to an ear and surveyed the room he had just entered, doing his best to ignore Evelyn's agonized screams form the hall behind. This room was a kitchen. The stove and refrigerator gleamed with the slick steel of modern appliances, but the remainder of the room was classic rustic European, down to the large pine table at the center of the room, covered with a dark green tablecloth.

A female voice came through the phone on Oliver's ear, speaking German with the practiced calm of an experienced emergency operator. Oliver thumbed the speaker phone function and said in German, "A woman has been injured at 7 Sibeliusstraße. Get here fast."

He slipped the phone into the pocket of his jacket and ripped the tablecloth from the table. He ignored the measured voice of the operator demanding more details, trusting that Evelyn's screams would be sufficient proof for the operator to send an ambulance, and strode back into the hallway. Evelyn still lay on the floor in the middle of a widening pool of blood. Oliver snatched up the sword and hurried towards Evelyn. Her eyes went wide as he hefted the blade, but she quickly relaxed as he smiled at her and began slicing the tablecloth into strips.

"Move your hands," he said in German, prodding at Evelyn's arm with the flat of the sword.

She hesitated for just a moment, then complied. Oliver laid a folded strip of cloth over the wound in her hip and ordered her to press her hands to it again. She did so, wincing as she applied pressure to the cut. Oliver spoke to her in German as he continued to fold the strips of cloth into bandages and pass them to her, "This isn't actually that bad, compared to what it could have been. A blade like this could have done some serious damage. There's a lot of blood, but that's just because the wound is deep, maybe to the bone, It isn't pumping out of you though, so I don't think there's any arterial damage."

His words seemed to calm Evelyn and before long she said, through gritted teeth, "You are surprisingly calm about this situation."

Oliver shrugged. There was little point in maintaining his cover at the moment, especially after she had seen him fight off the cloaked figure and calmly administer first aid to a sword wound. "I'm not exactly what you would call a pure academic," he admitted. "In fact, I haven't worked at a university in nearly fifteen years."

"You could have fooled me," she said in English.

Oliver grinned at the joke and shrugged before passing her one last bandage. "That's good. Keep that sense of humor and you'll be back on your feet quick. You're going to need a new copy of that score though," he said, spotting a blood soaked page of music resting at the foot of the steps.

Once Evelyn's wound was bandaged sufficiently that Oliver was no longer concerned that she might die of blood loss, he stepped closer to the open door to better examine the sword in a bright shaft of daylight. The blade was about two and a half feet long and only two inches wide at the hilt. The flat of the blade ran straight until an inch from the end, where the two razor sharp edges cut inward at a forty-five degree angle to meet at a wickedly sharp point. The blade was forged from a grey metal that had a dull, almost mottled appearance, except for the glittering edge and a series of angular runes that were etched into the flat of the blade. These gleamed as bright as the cutting edge, the glimmer of reflected sunlight against the surrounding matte grey metal making the runes seem to burn with a twinkling silver and gold fire. Oliver rested the flat of the blade against his left palm and opened his right hand to reveal a grip of wrapped leather. The stained brown strips twisted in tight spirals of mahogany, stained a deeper brown in places with what Oliver imagined to be the blood and sweat of a hundred battles, from the cross guard to the pommel. Both of these were crafted of the same flat grey metal as the blade.

"That looks like a very old sword," Evelyn remarked. Oliver glanced away from the blade and saw that she had pulled herself into a seated position, leaning against the splintered paneling of the wall.

"Yes. I believe it is," he replied. He rested the sword on the floor and pulled his phone out of his pocket, ignoring the shrill demands of the emergency operator that he reply to her requests for information, and began photographing the sword from several angles. He was careful to capture close shots of the runes on both sides of the blade, as well as an image of a mark, whether a rune or battle scar he could not say for sure, on the end of the pommel.

Oliver finished his photographs just as the wail of sirens reached their ears through the garden. He ended the call and put his phone away, then looked up at Evelyn and said, "I don't suppose I could convince you to say this is your family's sword and the intruder attacked you with it?"

She looked back at him with her mouth wide open, her head shaking mutely back and forth. She raised a trembling hand and pointed it towards him.

Oliver looked down and cursed. The sword had disappeared, replaced by a shimmering haze of silver mist.

Oliver looked back to Evelyn and shook his head. He had no idea who the cloaked figure was, but it was painfully obvious, to him at least, that it had not been the sort of person who would leave a trail for police to follow. The more he thought about it, the more Oliver was beginning to suspect that the intruder had been waiting for them. He waved away the mist and slid towards Evelyn.

"What did he ask you?" Oliver asked her.

Evelyn started at the question and looked at him, her mouth moving in quiet jerking motions.

"He's gone, Evelyn. He's gone and the police will be here soon. Just tell me what he wanted to know and maybe I can stop him from coming back."

She looked at him with pleading eyes, "How can you?"

"Like you said, I'm no academic. Let's just say that I'm in the business of finding very special artifacts, and at times I've crossed paths with people who wanted to hurt me. So far, I've always come out on top. Me, and the people I care about," Oliver said. He tried to give her a reassuring look, but doubted that it was effective.

She shivered and pulled her arms tight around her body, looking away from him and up the damaged and blood spattered stairway. She winced, though Oliver could not have said whether it was because of her bandages or the memory of the fight. The sirens grew suddenly louder and Oliver knew they would not have long until she was taken away in an ambulance.

He laid a land on her shoulder and spoke softly, "Please."

She looked back at him and said, "He asked where my father's collection went."

Oliver nodded, encouragingly.

"He wanted to know about the Wagner folio."

"Did you tell him where it went?" Oliver asked.

She nodded. The sirens had reached their apex and Oliver could just hear the sound of shouting voices beyond the screen of garden foliage.

"Tell me, please."

"I sold it, to the collection of Schloss Neuschwanstein."

CHAPTER FIVE

Recovery

It took nearly three hours for Oliver to extricate himself from the fallout of the fight in Dietrich Marby's home. The police, who arrived shortly after the paramedics, were especially irate that he had not responded to any of the emergency services operator's requests for information, but Evelyn's repeated assertions that he had saved her life dissuaded them from pressing him too hard for answers. After that, the ambulance had carried them both away to a local hospital, where the wound in Oliver's arm had been cleaned, patched with liquid stitches, and he had been released into the custody of two waiting detectives. He had answered their questions in a cramped hospital conference room while sipping bitter coffee from an automated dispenser, answering in terse German as they questioned him in clipped English and smiling to himself each time he detected a gleam of frustration in their eyes.

Oliver took a taxi to his hotel, a three star Regent located mere blocks from the Munich train station, and closed his eyes as the car threaded through late afternoon traffic. He allowed the events of the afternoon to play out behind his eyelids. He hadn't even seen the bandages beneath the deep hood of the intruder's cloak, let alone recognized a face, and the voice had been an unrecognizable rasp, but there had been something familiar about the intruder. Something in the turn of its body or the cadence of its guttural voice.

The taxi eased to a stop at the curb outside his hotel. Oliver paid the driver and hurried through the lobby and up to his room. The door locked behind him, Oliver shrugged out of his torn jacket, wincing as the stitches in his arm strained with the movement, and collapsed into a chair by the window. Outside and several floors below his window the fading sunlight had set the autumn leaves on fire. He gazed out at them for a while as his mind paced a slow spiral around the problem of the day.

His fingers traced the edges of the cut in his leather jacket. It had been sliced cleanly, with no sign of tearing, except at the corners where he had stretched it in the hours since the fight. The blade had been extraordinarily sharp and the cloaked figure had been remarkably strong, if a little unbalanced by whatever injuries had caused him to bandage his face. There had been something eerily familiar about the stance of the figure as it stood silhouetted in the doorway, but Oliver couldn't place it. He was accustomed to facing danger in his line of work, and to fighting for his life against a wide variety of foes, so it might take him days to recall the identity of the swordsman. And that was assuming that he hadn't just fixated on some common feature of sword-wielding madmen.

Oliver had come to Germany looking for clues in ancient manuscripts, but had now crossed paths with someone else who was seeking a specific document. Whether the intruder was a mad collector, a supernatural guardian, or something altogether stranger, he could not say, but Oliver could feel a jealous hunger rising up within him. It would be several days at least before he could return to the Marby residence to view the collection, and that was assuming that Evelyn was willing to help him again, so there was time to consider an alternative course.

He pulled his phone from the inside pocket of his jacket and tossed the jacket to the floor beside the chair. A few flicks and taps later and he was waiting impatiently for Hank to answer his phone.

"Did you find anything?" Hank asked, the moment he the call connected.

"Somebody is impatient," Oliver said, smiling to himself.

"I'm finally involved in one of your adventures, of course I'm impatient to see how it worked out. That, and I've got a few people over, so if we could get to the point..."

"Dinner and a movie at Hank's place?"

"What else on a blustery Saturday evening? Tonight it's ratatouille and Ratatouille." Hank paused, as if he sensed Oliver's wry smile over the cracking phone connection, then said, "Everyone had to bring their kids along this week, so we decided to... anyway, why am I defending my taste in films to you of all..." He blustered incoherently a few more times, then fell silent.

Oliver waited.

"So, did you find any clues or not?" Hank demanded.

"No. I don't want to say too much over the phone, but I'll send my cousin an update and you can get the details from her. Listen, Hank, I've got another reason for contacting you now. I need your help with something."

"Oh, what would that be?" The phone cut out as it squelched a loud creaking noise. Oliver could picture Hank settling his bulk into one of the heavy old wood and leather chairs in his library.

"I don't know for sure yet, but I think this search just took an abrupt turn towards Wagner, and since I know you're a great fan of his works, and already in the know on this particular quest, I thought that you could provide some background for me."

"Certainly. What do you need?"

"Whatever you can get me about Wagner and German mythology."

Hank spluttered and began to laugh, the hearty expulsions of mirth cutting out as his phone attempted to filter the volume. He laughed for so long that Oliver first rolled his eyes, then shook his head, then jumped to his feet in exasperation as he shouted, "Hank, get a hold of yourself. I just want a little help here."

Hank stifled his laughter just long enough to say, "Oliver, you do realize..." Then he started laughing again. Oliver paced the hotel room a few times, then settled down on the foot of the bed and began to remove his boots while he waited for Hank to collect himself. As Oliver was pulling off his second boot Hank finally said, "Oliver, that's like asking me for a brief summary of how Ansel Adams influenced landscape photographers, or what Stanley Kubrick had to do with American cinematography. It's a really big question, Oliver."

"I know that. Remember that I investigated the possibility of a shard being behind elements of Norse mythology years ago. I encountered Wagner's works then, but considered them too modern to be worth my time. Now I'm rethinking that assessment."

"So where should I start?"

"Anything you can give me on Wagner's source material should be a good start, as well as information related to any particular obsessions of his."

"Give me a few days. I must get back to my party tonight and I'm in the middle of a delicate Polaroid reconstruction project at the camera shop, but I should have something for you before long," Hank said.

"Thanks. Just call Amber when you're done and she'll

come by the shop to pick it up."

"And you?"

"I'm going to Neuschwanstein castle."

Oliver disconnected the call and switched to his Twitter app. He selected the secure account that he used for communicating with Amber while out in the field and send her a direct message:

In Germany. Need you to transfer data from Hank to me at some point. New leads on the Norse shard.

It might take Amber some time to reply if she was busy, which was more often the case these days, but Oliver knew he could rely on her to reply. His cousin had grown less involved in his adventures since they had returned together from the jungles of South America. That quest that had been Oliver's first, and Amber's only, adventure to recover a relic, and it had had vastly different effects on the two cousins. Amber had returned with the mystery of her parents' death resolved and a strong impulse to settle down into suburban comfort, while the deadly thrill of the journey had kindled a fiery hunger for exploration in Oliver and set him on his quest to recover the remaining shards. Since then Amber had been both Oliver's contact in America when he went off on wild adventures across the globe and his touchstone for when a quest showed the potential of going overboard.

Oliver stepped into the cramped bathroom and cranked the shower to full heat, then began undressing. The stitches on his shoulder ached as he pulled his undershirt shirt over his head and, with frustrated glance at the bloodstained fabric, threw it into the trash can beside the bed. Normally he would have been more circumspect about disposing of bloodied, or otherwise suspicious, gear, but both his presence and injury during the attack at the Marby home were on record with the Munich police, so he wasn't overly concerned about the maids reporting the discovery of a bloody shirt in his room. By the time he finished undressing steam was beginning to billow out of the bathroom. He checked his phone, still no message from Amber, and strode through the steam to wash the aches and filth of the day from his abused body.

CHAPTER SIX

NEUSCHWANSTEIN

Early the next morning Oliver walked from his hotel to the train station and used cash to purchase a rail pass. He boarded the blue Munich intracity metro train and rode twenty minutes to a transfer station at the edge of the city. He waited in the passenger lounge there for about half an hour, then switched over to a slick high speed train that carried him in luxuriant comfort, at least by the standards of American railways, to the city of Füssen, two hours south-west of Munich. According to the travel searches he had conducted the night before, Oliver could have rented a car and driven to Füssen in half the time, but he had elected to travel by rail instead for two simple reasons: The first was that he could spend his transit time absorbing information about the connection between Wagner and Norse mythology through his phone. The second was that he had a vague sense that this journey, like so many others he had undertaken in recent years, might take a turn towards the distasteful, if not outright illegal. If that were the case, it would be best if he could claim to be resting in his hotel room after a brutal, and fully documented, attack the day before. Not the strongest of alibis, perhaps, but it would be better than nothing. Arriving in Füssen, Oliver hired a taxi to drive him to Neuschwanstein Castle, then settled into the back seat to watch the countryside roll by.

The taxi carried Oliver through the center of town, past

dozens of stucco and stone houses, shops, and government buildings, each painted in a variation of soft pastels and topped with red tile roofs. The road passed over a narrow bridge of blacked steel and white concrete, which spanned the meandering waters of a river so calm that the brilliant greens, yellows, and golds of the autumn foliage were reflected against it in impressionistic perfection. Above the trees Oliver could see the snowcapped peaks of the Alps marching along the German-Swiss border to the south. The road meandered through two or three villages, little more than collections of houses and shops gathered around a school or church and surrounded by vast swathes of farmland, then began climbing the face of a mountain towards the towers of the castle high above.

Tucked in between the green flecked rocky peaks of higher mountains on three sides, the foundations of Neuschwanstein Castle rose up atop an outcropping of solid rock that emerged from the surrounding evergreen forest. Gleaming walls and towers of white stone surged upwards to meet the soft green grey of the copper roof. Perched atop the mountain like a proud eagle, displaying its plumage as it gazed down upon the valley below, Neuschwanstein was the picture book image of a fairytale castle. In fact, Oliver had learned on his train ride from Munich that the castle was rumored to be an inspiration for the design of several fictional castles, including Disney's iconic interpretation of Cinderella's castle.

The taxi deposited Oliver at the base of a sweeping approach that led up to the tall curved gateway of rich oak studded with iron, which was set into the towering walls of red brick accented with large blocks of white stone. The same white stone formed the curving walls of the corner towers and the soaring expanse of the other castle walls. He paid the driver, once again in cash, and joined the crowd of tourists meandering towards the entrance.

Oliver was not sure what course he would follow in continuing his investigation, but Evelyn Marby had told the cloaked intruder, and him, that she had sold the Wagner folio, whatever that might be, to the collection here at Neuschwanstein. He snagged a brochure from an oak paper rack beside the wicket gate and flipped it open as he stepped into the inner courtyard. Before he could begin to read, though, Oliver's hands fell before him and he nearly dropped the glossy paper pamphlet as his gaze drifted upwards in slack-jawed wonder.

Before him and to his right the white castle walls climbed upwards into a cloudless sky of a glorious pure azure blue, broken only by tall windows of thick glass, which reflected the sky with golden hue. Stone steps in front of him mounted to a second level of courtyard that marched away to the walls of the castle itself, while a narrower staircase, to his right, climbed up to to a third floor arcade that led to a set of red stained oak doors leading into the castle. The one place Oliver could look without being overwhelmed by glorious architecture was to his left, but that was no true relief from the visual assault as looking in that direction afforded him a sweeping view of the mountains of the Swiss border, marching upwards and away in successive rows of green pines, grey stone, and glistening white snowcaps as far as he could see.

Oliver felt a hand on his shoulder and turned to see a tall woman dressed in a blue velvet uniform motioning him to step out of the way of the small crowd that had gathering in the gateway behind him.

"Please step aside," the woman asked him in German.

He smiled apologetically and stepped over to lean against

the wall beside the gateway, permitting the other tourists to pass him as he continued to gaze upwards. Despite outward appearances, Oliver's examination of the courtyard was not entirely captivated reverie. He was also searching for weaknesses in the castle security and, much to his frustration, seeing none so far.

He glanced down to the brochure in his hand. The glossy paper was dark blue, printed with gold lettering, and bore several full color photos of a series of documents and wooden idols. The German text at the top of the folded paper proclaimed, "Wagner's Inspiration." The text beneath the photos went on to describe an exhibition of artifacts and documents that related the earliest known versions of the myths that had formed the basis of Wagner's Ring Cycle. When he unfolded the brochure Oliver nearly laughed out loud with glee at his good fortune. Spread across two panels of the inside of the brochure was a photo of a battered velum folio, the brittle, stained pages unfolded to reveal lines of faded brown ink. The left edge of the document faded into the rich blue backdrop and, much to Oliver's disappointment, the artistic photo filters and wide zoom angle conspired to make it practically impossible for him to read the text on the folio. The gold text on the inside of the rightmost panel exclaimed the value of the centerpiece of this exhibition, a folio that had belonged to Wagner himself, and which had been only recently recovered from a private collector after being lost to history in the years leading up to the second world war.

This had to be the folio that his fiendish attacker had sought.

Oliver closed the pamphlet and slipped it into a jacket pocket, then strode towards the ticket booth discretely nestled into one of the narrow arcades beneath the stairs to his right. It was starting to look like finding Marby's Wagner folio might be easier than he had expected.

"Has this display started yet?" Oliver asked the attendant, speaking in German, when he reached the front of the ticket line.

The attendant, an elderly man with half-rim glasses under a thick head of gray hair, dressed in a velvet blue uniform much like the one of the woman who had hurried Oliver along, examined the brochure, then shook his head. "No, not yet."

"That's disappointing," Oliver said. Acting on a hunch, he continued, "I traveled here from Munich especially to see the idols. I thought they were to be the centerpiece of the display."

The booth attendant glanced downwards, checking a schedule that was hidden from Oliver's view. "This looks to be the announcement brochure that we put out this morning, which," he leaned closer to Oliver and shook his head slightly as he spoke, "was produced in something of a hurry. The manuscript it highlights was only recently acquired by the institute and there's been quite a rush to rearrange the exhibition around it."

Oliver sighed in mock exasperation and shook his head, then asked, "Do you know when this display will actually open?"

"Next Thursday."

"There wouldn't be any way for me to slip in early, would there? I'm writing a book on the development of..." Oliver trailed off as the man shook his white head gravely.

"No. I'm sorry, sir, but if you need academic access you could to contact our director of research. Would you like her phone number?"

Oliver knew when it was impossible to go any further. He

had spent enough hours bartering in crowded marketplaces across the globe, and shouting down his father over his career plans on the richly manicured lawns of Fairfax county golf clubs, that he knew when he was facing the end of a conversation.

He accepted a card with the phone number of the director of research hand printed across it in precise lettering and purchased a ticket to the next castle tour. Though he would not be able to see the documents today, Oliver thought it wise to take advantage of the opportunity to scope out the castle's security. That, and it never hurt to pause and admire great works of art.

The tour, which lasted about half an hour, wound throughout the first and second floors of the castle, pausing to allow the guests to gawk at the gold encrusted pillars and furniture, the murals of European monarchs, knights, and mythic characters, and the sheer grandiosity of the architecture itself. The tour guide, an elderly woman dressed in the same royal blue uniform as the guards and ticket booth attendants, explained the history of the castle to the group. Oliver only paid the guide passing attention. Instead he focused on searching each room and corridor for security devices. It was growing increasingly difficult to spot cameras, microphones, and pressure sensors these days, Oliver had spent enough money securing his own apartment that he was familiar with the state of the art in consumer spy gear, but in his experience the average museum security director preferred to spend their budget on visible security measures intended to deter thieves, rather than on more readily concealed devices that would merely record the theft. The Neuschwanstein castle staff was no different. Each room Oliver entered was watched over by at least two cameras, their black lenses surrounded by the milky white bubbles of infrared emitters, all neatly tucked away between the gilt cornices.

Oliver was not a professional, or even amateur, thief. He made a living of uncovering ancient secrets and slipping, slashing, or shooting his way into ancient ruins where what passed for surveillance was more likely to consist of a deathtrap or ancient curse, but cautious observation of his surroundings had become an ingrained habit over the years.

It wasn't looking good for him breaking into the castle, even if he found where the folio was kept.

When the tour ended, Oliver found himself in the brisk air of the courtyard once more. He wandered the perimeter of the castle for another quarter hour, doing his best to remain close to clumps of tourists as he used his phone to photograph the exterior. He mentally kicked himself for leaving his professional equipment in the hotel safe, rather than bringing it along. With a better zoom lens he might have been able to get a better look at the security on the second and third floors of the castle. Eventually he jumped aboard a tourist shuttle bus to ride back to the train station.

Oliver arrived back at his hotel in Munich in the early evening. He was in a foul mood, having spent an entire day, and a sizable amount of money, to learn almost nothing. A rational voice at the back of his mind told Oliver that he had made the journey out to Neuschwanstein purely on speculation, but that did little to assuage his mood. This entire venture was based on the supposition that a rival had been more successful than he in tracking down a shard, one which Oliver had long ago given up finding, and his repeated failures since arriving in Germany had brought back the feelings of failure that Oliver bitterly recalled from the days when he had given up on the search and thrown his research notebook into a box.

It didn't help matters that he still had not heard from Hank or Amber.

He slammed his keycard into the hotel door, waited for the light on the handle to blink green, then ripped the card out and pushed through. Oliver shoved the door shut behind him and was surprised at the darkness of the room, as the autumn sunlight had still been gleaming off the windows of the office towers surrounding his hotel when he had entered the building. "Damn it," he muttered, "do not disturb means keep out."

He reached out blindly and found the light switch on the wall beside the bathroom door.

A man in a tattered black cloak lounged in the chair beside the window. He face was lost in the inky shadow of his cowl. A hand emerged from the cloak to drape over the pommel of a long sword of gray metal, which leaned against one knee. On his right shoulder perched a large raven, its eyes glinting at Oliver in the bright lamplight.

"Good to see you alive, Oliver," he said in a voice like a glacier crushing gravel beneath its mighty weight, "I believe you will be of use to me."

CHAPTER SEVEN
MEAD HALL

Oliver reached instinctively for the gun under his leather jacket, only to remember that he was unarmed as his fingers slid across the fabric of his shirt. Damn, he thought. He spun to pull the door open and escape into the hallway, but the sleek white metal door of the hotel had vanished, replaced with a heavy double door of rough-hewn oak, flanked by flickering torches held to the wall in iron-banded brackets. A gust of cold air blew in beneath the door, disturbing the filthy mat of straw and mud beneath Oliver's feet, carrying with it the heady scent of wood smoke, animal dung, and human sweat. He turned again and saw the cloaked man, now lounging in a large seat made from stripped branches of white ash wood, bent, twisted, and pegged together into the form of a sprawling throne.

The man laughed. His deep voice croaked out from the fold of his dark robe in harsh gusts. He reached down into the shadows beside his chair and hefted a horn tankard brimming with a foamy golden brew. He plunged the vessel into the shadows of his hood and raised it, drinking deeply with loud, slurping chugs that sent cascades of yellow foam dripping down the front of his black cloak.

Oliver slapped himself hard across the face and shook his head. He looked around, hoping that the hotel room would have returned, but still found himself standing at the entrance to a drafty longhouse built of hewn logs, mud, and straw. As his eyes adjusted to the smoky half light of the flickering torches he discerned the shapes of dozens of men, women, and dogs heaped together in gently heaving piles of sleeping flesh beneath thick rugs of wolf hide.

"I've got to be imagining this. I've been knocked out, or drugged, or..." Oliver muttered. He staggered forward and poked tentatively at the thick pine slabs of the long table that occupied the center of the room. The wood was cold, rough, and as real as anything he had ever touched. Oliver placed both palms against it and leaned forward heavily. His head was pounding and, despite the seeming cold reality of the place, he was increasingly certain that he was hallucinating.

"Or what?" the cloaked man growled. He set the tankard down on the split log table beside him and swatted at the raven on his shoulder with a large, scarred and callused hand. "Perhaps you're dead. Did you think of that? I might have welcomed you as a living man, but to tell you the truth, most of the mortal souls I have brought to this place have been close to death, so perhaps you are dead. Imagine that, you rogue, your body laying on the carpet of that miserable hotel room, blood gushing from a mortal head wound, hallucinating this whole experience as the thief who struck you rifles through your pockets for credit cards and cash."

Oliver shivered at the thought. He was certain that he was still alive, but the dark gravity of the man's voice sent shivers of fear down his spine.

The man laughed again and grasped the hilt of his sword with one scarred hand. He slammed the metal-tipped scabbard into the morass of filthy straw at his feet and used the sword as a cane to lever himself upright. The raven squawked and flapped its wings loudly, turning a lazy circle around the rafters of the longhouse before diving down to perch on the man's shoulder again.

"Who are you?" Oliver asked. His voice cracked half way through the question and he coughed, hating the weakness he had shown, stood upright, and demanded, "What is this place and why have you brought me here?"

"You do not recognize me, or know my home? Bah, what is the world coming to when a man can be plucked from the dreary sterility of his modern surroundings and carried to the most famous mead hall of all time and he can do nothing but complain," the man growled. He stooped and lifted the tankard, which Oliver noted was once again brimming with a frothy brew, from beside his seat, then drank from it again. Thirst satiated, he strode forward and slammed the tankard on the slab tabletop, causing the dark yellow liquid within to slosh up and over the edge of the cup. It splashed out onto the waxed pine and sloshed outward like a puddle of liquid gold in the torchlight.

"I've never seen you before," Oliver countered, "though perhaps I might recognize you if I could see your face. For all I can see, you're the man who attacked me yesterday, though from your voice I'd wager that was another madman with a cloak and sword. Are there a lot of you about here in Munich?"

"Do not jest about such matters!" the man roared, slamming his fist down on the table with such force that another wave of golden brew spilled out across the table. "There are few enough of us left these days and fewer still who remember what they truly are."

"And who are you then?" Oliver said. If this was a hallucination, it was a damn convincing one. The moment of panic had passed and Oliver was now beginning to grow angry. It was time for the old bastards across the table from him to provide some answers, or Oliver would walk out of this place into whatever cold dark night lay beyond. The worst that could happen, he supposed, was that he would slip out of whatever hallucinatory fit he was experiencing, die, and be found in his hotel room by the cleaning staff. Not the best option, to be sure, but it was there.

The man gave a dissatisfied grunt and raised his scabbarded sword. He held it aloft for a moment, pointed towards Oliver as if he we considering ripping off the scabbard and leaping across the table to skewer Oliver on the long blade, then he slammed the blade down on the table and sighed. It was the sigh that told Oliver what, if not who, the man was. He could not have explained it to anyone, but there was such a world weary quality to that sigh, such a tone of exhaustion and disgust with the entirety of the mortal realm, that something deep within Oliver's soul recognized what he was dealing with before the man said another word. The man reached up then, with fingers so thick and scarred that it was a wonder to Oliver that he could even bend them anymore, and pulled back his hood.

The face that was revealed was not ugly. Nobody would ever have dared to call it beautiful, or even handsome, but it could not be called ugly either, despite the ragged scar that ran across the forehead and the drooping hole of dark, empty flesh where his left eye should have been. The man's face was set in an expression of resolute self-determination and certainty, which was only enhanced by the scars and missing eye. His remaining eye was a deep, cobalt blue, which transfixed Oliver with a gaze that bespoke not a threat of violence, but a promise of utter annihilation if Oliver were to bring this man to anger. The face was framed with a beard of thick snowy white hair, which curled tightly against his chin and neck, despite being trimmed short.

"Do you know me now?" the old man asked, his voice low and rumbling like the sound of a distant freight train.

Oliver shook his head. He had good idea of who, or what, he was speaking to, but he would not say it aloud. "I feel as if I should, but I cannot name you."

The man sighed again and his expression fell to such a glower of sadness and world weary exhaustion that Oliver felt as though all the joy had been drawn out of his own soul just from watching the transformation. The man shook his head and sank to rest wearily on one of the log slab stools arrayed beside the table. He rested his elbows on the pine slab and reached despondently for the tankard that sat a few inches from his right elbow. He pulled the tankard towards him and lowered his gaze into it, long strands of white hair falling from the folds of his robe to surround his face.

Oliver stepped hesitantly forward as the one eyed man slurped unenthusiastically from his tankard, which was once again full to the brim with a golden liquid. He settled onto a stool across the table from the man and watched him drink in silence for a while. A cold wind gusted in under the door, playing with the flames of the torches and bringing with it the bracing scent of pine and woodsmoke.

"Tell me who you are," Oliver said.

The one eyed man looked up from his drink and now the froth of yellow foam around his mouth made him look less like a rabid dog and more the sorrowful terrier soaked to the skin in the midst of an unwanted bubble bath. "What does it matter to you, mortal fool?" he growled.

"It matters because you've brought me here and I have no idea how to return to my home. I want to know who you are and what use you would have of me, then I want to go back to my hotel room," Oliver replied.

"If you, of all people, don't know me, then what hope is there? In all the worlds, what hope remains for a wretched old man like me, when even an expert in the old ways doesn't know who I am?" He took another pull from his tankard and looked as his he were trying to fix Oliver with that same piercing gaze from before, but his solitary eye wandered and soon he shook his head and gulped from his cup again. When he had swallowed and wiped the foam from his mouth with a filthy, craggy hand he said, "I bet you didn't even know what you were doing when you set the bastard on fire."

That got Oliver's attention. He'd done a lot in the course of his relic hunting, destroying ancient traps, killing supernatural guardians, even shooting a few rivals in the kneecaps so they couldn't chase him down, but he had only ever set one person on fire. "How do you know about that?" he whispered, leaning across the table and trying to catch the old man's eye.

His eye came to rest on Oliver and he squinted, the cavern of his empty eye socket drooping until it was nearly shut, and examined Oliver for a while. Oliver waited quietly, holding his breath in anticipation. Just when his lungs were beginning to burn from the effort the old man said, "He told me." He nodded one head towards the raven, which had hopped down from his shoulder and was strutting across the tabletop, pecking at scraps of meat and bread that had been spilled by the now comatose revelers.

"The raven?" Oliver asked, his voice more incredulous than he had intended it.

"Of course. Munin tells me everything he sees, and these days that's mostly gossip about what others like me are getting up to." The old man sighed again and shook his head. "Makes me long for his brother. Old Hugin was always the wiser of the two."

"You have a talking raven named Munin?"

"Used to have two of them. If you were listening to a word I said, you'd know that by now, but old Hugin vanished on me nigh on four hundred years back. Damn, but I miss that bird," the old man muttered, wiping his nose on the sleeve of his robe.

Oliver sat back and pounded a fist on the table. He pointed an accusatory finger at the old man and shook his head, saying, "No way. I'm not going to fall for this. You must have drugged me and brought me here."

"And where do you think 'here' is, boy?"

"I have not the slightest idea, but I am not going to sit here and listen to an old drunk tell me that he is Odin." Oliver stood upright and looked down at the old man, his heart thudding in his chest as he tried to convince himself that this was all an elaborate hoax. "It's really quite pathetic. Now let me go or tell me what the hell you want with me. You can start by telling me the truth about how you know about the explosion."

"Finally, he gets something right," Odin said to the raven, which squawked, turned away, and strutted down the table to peck at a chicken bone. Odin shook his mane and growled, "Yeah, you and your mother too."

He looked back to Oliver and said, "I already told you how I know. Now, stop behaving like a child and sit down, we have much to discuss."

Oliver obeyed him. Despite his tirade, he did not truly believe that this situation had been manufactured. Not that he had any rational idea of how he had come to be in this place.

"Good boy, now tell me: do you have any idea of the import of your actions on that Pacific isle?"

"I think I do, though your..." Oliver paused and glanced askance at the raven known as Munin, which was busily battering a chicken bone against the edge of the table with its beak, "...your raven might have told you less than the truth. I was on a certain island in the Pacific when an explosion occurred, and to tell you the truth I still don't quite know how I survived it myself, but I did not cause it."

"You can tell me the truth, Oliver. We're both men here. I've killed more men in my lifetime than you're likely to have met, and I'm not even exaggerating. Back when I was young I started counting the number of times I beheaded a man in battle with this very sword, and you know, I lost count somewhere over seven hundred. So don't be bashful, boy, just tell me the story of why you torched that bastard Loki and then we'll share a mead."

Oliver frowned at that. He pursed his lips in thought, then shook his head slowly as he said, "I really don't know what you mean. The other person in the cavern with me was named Leo. Leo... well, I never knew his last name. But I would have remembered if he was named after a Norse god."

"Not named after, you fool," Odin guffawed. He slapped the table, sending Munin flapping up into the rafters with an angry screech. "I'm telling you here that the man you torched in that cavern was Loki. The brother of lies. The husband of Hel. The mother of my own damned horse, if you believe that particular bit of myth."

"I still don't believe that I am talking to Odin, so I don't know how you expect me to believe that the man I knew as Leo was actually a mythical Norse god named Loki, especially on your word."

"Believe what you will, but I am Odin, and that was Loki down in the cavern with you."

Oliver rose from the stool and glared down at Odin for several long seconds, then shook his head in disgust and strode back towards the heavy doors at the end of the mead hall. He pushed the locking bar up from its resting place and pulled the door open.

Outside, the land fell away from the mead hall in steep angles of snow covered rocks, broken only by the upthrusts of lone trees, until the mountainside met the wide plane of a valley far below. Dotted across the valley were the dark forms of small cabins which stood out beneath the rising sparks and flickering glow of firelight from their chimneys. Looking up from the crude village, Oliver gasped at the sight of the sky, which shone like a jeweler's table, with stars and planets twinkling brilliantly in gleams of white, blue, and pale red against a velvet black background. Oliver stood motionless in the doorway for a long while, uncomprehending of the cold wind that drove flecks of blown snow against his face, staring up at the sky in awe. He had traveled to the most remote parts of the earth on his quests to capture relics and track down shards of the mysterious mechanism, he had gazed up at the sky from deserts, glaciers, and jungles so remote that no other human was within a hundred miles of his camp. Never, though, had Oliver seen such a brilliant sky as he did standing in that doorway.

A heavy hand fell on his shoulder and Oliver looked around to see Odin standing beside him. The flickering light of the torches behind them shone against his white hair, turning it to fire against the shadowy billows of his cloak as he gazed up at the sky outside.

"That's my wagon there," Odin said, gesturing up at the constellation Oliver had always known as the Big Dipper. "Traveled long in that I did, back in the days before trains and cars. Eventually I couldn't get anywhere in it without attracting too much notice, so I gave it to a farmer somewhere in Bavaria and bought myself an automobile. That must have been, what, nineteen twenty or so by the Christian reckoning?"

Oliver looked from the brilliant stars down to the one eyed old man and said, his voice a barely audible whisper, "Are you really Odin?"

"That I am, boy. At least, I'm what became Odin, back when people believed in such things."

"What about the others? Thor? Freya? Are they also alive today?"

Odin slapped Oliver heartily on the shoulder and growled, "It's cold out here. Can I offer you a drink? Like I said, I may have use of you, and a cup of mead is good fuel for telling stories."

Oliver hesitated for a moment, glancing between the stars and black landscape, swept with bitter gusts of wind, and the warm glow of the mead hall, then he nodded and followed Odin back to the rough-hewn pine table.

CHAPTER EIGHT
ODIN'S EYE

Oliver sipped the cold, golden liquid from the horn cup, savoring the rich taste of honey washing over his tongue. The mead warmed his throat and brought a flush of blood to his face.

"That's from my own brewery," Odin said, tipping his own massive tankard towards Oliver in salute. "I tried my hand at many things after the Christians arrived in my lands, but the most successful of all was brewing. There was a time when I served in their monasteries, teaching what I knew to the brewing monks and learning their own innovations. Those were good days, boy. Good days." His eye drifted out of focus for a moment as his mind wandered back a thousand years or more.

"You said you would tell me a story," Oliver said. He set down his cup and looked across the table to Odin's rugged face. There was a story in that face, he knew. The deep wrinkles etching out from his eyes bespoke a long life of laughter. Above that his brow was crossed with deep scars, one of which cut down through a bushy white eyebrow in a jagged line.

"That I did. Let me tell you, boy, I've been alive on this earth a long while. There are not many who could live as long as I have and stay sane. I've known others like me who gave up and died as soon as their cults withered away. There were some who lasted a few hundred years, then went out the same way, or who let themselves get caught up in the wars, the crusades, a few of them even died in the plagues. Not that there are many like me. You need to understand, Oliver, I'm an anomaly. I actually get to live forever, and have a touch of what you might call magic, as you probably guess from being brought here. The others though..." he trailed off and sat in wistful silence for a while, then shook his head and took a sip from his tankard.

"The others?" Oliver prompted.

Odin blinked, set down his tankard, and continued, "Yes, the others. You asked about Thor. I knew a man who claimed to be Thor. For all I know he might even have been the source of some of the myths. He fought with a war hammer that must have weighed sixty pounds, drove around in a chariot pulled by goats, even killed a few giants, but all that lasted only about twenty years. Last I saw him he was near sixty, frailer than a dry bone, and was tottering around a small goat farm in what's now called Norway."

Oliver nodded and sipped at his mead. That was the way of things in the world of myths, he had long ago learned. For every bit of truth he uncovered in the tales of the ancient world, for every holy staff, living Norse god, or genuine fairy, there were a dozen half truths built on the deeds of stupendous, but ultimately mortal men and women. Still, he mused, assuming that all of this was really happening he had hoped that there would be more truth to the Norse myths than a single old alcoholic with a missing eye.

"There's where things get strange, actually," Odin continued. "Like I was telling you, Thor and a lot of the others were little more than mortal men who earned a name for themselves, or took on the names of gods that the common folk already believed in to exploit their devotion. Loki and I though, we're special. Hel too, but she doesn't come into this."

"How so?"

"I'm getting there, boy. I've been on this blasted earth longer than whole empires. Damn it, the only things older than me are a couple of religions and philosophies that survived Christianity spreading out across the globe, and they don't live, and breathe, and drink like I do. Which is to say, if I meander a bit in my tale, I think I've earned that," Odin growled. Despite his tone, Oliver sensed that the old man was speaking more from a long rehearsed script of his role as an indignant grandfather than from actual frustration.

"Sorry," he said.

"Now, where was I? Oh, right, Loki. You see, Oliver, I was what you might call a warlord these days. I had over three hundred men under my command, with at least as many women and the Fates alone know how many filthy kids running about in the squalid mud holes we called villages back then. This was, oh, about four thousand years back, if I'm remembering right. Now, I wasn't happy with the mundane things that warlords get up to, like leading men in battle, settling squabbles between farmers, and bedding any woman who took my fancy. Those pleasures carried me through my youth, to be sure, and it was my skills in both battle and the bed that won me, and kept me in, the throne of my people, but by the time I reached forty winters I knew that my best years were behind me. That's when I turned my attention to seeking the thing that no man can steal from you in battle, and no woman can make you feel ashamed for as you grow old: knowledge."

Oliver nodded solemnly and took a sip from his cup, but did not interrupt the old man's tale. Meanwhile, Odin continued to speak, gazing into the shadows of the rafters behind and above Oliver, telling his story more as if he were speaking to himself than explaining it to another person sitting across from him.

"For nearly twenty years I searched for knowledge. I consulted the witches who lived in the bogs to the west of our village, shamans who dwelled within my lands, reading entrails and throwing bones to foretell the future for my subjects, I even spoke with an astrologer who came back on one of our trading ships from the southerly lands, what you would now call the middle east. None of them could give the knowledge I sought. Then Loki showed up."

At the mention of Loki, Odin grimaced and took a deep swallow of his mead, smacking his lips several times and shaking his head before he continued.

"I should have known there was something wrong with that boy from the beginning. All sly he was, speaking exactly what I wanted to hear and never once raising a breath of suspicion. That should be a warning to you, Oliver. Never trust a man who seems completely trustworthy, the bastard is probably just playing you for a fool, saying only what he thinks you want to hear, luring you in to trust his every deceitful, damnable word. If I had it all to do again I would have ducked that bastard in a pond the moment he performed a bit of witchcraft in my mead hall and been done with him, though I guess we didn't really take to doing that until a couple of Monks showed up a few hundred years later, but if I would have just killed him then I would have died an old man. And I would have been happier for it."

Odin spoke the last part in a softening tone, his head drooping and his eye flickering shut as he appeared to contemplate the distant, mythic past.

Oliver waited, patiently, sipping his mead and still trying to decide how much of the old man's story to believe. Even if he accepted that the man was Odin, or some other being with sufficient powers to conjure up this mead hall in Oliver's hotel room, or to transport Oliver here from that room, it would be wise to take his words with a measure of skepticism. Though he had little experience with them, outside of a few undead guardians he had encountered, and generally killed, Oliver imagined that anyone who had marked time by the rise and fall of entire empires and religions might well have hidden intentions.

After a time, Odin stirred and looked across the table at Oliver, who met his gaze levelly and waited for him to continue. Looking directly into Oliver's eyes with his one solitary eye, Odin growled, "That's right. Look right into it, boy. Face down the endless maw of time and deny your own mortality. Who knows, maybe you'll find a way to live a tenth as long as I have. Perhaps, if you complete the task I have for you, you may even gain immortality yourself, not that I recommend it."

He blinked, releasing Oliver from what he knew to have been a contest of wills. Though he had not surrendered, Oliver was sure that he had not won either.

"Loki proved himself a master of court politics, which was no mean feat back then I will tell you. Most politics then amounted to who had the faster sword or most voracious appetite, but Loki managed to insinuate himself into my counsel with neither. A master of words, he was, and it's true what the stories say about him being able to change his shape, though the transformation was always slow and, so far as I could tell, quite painful. It was with words that Loki trapped me. He dropped just enough hints, into just the right ears, that I was able to find my way to the secret door, descend the steps to the roots of Yggdrasil, and drink from the well of Mímir. It cost me though."

Odin drained his tankard and threw it to the floor before

his ashen throne. He rose and leaned across the table until his face was mere inches from Oliver's, fingers curling hard against the surface of the slab tabletop. He thrust his empty eye socket into Oliver's face and jabbed a calloused finger at it, pulling down the scarred skin to reveal a gaping hole of pink flesh. Deep within the gaping flesh, Oliver saw the dull form of a shard of gray metal, encapsulated in tendrils of angry red flesh and glistening with a thin sheen of mucus, sweat, and tears.

"Oh my god," Oliver breathed.

"Ha!" Odin bellowed, dropping back on his stool and slapping the table a hearty blow that made his sword clatter. He continued to laugh, the table shaking with the force of his convulsions as tears began to streak down his face.

Oliver grimaced, glancing about them at the tangled bodies curled up beneath piles of animal skins.

Odin wiped the tears from his face with the edge of his hood and said, "Don't worry about them, boy. Not a one of them is even real, in what you might call the traditional sense. Most of them I dreamed up myself, just to give you a feel for how the old place used to be, though a rare few are genuine souls that have clung on to me throughout the ages, even after better offers came along."

Oliver nodded and turned away from the surrounding bodies. He looked at Odin's missing eye again, hardly believing what he had seen there. Eventually he said, "How did you come by that shard?"

"Recognize it do you? I expected as much, especially after your encounter with Loki a couple weeks back. Don't think I haven't had an eye on you, Oliver. There have been many treasure hunters over the ages, some far more prolific than you can ever dream of becoming, but you're the first to successfully gather more than two of these little devils together, or to realize their true significance." Odin tapped at the corner of his missing eye as he said this, indicating the shard buried within his skull. "You've heard of my journey to the well of Mímir, of how I plucked out my own eye and placed it into the well, then drank from it and received true wisdom? That story, at least, is true. And it's why I need you."

"What could I possibly do for you?" Oliver asked.

"There's one thing that the myths never quite made clear: I never went back. Oh, some of them say that I killed Mímir in battle, but the truth of it, Oliver, is that only a mortal can pass into the realm of the ash and serpent. That's why Loki gave me the clues I needed to get there, he was hoping that I would bring back something for him, but the moment this shard of metal became lodged in my skull, I ceased to be mortal. Loki wasn't happy about that, but by the time he learned what had happened it was too late for him to do anything about it. Not that he didn't try to kill me more than a few times, but I always just healed right up again before he could pluck this metal from my head. And now, now I hope that you will be able to help me outsmart that bastard once more."

"No need for that. If you're right about Leo and Loki being the same person, he died in that explosion almost two weeks ago."

Odin gave Oliver a look as if he had just suggested that the fine mead they had both been drinking was nothing more than sour lemon juice. He shook his head and said, "You really are just a boy, aren't you. Do you really think that someone who has lived through so many ages of this world would be done in by a mere fire? Or are you forgetting that you, nothing more than a foolish mortal man, survived that same explosion, merely because you happened to be carrying the right relic in your pocket?"

Oliver felt his face growing hot at that and knew that he would soon be blushing nearly as red as his hair. He glanced up at the rafters and wondered if the raven Munin had been in the cave that day, or if Odin's mysterious pet had simply perched outside his apartment window.

"No, Oliver, Loki is still alive, and you would be a fool to discount his involvement in this game."

"Then why hasn't he duped some other mortal in to capturing whatever it is he wants?" Oliver demanded.

"That I do not know. We haven't been on what you might call speaking terms for several hundred years."

"So what do expect of me? I'm not saying that I will help you, not yet, I just want to know how you think I can help."

Odin tapped his face, just below the hold of his missing eye, and said, "I need you to step beyond the veil and retrieve the eye I left in the well beneath the roots of the world tree."

"What will that accomplish?"

"I am old, Oliver, older than you can imagine. I don't just call you boy to insult your manhood. You, and every living mortal on this planet, are mere children to me. I have longed to rest in the peace of death since before your grandfather was born, or his grandfather before him, but I could not find any way to make it happen."

Oliver considered that for a while before responding. He studied the deep wrinkles of Odin's features, the craggy lines etching down from the corner of his ruined eye like canyons, the thick hair as white as fresh fallen snow piled up around his neck, the dull glimmer of his one good eye, which drew Oliver so deeply into its own depth that he felt as if he might lose himself in its sorrowful weariness. He knew that he was looking at a man for whom life had reached an end, yet he could not justify bringing an end to it.

"You're asking me to help you kill yourself," Oliver said.

"Nothing so simple as that, boy. Oh, I see that righteousness in your eye. You think that this is somehow morally wrong, that you'd be complicit in a suicide. You don't know if you could sleep at night, knowing that you aided an old man to his death."

"Perhaps."

"It's not that simple. I am not mortal, Oliver. I don't have a limited number of years to live on this earth. As far as I know, this damned shard of celestial steel lodged in my skull will preserve me in this exact form until the day that the sun explodes. By any right I ought to have died over three thousand years ago, but I found this key to eternity and knowledge." Odin's hands shook with passion as he spoke. His voice rose from a harsh whisper to a roar. He rose to his feet, towering over Oliver as he sat in stunned silence at the outpouring of rage from the old man. "Let me tell you now, you self-righteous fool, eternal life and knowledge of all things aren't as desirous as you might expect, once you've experienced them. I have seen billions of people die. I've watched as my own life was transformed into the centerpiece of a religion that spanned hundreds of years, then watched it all crumble to dust as other faiths, some closer to the truth, others just another variety of my own cult, rose, were corrupted, and fell. After all of that, I think that I deserve the right to decide if I am to go on living as the human race accelerates to its glorious self destruction, or if I get to step off this ride and return to the dust, before I have to see the whole of humanity commit mass suicide through its own stupidity and pride. I wrote the tales of Ragnarok, I heard them sung around campfires and in mead halls, and I have no desire to witness it for myself."

Odin fell back into his seat and grasped the hilt of his

sword, where it lay on the table between them. A gust of wind battered against the door at the end of the mead hall and Oliver saw light streaming in through the cracks. A second gust blew the doors open, revealing the hallway of his hotel beyond.

"I am not threatening you, Oliver, I merely offer you a choice: You can help me to rid myself of this curse of immortality, and possibly come through the quest with some measure of wisdom about what it is you are facing, or you can walk out that door and spend the rest of your life wondering what might have happened."

CHAPTER NINE
BACK DOOR

Oliver shivered as a gust of cold air blew down the mountainside, carrying with it the chill of the snowcapped peaks far above. He pulled the gray cloak more tightly around himself and cursed his foolishness for not dressing more warmly. He glanced about him, checking his progress up the mountainside as best he could through the smattering of thickly branched pine trees that grew up the mountainside. Down below, the lights of the farms and villages glinted against the dark plane of the river valley, while the rippling ribbon of the Lech River glowed a pale white with reflected moonlight as it wound through the fields and poured out its brightness into the black expanse of Lake Forggensee. Up above, the stars were blacked out by the ridge of the mountain, but their absence only highlighted the gleaming lights of Neuschwanstein castle, sparking against the black shadow of the mountainside.

"I hope this is worth it," Oliver muttered, tucking his gloved hands under the folds of the cloak as he continued to climb upward through the band of trees that lined the side of the road leading to the castle gates.

After agreeing to help Odin, the old man had pulled off his cloak, revealing a thick layer of padded and cross-stitched leather armor beneath it, and handed it to Oliver. "This will hide you from all but the most prying eyes," he had said.

"A magic cloak?" Oliver asked, eyebrows arching

skeptically.

"After a fashion. It won't hide you completely, and cameras will still capture your image, but the gaze of most observers will slip past you. So, cover up that red hair of yours, make sure the cowl keeps your face in shadow, and move quickly. "

"What do I need this for anyway?"

Odin gave Oliver an exasperated look and shook his head, as if Oliver alone were responsible for his lack of faith in the entire human race. "You need to steal something, don't you?"

"No," Oliver said, automatically.

Odin glared at him.

"How did you know?"

Up in the rafters the raven named Munin squawked angrily and dropped a chicken bone, picked bare and pocked with beak marks, to clatter across the table between the two men.

"You were on the right path, Oliver. That's precisely why I have chosen you to aid me. Go back to the castle and use my cloak to help you secure the Wagner folio. I'll need it back though, so don't get too used to having it."

After accepting the cloak from Odin, Oliver had blinked and found himself seated at the table in his hotel room, still holding the gray cloak. The scent of unwashed bodies, smoke, and spilled mead lingered in his senses for a moment, before dissipating into the familiar hotel odor of industrial cleaning fluids and air freshener.

He spent the next twenty four hours desperately trying to gather information and, later, supplies. He had called the historical institute at Neuschwanstein a dozen times, using four different anonymous SIM chips to mask his identity, only to be rebuffed each time by the iron walls of bureaucracy. He had tried to contact Evelyn Marby to see if

her lawyer could arrange a more legal method of examining the portfolio, but the one time his calls were actually answered her brother firmly instructed Oliver to never contact her again. His frustrations were compounded by Amber continuing to ignore his messages.
Not that any of these problems surprised him. None of the fake names he gave to the operators at Neuschwanstein carried any weight in academia, he was indirectly responsible for Evelyn's severe injury, and it wasn't uncommon for Amber and him to go days without speaking, though she usually monitored their private Twitter link carefully for any sign of trouble. Finally, he did catch a break in the form of a talkative personal assistant, who mistook Oliver for the secretary of a particularly insistent donor. Through that conversation, Oliver learned that there would be a costume party the next night for donors who had funded the rental, purchase, and transport of various artifacts.

The perfect opportunity for an unscheduled visit, Oliver thought.

And that was how Oliver found himself on this mountainside, wrapped in an old grey cloak, hoping that he was not mad for attempting such an audacious raid. It wasn't the first time Oliver had attempted to sneak into a site to gain access to documents or steal a relic, but it was certainly the first time that his plan had hinged on the efficacy of an ancient magical cloak, rather than a carefully forged identity or an unsecured entrance.

He continued to hike up the steep mountainside, moving slowly so that he did not trip over any unseen obstacles in his path. He had a flashlight in his coat pocket, but he left it there, not wanting to attract any attention from guards at the castle. As he approached the point where the trees thinned out around the castle foundations, Oliver heard the sound of an approaching car and ducked deeper into the woods to watch as a large black sedan eased by, headlights cutting through the darkness to reveal the ascending curve of the road leading up to the castle gates. He followed the car with his eyes, watching as it paused outside the high oak gate of the castle to disgorge a man and a women dressed in expensively impractical evening attire, then continued on to disappear around the rear of the castle.

"That might do it," he muttered. If there was a service door around the back of the castle, he might be able to slip in and make his way into the administrative wing unobserved. From there he hoped to find evidence of where the folio was kept.

He hurriedly crossed the road and darted up the rocky incline, pulling himself up by tree branches where he was able, scrabbling on hands and knees across the bare rock when necessary, until he reached the wall of white stone rimming the castle parking lot. Peeking over the top of the wall, he saw twenty or more cars, mostly expensive sedans in stark shades of polished black and pearly white. Chauffeurs, some dressed simply in warm woolen coats, others decked out in ornate costumes complete with gold braid and peaked caps, congregated under a buzzing halogen lamp, smoking cigarettes and carrying on an animated conversation in German. Beneath the light a small iron door was set into the white stone of the castle wall.

Oliver checked that the cloak was pulled over his shoulder and that the hood was drooping low around his face, then pulled himself over the wall. He paused then, waiting for any of the chauffeurs to notice him and call out or raise an alarm, but they continued their conversation uninterrupted. Oliver waited for a few moments, listening as they debated the performance of several footballers in last weekend's game, until one of the chauffeurs stubbed out his cigarette against the wall beside the door and said, "Screw this cold. I'm going to the kitchen for a coffee. Anyone else?"

All but two of the other nodded, dropped their cigarettes to the tar, and ground them out under their boots. The one who had suggested the drink pulled at the handle of the iron door, opening it to reveal a dimly lit corridor that tunneled into the foundations of the castle. He slipped through the doorway, followed by most of the other chauffeurs. Two of them, a short man in a grey coat and a tall woman in padded brown leather, remained outside. As the door closed behind the others the man muttered something to the woman, who laughed and nodded before pulling a pack of cigarettes out of her jacket pocket and offering him one.

Oliver smiled to himself. That was his way in. He skirted around the pool of light cast by the halogen lamp, staying in the shadows behind the cars whenever he could so that his cloaked form would not be silhouetted against the moonlit valley below. He crouched beside the wheel well of a pearl white Mercedes and listened as the pair by the door continued to smoke and chat, their conversation turning from footballers to speculation as to whether their respective employers were carrying on an affair, or simply putting together a covert business merger.

Finally, just as Oliver's legs began to protest from squatting in one position for so long, the woman sent her cigarette spiraling off into the night and announced that she was ready for something warm herself. The man nodded agreement and they both turned to enter the castle.

As soon as they both disappeared through the doorway, Oliver sprinted out from behind the car to catch the door handle before it swung shut. He levered the door slowly open and saw the backs of the chauffeurs retreating down the hallway. He pulled the door open and slipped inside, allowing the heavy iron door shut to ease shut behind him on its pneumatic hinge.

It was at that exact moment that his phone pinged with the sound of an incoming message.

"What was that?" the woman demanded, spinning around and peering back down the hall.

Oliver froze. Every instinct screamed at him to run back out the door and lose them in the forest, but he forced himself to remain still, half pressed against the wall of the hallway. He moved his left hand slowly towards the pocket containing his phone, hoping that it would not ping again, while silently cursing himself for not setting the phone to vibrate. Silencing his phone was not generally a priority when sneaking into ancient temples, where caution was more a matter of avoiding traps and spotting the occasional supernatural guards before they noticed you, rather than avoiding the notice of other people. Clearly, though, the cloak was having some effect.

"What?" the man asked, pausing and glancing back at the woman.

"I thought I heard a phone."

"You sure it wasn't your own?"

The woman shot him a withering look. "I'm not an idiot, Karl. I know what my own phone sounds like."

"The hall is empty, Bridgett," Karl said, waving back towards where Oliver stood.

Oliver snapped the silence switch on his phone just in time, as he felt the phone buzz four times in quick succession.

"No. I think I see..." Bridget began.

Karl interrupted her, "Maybe it's like when you feel your phone vibrate, but when you pull it out of your pocket it was just a muscle spasm. You told me about that happening just last month."

Bridget shook her head and blinked as if to clear her eyes, then turned back and continued striding down the hallway, shoving Karl out of her way and spitting an indistinct insult at him as she moved past.

Oliver waited until they turned a corner in the hallway, then hurried forward, pausing at the corner. To the left he heard the sound of loud voices and smelled fresh coffee. To the right he saw a series of narrow doorways, labeled with black and gold tags indicating changing rooms for men and women. He strode to the door of the men's changing room, pushed it open, and found himself in a long, narrow room lined with battered red lockers. A bulletin board hung on the wall beside the door, filled with birthday cards, sale fliers, and reminders from castle management. A second door stood half open at the far end, revealing the dark interior of an unoccupied bathroom.

"That was too close," Oliver breathed. He was still struggling to assimilate the fact that the chauffeurs had stared directly at him and not noticed that he was standing in the hall. He had seen a hundred truly amazing, seemingly impossible things in his lifetime, but this was a first.

He stepped into the small bathroom, flicked the light on, and pulled the door shut behind him, then leaned against the wall and pulled his phone from beneath his robes. A string of messages glowed across the lock screen.

Amber: Sorry I've been out of touch. Big news here.

Amber: You're going to be an uncle.

Amber: So don't do anything too stupid.

"Oh, just perfect," Oliver muttered, shaking his head in bemusement. He unlocked his phone and tapped out a quick reply.

Great timing cousin. Your warning almost got me killed. Congratulations on the kid. And thanks.

He pressed send and looked up from the phone to inspect himself in the round mirror over the grimy porcelain sink. There didn't appear to be anything unusual about the grey cloak in which he was wrapped. No shimmering, magical auras. No oily blackness. No vaguely distorted vision of the wall behind him visible through the folds of the cloak. He was simply a thirty-eight year old man in a gray cloak, face silhouetted in the campfire horror story glow of a smartphone held at chest level.

"How the hell did they not see me?" Oliver wondered aloud.

He shook his head in wonderment and looked back down at his phone to pull up a floor plan of Neuschwanstein castle, which he had found on a website run by a fan of the Disneyland castle. Recognizing the link between the two palaces, the fan had pieced together extensive information about the history and design of Neuschwanstein. The simple vector illustrations revealed little detail beyond the publicly accessible rooms which Oliver had already visited on his tour the day before, but they were better than nothing, and certainly an improvement over the information available on the castle's official website. He spent several minutes memorizing the layout of the galleries, courtyards, and connecting balconies, attempting to guess at the location of the director's office from the blank places on the map. Unfortunately, neither the fan made maps nor the official maps of the castle revealed any information about the layout of the castle's basement or first floor levels, as they were completely closed off to the public, and had been for decades.

A message from Amber arrived while he was perusing the

maps: How stupid?

He grinned, double checked that they were communicating via the encrypted Twitter link, and replied: Crashing a party of the German elite to steal an artifact for a defunct god.

He heard the outer doorway of the locker room open with a squeak and bang as Amber's reply came: So, a normal day then. Be careful. Still waiting on Hank to get me his data.

The doorknob rattled and Oliver heard a muttered German expletive, followed by a male voice saying, "Franz, if that's you in there again, I'm going to tell Marta you're slacking. We all know you dodge prep work by taking extra bathroom breaks just when..."

Oliver didn't let him finish. He twisted the handle and slammed the bathroom door into the face of the man outside. The man gave a brief cry of surprise, cut off with a painful exhalation as Oliver's fist hammered into his belly, doubling him over. A second blow to the stomach, followed with a sharp twist to the nerves at the base of the man's neck sent him to the floor, twitching and barely conscious.

From his dress, Oliver guessed the man to be a waiter, which was exactly what he had been hoping for. He pulled the man's limp body into the bathroom and quickly shut the door behind them. A quick check of the waiter's pockets revealed a pack of cigarettes, a key, a cheap plastic lighter, a small smart phone, and a wallet with several credit cards, fifteen euros in cash, and several membership and identity cards.

Oliver pinned the man against the wall beside the toilet and pressed the thumb of his right hand into the hollow of his throat as he flipped through the wallet with his left hand. He held up the German driver's license, glanced at the name, and looked the terrified man in the eye and spoke in his best German, "Good evening, Sylvester. I am going to assume that you are willing to answer a few questions for me. Am I correct?"

Oliver increased the pressure from his thumb ever so slightly and the waiter named Sylvester nodded frantically.

"Good. Now, do you know where the director's office is?"

Sylvester nodded.

"That is good for you, very good," Oliver said. He lessened the pressure on Sylvester's throat ever so slightly and continued, "Do you know anything about this new acquisition, the Wagner folio?"

The man named Sylvester swallowed, eyes darting around the cramped bathroom, then croaked out, "Just that the director is excited to have acquired it. She has been pushing all the curation staff work overtime so they can reorganize the new exhibit around it."

"I see. And what about right now? Do you know where the folio is now?"

"In Singers' Hall, on the fourth floor. That is where the exhibit will be when it opens next week."

"Is it guarded?"

Sylvester's eyes widened and he looked into the shadowy depth's of Oliver's cowl in visible surprise. He shook his head and said, "No way. You are not thinking of..."

Oliver tightened his grip on the waiter's throat and leaned forward so Sylvester could see the glint of his eyes, then said, "I am asking the questions, Sylvester. Now tell me what you know about the security around here or I will crush your windpipe."

He waited until Sylvester attempted to speak, and failed, before loosening his grip. The waiter coughed and dragged down a deep breath before saying, "I do not know anything about the security systems. I am just a waiter. I work in the café. I serve at special events."

"And the folio?" Oliver demanded, determined to extract whatever information he could from this man.

"It is at the far end of the Singers' hall from the staircase. I saw it while delivering food. They have it on a big table, with a preservationist standing by to turn pages so the donors can examine it through a big magnifying glass."

"How many people are up there?"

"The chefs were told to prepare food for two hundred."

Oliver muttered a curse and threw the waiter's license into the sink. While it was an unexpected advantage that the folio was being kept out in the open, without even a glass case covering it, it was going to be next to impossible for him to steal it from a room filled with two hundred partygoers. The thought back to his encounter with the chauffeurs in the hallway. The man had not even noticed him, but the woman who had heard his phone had thought she saw something before she changed her mind and turned away. Whatever its powers, the robe that Odin had given to Oliver certainly did conceal him from view, but it seemed to grow ineffective under direct and intentional scrutiny.

"What about guards? Are there any bodyguards or armed security up there?"

Sylvester nodded.

"How many?"

The waiter shrugged. "Many donors brought bodyguards. They patrol the perimeter of the party, keeping an eye on their bosses."

Oliver nodded, the outlines of a plan beginning to come together in his mind. It would be dangerous, but he had to capture the folio soon, before Sylvester was found and raised the alarm or, God forbid, the cloaked man from the Marby home came here and stole the folio himself.

He held up Sylvester's phone and said, "Unlock this. Do not even think of calling for help."

Sylvester hesitantly raised a hand and tapped out his unlock code.

"Now set an alarm for nine in the morning."

Eyes filled with uncertainty and fear, the man complied with Oliver's instructions.

"Good. Now here's how this is going to work. I am going to tie you to this toilet. If you make a fuss, even after all your work friends come back in here, I promise that I will hunt you down and kill you." He glanced down at the license again, then tightened his grip on the waiter's throat before saying, "Do you understand what I am saying, Mister Sylvester Schuler of Ritterstraße in Füssen?"

The waiter's eyes widened and he nodded as forcefully as he could with Oliver's hand around his neck.

"Good. Your alarm will sound at nine in the morning. When it does, feel free to do whatever you want to escape, but until then I do not want to hear a word. Clear?

He nodded again.

Oliver rammed a knee into Sylvester's stomach and once again squeezed sharply at the pressure point in his neck. The man sagged against Oliver's restraining hand, twitched twice, then went limp again. He pulled off the waiter's shirts, then used his undershirt to gag him tightly. He propped Sylvester up against the toilet and used his outer shirt and belt to secure his hands and legs around behind the bowl. That completed, Oliver slipped out of the bathroom and locked the door shut behind him. He pulled black marker out of his jacket pocket, stole a flier from the board, and scrawled, "Bad geschlossen. Es ist Franz Schuld." across the back of it, then stuck it into the door frame.

"That ought to keep him out of my way for a few hours,"

Oliver mutter to himself. "Now to get up there without being spotted."

Oliver pushed the locker room door open and peered down the corridor in both directions, then darted out into the hall and turned left, away from the enticing scents wafting down the passage from the kitchen and towards a doorway that he hoped would open onto a staircase leading up. The door opened to reveal a tight spiral staircase of rugged iron, illuminated in crisscrossing slats of bright light and deep shadows cast by red lamps bolted to the stone wall every two revolutions of the staircase. Oliver climbed the stairs quickly, knowing that if anyone entered the staircase he would certainly be found. The robe might hide him from view, but he was certain that anyone pushing past would still feel the rough woolen fibers and the bulk of his body. He passed the second floor landing, a tight closet space with no light shining from under the door, and continued upward, towards the third floor of the castle. As he approached the top of the staircase, Oliver began to hear a thumping beat resonating through the iron rails and echoing down the staircase.

The staircase twisted up through a passage cut into stone and Oliver stepped up into a small alcove with a white stone floor and walls paneled in rich, brown mahogany panels. An iron railing surrounded the hole from which Oliver had emerged and a line of multicolored light shone into the tight space from under a door. The music was louder here, but still muted from its passage through the heavy door of solid hardwood. Oliver stepped up to the door, twisted the handle, and pushed it forward just enough to peek out into the room.

CHAPTER TEN
LIFE OF THE PARTY

A pulsating rhythm slammed into Oliver's chest as he stepped from the dimly lit stairway alcove into a long, hallway with an arched mosaic ceiling curving just two feet overhead, stained oak paneling lining the lower three feet of the walls, and brilliantly lifelike murals of scenes from German folklore splashed across every wall. Just to his left, a wide staircase covered in opulent, but well-worn, red carpet wound up to the floor above. The thumping sound that filled the hall was accompanied by a lurid throbbing of colorful lights, their flash sequence seemingly beat-matched to the tempo of the music as their colors shifted in time to the rapidly modulating audio frequency, which poured into the hall through an open doorway up ahead on his right. Oliver felt as if he had just stepped out into an industrial rave venue, even though he now recognized this place as the Lower Hall of the castle, in which he had briefly paused on the tour two days previous.

Oliver quickly pushed the alcove door shut behind him and slipped along the wall towards the source of the noise until he reached the open doorway, which he knew would open into the Throne Hall. He risked a peek around the corner and saw, under the glittering refractions of light from the twelve foot wide gold plated chandelier, a crowd of at least a hundred people dancing to the electronic static, pulses, and trills being produced by a man dressed in an oversized Thor costume, who stood behind a bank of audio equipment on the upper balcony of the Throne Hall. The strobing lights had been placed between the columns of the banisters which ringed the fourth floor balcony, shining down to play their light across the dancers below, many of whom were also dressed as gaudy interpretations of mythological figures. Many of the men were dressed in leather and chain mail, with short swords or axes strapped to their waists and helmets on their heads. Those who had the muscle tone for it, and more than a few who did not, sported minimalistic leather or drapes of vivid blue cloth over bare chests. Most of the women were dressed in flowing white dresses sewn, or simply draped, from gauzy fabrics that shimmered as the varied hues of light slipped through the delicate layers. The dresses were secured at the waist with simple belts of gilt chain, which clasped at the belly with large enameled clips.

Oliver grinned as he counted no fewer than five men dressed in gray robes milling about the edges of the dance floor with drinks in hand. Odin as the gray wanderer might not have been the most popular costume at this party, but it certainly was common enough that Oliver would not stand out if he were somehow spotted. He stood, straightened his robe, and strode through the passageway into the throne hall as if he belonged there.

Nobody paid him any mind. Oliver adopted an unsteady gait and angled his way towards the nearest waiter, who was standing beside a pillar not far from where Oliver entered the hall, to the side of the crowded dance floor. Oliver snagged a glass of champagne, frowned at the feel of cheep plastic crystal between his fingers, and tottered away. These sorts of parties were the same the world over, he decided. Cheap thrills dressed up to look fancy so that the donors could feel as if their money had bought something.

He moved on through the crowd without visible purpose, bobbing his hooded head in time with the screeching music as it approached a crescendo, then broke into a stuttering tangle of sampled symphonies, the familiar strands of classical strings twisting and churning into a new form that was at once familiar and utterly alien to Oliver's ears. Always, though, Oliver was scanning his surroundings, searching for guards, paths to his target, and possible exits.

Other than the passage through which he had entered the throne hall, Oliver did not see any clean exits, but he had anticipated that from when he had taken the tour. Still, it was worth checking carefully, since all of the velvet ropes and Plexiglass barriers that had been up during the tour to direct the flow of tourists had been removed to make room for the party. Along one side of the hall, opposite from the passageway through which he had entered, three sets of wide glass doors opened onto a long balcony that ran most of the length of the hall. Through the doors Oliver saw a small group of costumed revelers smoking and sipping their drinks under the gaze of two hefty guards. Under the DJ's booth, and at the opposite end of the hall, behind the raised altar and throne dais, Oliver spotted four single windows, all of which were virtually useless as exits as they consisted of thick panes of glass glazed into heavy wooden frames.

Over the course of a quarter hour, Oliver mingled with the crowd and checked each window to determine whether it might provide an escape route. Unsurprisingly, he was disappointed. The windows under the DJ booth opened over a thirty foot drop to the gray stone courtyard and that, while certainly not a safe exit route, was safer than the windows behind the throne, which looked out over the valley below in a sheer drop of over a hundred feet.

"So, it's a fall, a fall, or back out through the hallway,"

Oliver muttered.

The couple that had been standing beside him, a young woman with blond hair dressed as, Oliver thought, a valkyrie and her companion, an elderly man dressed in leather armor, both started and looked straight at Oliver. "Where did you come from?" the man demanded in German.

Scheiße, Oliver thought. It was one thing to talk to yourself when alone in the jungle, or in a crowded city, but it was plain stupid to mutter in English when attempting to blend into the background at a German masked ball. He waved his half empty champagne flute at them and asked, also in German, "Do you know where the drinks are?"

The man snorted and pushed past Oliver, back out onto the dance floor, pulling the woman along with him.

Oliver breathed a sigh of relief and moved quickly around the border of the dance floor towards the passageway through which he had entered the room. Sylvester had told him that the Wagner folio was on display in the Singers' hall and, according to the maps he had downloaded that afternoon, that was located on the fourth floor, just off the Upper Hall. He looked upwards to the railing that separated the Singers' Hall from the soaring vault of the Throne Hall at the level of the chandelier, but could see little more than the suited forms of seven security guards, one standing beside each pillar along the railing, so he continued towards the exit from the dance hall.

He moved slowly through the main hallway, keeping up the persona of the tottering drunk for the sake of the cameras that were wedged into the corners of the room and any partygoers or guards who might come upon him. Once he had returned to the Lower Hall, Oliver was found himself drawn to a large mural which occupied the wall between the entrance to the Throne Hall and the small door that concealed the staircase that he had taken up from the first floor.

Oliver had first spotted this mural on his tour of the castle, as the tour group assembled between the rope barriers, awaiting the guide who would take them through the tour of the castle. Now, granted the time to examine it more closely, Oliver thought that he recognized the scene depicted in the painting. Deep shadows and glowing firelight bathed the scene in a dramatic glow as a bare chested Regin worked at his anvil to reforge Gram, the sword of Sigmund, which his son Sigurd would eventually use to slay an evil dragon. As he examined the mural, Oliver felt a strange discomfort settle over him, as if he were picking up on an artistic detail that could be important to his quest, but which eluded his conscious mind. He searched the mural a second time and found no clue except that he felt the most uncomfortable when he looked at a shadowy figure who watched Regin and Sigurd from the darkness. Something about the mural, and that shadowy figure, disturbed him, but he could not quite identify why. After a few minutes, he moved on, climbing the wide spiral staircase up to the fourth floor.

As he climbed, Oliver felt the physical impact of the music against his body lessen as the sound of it grew fainter. It was still loud at the top of the staircase, but by the time he passed the carved stone dragon, which lay open mouthed at the top of the steps, the noise was no greater than if he were standing in the lobby of a concert venue during a performance.

A dozen people stood about the hall, some dressed in full costume, others attired more conservatively in tuxedos with only a sword or winged helmet serving as concession to the theme of the party. They were clustered into groups of two or three and speaking animatedly as they drank their champagne. All around them the hall was decorated in an even more lavish fashion than the lower hall had been.

Oliver smiled grimly to himself at the sight of the murals, which depicted the funeral feast of Gudrun, a fierce queen who was said to have married Attila the Hun, then killed him at a funeral banquet she held in honor of her brother, who Attila had killed. According to the legend, she had been so outraged at the murder of her brother that Gudrun had killed her own sons, fathered by Attila, and served their flesh and blood to him at the funeral feast. Only after he finished eating their hearts and drinking mead flavored with their blood did the fierce queen tell him what he had eaten. She then killed the famous Hun and burned his body. It was, Oliver thought, a fitting setting for whatever cutthroat business deals might be taking place here on the fringes of the party.

He crept past the groups, pausing near each one to see if they noticed him. None did. It appear that the robe was continuing to conceal Oliver, though his encounter with the couple down in the dance hall, and the chauffeurs in the first floor corridor, indicated that whatever power the robe possessed was better described as deflecting attention from its wearer than actually making them invisible.

A guard stood at the door of the Singers' hall. A short, burly man with short cropped blond hair and a chiseled nose. He was dressed in a black suit, white shirt, and tie, and carried himself with the comfortable tension of a professional who was prepared to do violence whenever it might become necessary. He did not challenge Oliver as he passed through the low doorway into the hall, but as Oliver approached their eyes locked and Oliver knew that this man could see him. That, he thought, might be the last secret to mastering the robe Odin had gifted to him. The old god had said that cameras would still see him, so perhaps the secret was in the vigilance and intent of the watcher. A bored chauffeur, merely reacting to an unexpected sound, would catch at most an uncertain glance. Partygoers, already distracted by their hedonistic pursuits, would be oblivious to his passing unless he interrupted their dalliances. A guard, however, one who was alert on his post and prepared to carry out his duties at a moments' notice, might still sight in on Oliver no matter how low he pulled the cowl.

He stepped past the guard without acknowledging his presence, tottering slightly and intentionally allowing some of the champagne in his plastic flute to slosh onto the man's black suit. If Oliver was visible to this man, he was determined to play his part to the fullest and ensure that he faded into the background of drunken revelers.

"Allow me to take that for you," the guard said in German, catching Oliver's wrist and extracting the flute from his gloved fingertips in a single easy motion. "It wouldn't do for you to spill any of that on the artifacts."

His eyes lingered on Oliver's face, piercing the shadows of his hood to examine his features. Oliver drew himself upright and pawed ineffectually at the arm holding the glass. He kept his eyes drooped and did his best to not think of how easily this man had captured his drink. Oliver was no slouch in a fight himself, but he had sensed a mighty strength in the man's grip and, judging from the speed with which he had snatched Oliver's glass, that strength was coupled with a swiftness that Oliver could not match.

Oliver summoned up a burp, tottered slightly, then pulled himself upright to stand as steadily as he could. He replied, "Thank you. It was getting a bit low. If you could have a fresh glass waiting when I finish in here that would be most appreciated." With that, he turned from the guard and walked into the room, giving the best impression he could of a drunken man attempting to walk soberly. The burly guard did nothing to stop him. Oliver assumed that the guards, whoever they worked for, had been instructed to allow the partygoers to enjoy their evening unhindered, so long as they abided by some sort of liberal ruleset.

The Singer's Hall ran the length of this wing of the castle. Four electric chandeliers, smaller than the one in the Throne Hall, but still larger than one would ever find in a home, or even most hotels or banquet halls, bathed the hall in a soft yellow glow. The golden hue was enhanced by the glitter of ten gilt candelabras standing noble sentries atop the ornate floor, which was comprised of interlocking triangles of deeply polished yellow ash boards. The walls of the hall were decorated as ornately as any of the other rooms which Oliver had visited, with colorful painted lines drawn into intricate knots sprawling across any surface not already decorated with murals, portraits, or gilded wood. When Oliver had first entered this room with the tour group, he had been mystified by the events depicted in the murals, which were starkly different from the Norse myths which adorned many of the other rooms. Only when the tour guide had said the name "Parzival" did Oliver recognize the tale unfolding around him. All around the perimeter of the Singer's Hall were painted murals depicting the Arthurian legend of Percival and the Holy Grail. With the identity of the characters revealed, Oliver had quickly recognized the series of events depicted in livid color on the walls, which retold the German variant of the famous Grail Quest.

Now, standing in the hall again, with only a perturbed guard, a white gloved museum attendant, and five costumed partygoers, Oliver took advantage of the moment to totter towards and examine a painting of Parzival, unhorsed and armed with only a spear, bravely confronting a knight in full plate, cloaked in a red tabard and riding a red horse with a flowing golden mane. Oliver might have felt a sort of kinship with Parzival in that moment, a lone hero in a dark robe, searching for a powerful relic, except that he couldn't see himself as especially pure of heart.

He was, after all, here to steal an artifact.

Oliver turned from the painting and strode towards the far end of the Singers' Hall, where the museum attendant stood beside a tall, narrow display table covered in a white cloth, beneath a painting of Parzival looking on in wonder as the Holy Grail was displayed in the court of King Amfortas.

Approaching the table from the side, Oliver saw a square of creamy vellum, about the size of an unfolded newspaper, scribed with short lines of painfully neat calligraphy, arranged in rectangles with narrow lines of blank page between each. About half of the lines appeared to be grouped into stanzas, with precisely drawn angular runes written above the first line of each. Around the edges of the folio, and between the blocks of neat text, were scrawled lines of darker ink in a looping German cursive.

One of the partygoers, a portly man in a studded leather doublet, trundled over to the table and leaned precariously over the folio. The attendant tensed and his eyes darted down to the man, but he remained the model of an accommodating host and did not move as the guest tottered over the table for several minutes, muttering to himself in slurred words, lips moving as he attempted to read the text. Eventually, the man looked up at the attendant and said, in slurred German, "Wagner bad handwriting."

The attendant nodded politely.

"And the folio, what's the age on this thing?"

"It has been reliably dated to the fifteenth century, sir, and we believe it to be a translation of an even older text that was smuggled out of Christianized scandinavia. If you look at the..."

"Yes, yes, it's old, but can you explain why the institute spent," he paused, pressing a hand against his face to stifle a prodigious burp, then continued, "As I was saying, the institute spent so much money to acquire this old scrap of sheep skin."

The attendant gave the man a thin smile and said, "The purchase was approved by the board of trustees, sir. Our director thought it a key element of the exhibit as much of Wagner's interpretation of the Ring Cycle, and thus much of the inspiration for this castle, was drawn from this very document."

"Are you serious?"

"Most, sir. The folio itself is a translation of an ancient legend, the plot of which is quite distinctive in the corpus of Germanic myth, though it bears some parallels to the Völsunga Saga. Do you see the cursive writing between the lines of calligraphy?"

"Of course. I'm drunk, not blind."

"Those words are written in Wagner's own hand and indicate that he drew inspiration for elements of Siegfried's quest from this portion of the folio. Specifically, the notes indicate that..." The attendant trailed off as the portly man turned and tottered away in the direction of the door to the outer hall. He glanced down at the sleek steel watch on his wrist, dusted his fingertips against one another, then arranged his mouth into a neutral smile and returned to gazing at the opposite wall.

Oliver recognized the expression of someone marking time until an unpleasant duty was complete and approached the display table wordlessly, not bothering to maintain his faux drunken shamble. The attendant continued to stare into the distance, though Oliver could not tell whether he was ignoring Oliver until he asked a question, or was unaware of his presence due to the effects of Odin's cloak. He glanced back and saw that the guard at the door had turned his back to the room again, while the few suited and costumed partygoers were distracted with their own conversations. If he crept into one of the cluttered alcoves in the eastern corners of the room, or up the narrow steps to the balcony seats above, Oliver suspected that the robe would enable him to remain concealed until the party had ended. But if the folio was taken to a locked room, or placed in a secure display case, there was no certainty that Oliver would be able to gain access to it. He specialized in retrieving artifacts from ancient sites by outthinking ancient traps and skirting around magical wards, not in breaking into museums like a common burglar.

He backed away from the table and walked around to the side of the dais on which the table stood, then slipped past a gold encrusted candelabra and up onto the platform, placing his feet carefully for fear of creaking boards. Not that the attendant was likely to notice a board creak with the constant murmur of conversation from the groups partygoers admiring the murals and the barely audible, but pervasive thump of music from the Throne Hall. He knelt down on the dais, about ten feet behind the display table, and lowered his head within the cowl to study the grain of the floorboards as he contemplated the situation.

If he could have got away with simply photographing the folio, Oliver would have gladly done that rather than stealing it, but he could not be certain that an image would be sufficient. Oliver was not even certain why this particular document was so important, so if he wanted to unravel this mystery he would have to take some time to examine the folio in detail. Perhaps, he thought, he could pull the folio from the tabletop and slip it under his robe while standing behind the museum attendant and nobody would notice that the folio was missing until he had already made it back out into the corridor.

A cold wind gusted through the hall, breaking Oliver's reverie.

"That shouldn't happen," he muttered, recalling the ornate glazed glass windows he had seen downstairs in the Throne Hall.

He looked up just in time to see a dark form in tattered, billowing robes leap from the corner alcove to his left and drive the attendant to the floor with a blow from the pommel of a short sword. Light glinted from the cutting edge and from runes carved into the matte grey metal of the blade. The attendant cried out and fell to his knees, then toppled forward to the floor. The guard at the door spun, reaching under his jacket for the pistol he carried in a shoulder harness. He pointed the gun towards the figure, then hesitated, seemingly unsure whether he was facing a true threat or an elaborate scene enacted for the amusement of the party guests. The cloaked figure vaulted over the prone attendant, the dull grey metal of his sword glinting in the golden light of the hall as landed in a tumble, and came up swinging the blade in a wide arc. The guard dove back into the hall and fired twice at his assailant. The figure jerked backwards as the bullets impacted its body, then surged forward again, spewing thick black blood on the floor as it pursued the guard out into the hall.

Oliver took his chance. Leaping to his feat he grabbed the folio from the display table and flipped it closed along the worn crease lines between the blocks of lettering. He tucked the folded square of vellum, now the size of a thin paperback book, under the gray robe and into the side pocket of his khakis, then darted past the stunned guests and into a short passageway to his right.

Another gunshot echoed through the halls, followed by a piercing scream, and Oliver dove out of the passage into the long, windowed hallway which ran parallel to the Singers' Hall down the length of that wing of the castle. He peered back around the corner and saw the cloaked figure striding down Singers' Hall with his sword gripped in one hand, now stained red with blood that still dripped from the familiar etching on the blade. Someone screamed and the figure turned, flicking its sword to fling a spray of red blood across the gilt walls. The screams halted, to be replaced with sobs and pathetic cries for mercy.

Oliver turned away and ran to the oak door at the western end of the windowed side hall, praying that it was unlocked. The knob refused to turn in his hand but, breathing deeply and keeping doing his best to remain calm, Oliver examined the mechanism and located the wrought iron lever which would unlock the door.

An inhuman scream of rage echoed through the Singers' Hall and down the passage in which Oliver stood. At the back of his mind Oliver knew that the cloaked figure had just realized that the folio was missing.

Oliver wrenched the door open and leapt through, then lost his footing in the pool of blood surrounding the dead guard, tripped over the man's slashed body, and fell to the stone floor. Dark red blood drenched the front cloak and Oliver heard someone shout and looked up to see two more guards rounding the corner of the staircase.

"He's got a sword!" Oliver screamed in German. He pointed towards the Singers' Hall and stumbled to his feet.

He didn't have to pretend that he was terrified. This was his second encounter with the cloaked thief in less than a week and, unless he was mistaken, the sword that the figure had wielded was the same one which had dissolved into a silvery mist in his hands back in Munich. The guards stormed past him, one entering the hallway Oliver had just escaped through while the other halted at the doorway to the Singer's Hall, then darted around the corner shouting threats.

Oliver searched around him, located the dead guard's gun, and grabbed it. Damn the consequences, he was not going to carry on another minute unarmed. He shook the sleeve of the robe down to cover his gun hand, then went down the stairs at a run, leaving bright red bootprints on the worn marble steps. In the lower hall he encountered two more guards, guns drawn and held at their sides, watching over the now closed doors to the Throne Hall. The thrumming rhythms of the music still pulsed from behind the doors, the revelers within apparently unaware of the violence that had taken place beyond the all consuming beat of the dance music. The guards shouted for Oliver to halt, but he ignored them, plunging through the small door beside the staircase and taking the spiral steps down to the lower floors of the castle as quickly as his bloodied shoes would allow. The guards shouted at him as he retreated, but did not leave their post.

Oliver burst out of the staircase into the basement hall to find it as barren as when he had passed through it before, after leaving the waiter tied up in the bathroom. He strode down the hall, running through his options, trying to plan out the best way for him to escape the castle and make his way back to Munich. Before he reached the side corridor which lead out to the parking lot, however, the door at the far end of he hall opened, spilling the warm light and tantalizing scents of a kitchen out into the bare hallway. A man in dress uniform backed through the doorway, calling out a jovial insult to the other drivers, who sat crowded around a formica tabletop. Oliver threw himself down, skidding to a stop full-length on the floor as he yanked the hood up over his head, and prayed that the robe would still conceal him if he didn't present the bloodied portions to an observer.

No such luck. The driver turned and shouted out in alarm at the sight of a robed man laying crumpled on the floor at the head of a streak of blood. He shouted in alarm and Oliver knew he had only seconds to react before he was mobbed by well-meaning drivers who would doubtless detain him and call for emergency services.

"This is why I prefer ruins," he muttered. "No damn people to complicate matters."

He tightened his grip on the gun, the warmth of the molded plastic grip lending him a modicum of confidence that he might escape, tensed his muscles, and waited until the first driver had approached to within ten feet of him. Then Oliver leapt upwards and slammed into the driver's right shoulder, pushing him back into a spin that set him off balance and spun him around. The man was a little taller than Oliver, but he reached up and wrapped his left arm around the driver's neck, then rammed his knee into the back of the man's leg, driving his knees out and dropping his head down to the level of Oliver's shoulder. He tightened his grip around the driver's neck and leveled the gun in the direction of the other drivers as the spilled out of the kitchen door.

"Don't move," he shouted in German.

The nearest driver, who Oliver recognized as the woman who had nearly spotted him in the hallway as he entered the castle, slid to a stop on the stone floor. Two others collided with her from behind and she threw out her arms to keep her balance. "What do you want?" she called, pushing the other drivers back behind her towards the kitchen.

Oliver ignored her. He ducked his mouth close to the ear of the driver he had captured and muttered, "Do you have your keys?"

The man nodded.

"I was just attacked by a business rival. I'm bleeding. Get me to a hospital without a fuss and I won't hurt you."

He hesitated. Oliver squeezed his neck more tightly and looked to the other drivers standing in the hallway just before the kitchen door. "I need to escape before an assassin finishes me off. Your friend will be safe if he gets me out. Don't believe me? Send someone upstairs as soon as we're gone. If everything hasn't gone to hell you can come after us." He eased up on the driver's neck just a little and said, "Are you going to take me?"

The man nodded.

Oliver walked him forward at an awkward gait, keeping the man's head at shoulder level so his knees stayed bent and he remained off balance and unable to fight. The other drivers backed up until all but the woman in front had retreated into the kitchen. Oliver caught a glimpse of one of them turning and running deeper into the kitchen, most likely to go up a servants' stair to the party and report that a madman was kidnapping one of the drivers at gunpoint. They reached the passage to the outer door and Oliver began backing towards the exit, pulling the driver along more quickly now that they were out of sight, glancing back occasionally to ensure that he was not stepping into a trap.

Outside a chill wind whipped through the mountain tops, carrying with it a chill that had not been predicted by the weather forecast Oliver had viewed earlier in the evening.

They reached the car, a long black Mercedes with silver trim and windows tinted black, and Oliver ordered the driver to open the driver's side door, put the keys into the ignition, and turn the headlights on, without getting into the car.

When the driver had complied, Oliver pressed his gun into his side and whispered, "Go stand against the wall. I'll have this pointed at your back the whole time, so don't try to run back into the castle until I'm gone. The car will be parked along the road into town. If you wait half an hour then get a ride down there there is no need for your employer to ever know of this. You wouldn't want him to know how willingly you gave up the car, would you?"

The driver grunted and shook his head. Oliver nudged him in the side with the muzzle of the pistol and the man stood, raised his hands above his head, and walked slowly to the stone wall, taking obvious care to move slowly and not approach the door.

Oliver waited until he had covered half the distance, then slipped quickly into the car, turned the ignition, and slammed the door shut. He wrenched the gearshift into drive and pealed out of the parking space before the driver had reached the castle wall. He took the tight turn to the castle drive as rapidly as he dared, then accelerated hard down the steep mountain road.

A cloaked figure stepped from the shadows of the castle gate. The wind whipped at its tattered black robe, obscuring the figure's shape, but doing little to conceal the pained heaving of its chest. The moonlight illuminated the stones around it, except for in places where a dark black liquid had dripped onto the ground from the gaping wounds in the figure's chest. It reached up and pressed the fingers of its left hand into the tattered edges of one of those wounds, wincing as torn flesh was pushed aside, then grunted as it extracted the flattened remnants of a hollow point bullet. It held up the leaden lump to inspect in the moonlight, then threw it aside into the brush.

It looked down the roadway at the receding taillights of the car and a smile crept across its face. "Finally the seeds begin to grow," the figure growled. "Soon I will reap what ought to have been mine so long ago."

It drew the tatters of the cloak around itself and slipped away into the darkness.

CHAPTER ELEVEN
THE ALL FATHER

Oliver awoke in his hotel bed feeling like hell.

He had successfully navigated the winding road from Neuschwanstein Castle to the village of Hohenschwangau, nestled into the fold of land between two mountains, at the end of a long blue lake, and swapped the stolen car for the one which he had rented under a false identity and driven from Munich earlier in the evening. So far as the German police were concerned, Oliver Lucas was still sleeping soundly in his hotel room in Munich, blissfully unaware of the escapades of James Croft, the Danish businessman who had just witnessed a bizarre murder and theft in the Neuschwanstein castle. Oliver could only hope that there were no security camera recordings of his face inside the castle. The drive back to Munich had taken four hours, with Oliver strictly observing every German traffic law of which he was aware and jumping in his seat each time a pair of headlights appeared in his rearview mirror.

Now, laying in the fine bedclothes, finally clean after sitting in the steaming shower for twenty minutes last night, Oliver blinked his eyes furiously and tried to piece together the events of recent weeks. Recent events, from the encounter with Leo, who might have actually been the Norse god Loki, to the strange interaction of the shard and the heartwood, to his evening spent drinking mead with Odin in a strange, in-between place that was both in his hotel room and not, were beginning to make Oliver think that he had crossed some critical threshold. He had always believed that there was an underlying structure to the world, a deep meaning that was truly seen only by the sort of religious visionaries that seemed so common in history books, but were strangely lacking in his own experience. The confluence of beliefs and sudden emergence of technologies, religions, and social movements across the world had seemed an impossibility to him without some external motivator.

Oliver had thought that he had found that catalyst in the shards.

Now though, Oliver felt as if he had fallen into the straits of Charybdis and was trapped between the deadly, snapping heads of the Creed kept flitting about at the corners of his perception on one side, and the gaping whirlpool of mad conspiracy theories on the other. Oliver closed his eyes and groaned at that thought, briefly toying with the idea that he might next encounter a literal Scilla and Charybdis while crossing the street outside his hotel. He rolled over and threw his arm out to pull a pillow over his eyes.

His hand touched something warm and soft, which rose and fell steadily under his questing fingertips. He opened his eyes and found himself gazing into the face of a woman. Her face was long and narrow, with a sharp nose framed by wide eyes, which were closed in blissful sleep, framed by long blond hair which flowed over her neck and shoulders in sweeping curves. Her hair seemed to glow in the light pouring into his hotel room, the yellow radiance of it accentuating the deep tan of her smooth skin.

Oliver rolled away from her and leapt out of bed. His eyes darted around the room, searching for some clue to who this woman was and how she had found her way into his bed.

"What sort of man are you, boy? I put a comely lass in

your bed and all you can do is run away. I'm surprised you didn't piss yourself."

Oliver turned and saw Odin sitting in a chair beside the wide window. He was dressed in the gray robe, which had seemingly shed all of the blood which had stained it when Oliver returned to the hotel the night before, and munching on a large green apple.

"I remember the days when a real man would have stayed there in that bed with her for hours. It's a proper celebration after a victorious campaign."

"What the hell are you doing here?" Oliver hissed. He stormed over to his suitcase and pulled out a pair of clean khaki cargo pants, then continued as he pulled them on, "And where did you get her?"

Odin took another bite from his apple and chewed it slowly as Oliver zipped his pants and glared at him. Finally he replied, "So many questions from one who should be enjoying himself. Did I misread you? Ought I to have brought one of her brothers instead?"

"No, you should not. And you should not have brought her. Where the hell is she from?"

"Please, don't call her that."

"What?"

"Hel. This is Bila, a beautiful woman who I've known many times, as is my right after fighting her father, and all of her older brothers, to win her and claim her family's land. Hel, on the other hand, is Loki's wife, or daughter, or sister, depending which story you believe. Maybe all three, for all I know. The ugliest woman I've ever laid eyes on, she is."

"Bila, Hel, whoever she is I don't appreciate waking up to her in my bed."

Odin sighed and shook his head, looking wistfully at the woman laying asleep beneath the covers. After a moment he nodded and she disappeared, her body seeming to dissolve into a cloud of mist, which dispersed out into the room carrying the scent of an ancient time: fires, sweat, blood. The bedclothes held their shape for just a moment, then settled down, drooping into the space where the woman had lain.

"Thank you," Oliver said.

He stepped over the table by the window and settled into the seat opposite Odin. Odin pushed a room service tray laden with breakfast foods towards him and Oliver selected a plate of scrambled eggs with buttered raisin toast. He cracked the seal on a bottle of orange juice and drank deeply from it, then began eating his eggs and toast in silence, watching Odin thoughtfully as he chewed each bite. After a few minutes he noticed a slow twitch in Odin's remaining eye. He ate more slowly, savoring each bite, then taking a slow sip of juice, then sitting in silence and contemplating the growing tension in Odin's face for a moment before taking his next bite.

Nearly ten minutes passed in this manner before Odin slammed a fist down on the breakfast table and shouted, "Damn it boy, did you get the folio?"

Oliver sat back from the table, the corner of his mouth quirking up in a sardonic smile. "I thought you said the woman was a reward for a job well done."

"And you rejected her. And now you sit here eating like you haven't a care. So maybe you didn't finish the job."

"Then why did you appear in my room with a naked woman? For that matter, how did you know I was back?"

Odin rose from his seat and leaned across the table with both hands braced on the tabletop. His eyes fixed onto Oliver's face and he growled, "I am the Allfather. Odin, the wandering god of old. I know your true name, Oliver Lucas, the name which is hidden to all others. With a word I could snuff out your life or grant you an eternity of ecstasy. Now, before I grow angry, tell me where that damn folio is!"

Oliver took in all of this with a cool consideration, his face remaining impassive as he listened to the old god rage. He had been afraid last night, when the cloaked swordsman had unexpectedly attacked the party at the castle, but in the fresh light of morning Oliver had come to a decision. He had been far too passive since starting this quest, simply going from place to place at the suggestion of others, never sitting down to determine what course of action he truly thought to be the best. That was going to change.

"You need me," Oliver said.

Odin blinked and cocked his head to one side.

"If you could do this yourself, you wouldn't have asked me to steal the folio, you wouldn't have loaned me your cloak, you certainly would not be asking me where I hid the folio. You've already told me that you can't go back to the well yourself. So, please, stop with the theatrics and tell me what you want."

Odin's eye squinted nearly shut and he held his breath for a long moment, then he let out a harsh guffaw of beer-scented breath and slapped the tabletop, rattling the silverware and sending his browning apple core skittering to the floor. He fell back into his chair and exclaimed, "Damn, boy. You were a good choice."

"Thank you, again. Can we get to the point now?"

"Sure. Did you steal the folio?"

"Yes."

"Munin spotted you coming out of the castle covered in another man's blood and watched as you stole a car to escape. Not very subtle, if I may say."

"Neither was the swordsman. Do you have any idea who that might have been?"

"If I had to guess, I'd say it was probably Loki."

Oliver thought about that, trying to fit it into the puzzle of recent events. If the man that Oliver had known as Leo and the infamous Loki had indeed been the same person, and Odin appeared certain that they were, then Loki had certainly been interested in the Wagner folio. But that didn't answer the question of why Loki had proven so ineffective at capturing the folio for himself.

"Why does he keep failing?" Oliver muttered to himself as his gaze unfocused and he stared out across the rooftops of Munich through the window. His fingers crept up past his bare chest to finger the heartwood from Moses's staff, which still hung about his neck on a leather thong.

"A worthy question."

He turned back to Odin and said, "You still haven't made it clear what you need the folio for, and I don't understand why Loki keeps showing up, attacking me, and failing."

Odin glowered. His right hand tightened into a fist atop the table and he growled, "I don't know for certain, but I suspect that Loki may have hidden clues to the ritual that unlocks the passage to the roots of Yggdrasil in that folio. Unfortunately, I have forgotten the ritual over the last few thousand years, thanks to indulging in so much wine and so many women. So, if you want what I've got up here," he jabbed a finger at the side of his head, where Oliver knew a shard rested deep within his maimed eye socket, "You're going to need to find a way into the roots of Yggdrasil."

"And you can't help with the translation?"

"You would trust me to help?"

Oliver stifled a yawn, then shook his head as he took a sip of orange juice. "No, I can't say that I would."

"That's just as well. It has been a long time since I read any ancient tongues. I've had other things on my mind these last few centuries."

"You're pretty much useless as a partner, other than having that nice cloak." Oliver pushed his empty plate away and crossed his arms on the table in front of him, leaning forward to meet Odin's eye. "I want the shard, and I'll do my best to give you your mortality back, but it would be very helpful if you had any more information to share."

"All I recall of the ritual is that I had to cut my thumb and press it to some runes. I have no idea what runes I touched or in what order. I can't honestly recall how many there were either."

Oliver nodded. That was at least somewhere to start.

Odin glowered at Oliver for a long moment, then nodded his shaggy head and stood, flicking a card onto the table. "We will meet again when you are finished then. Contact me at the brewery when you are prepared to continue. I've lived on this earth nigh four thousand years, I can tolerate a few more days."

Oliver picked up the card, glanced at the number embossed in the heavy paper beneath the printed words "Ash Spear Brewery," and set it down again in front of him. He waited until the old man had paused to open the door to the hall before he said, "Odin."

Odin turned and fixed Oliver with his single eye.

"Do you have any idea what that shard in your head actually is?"

Odin shook his head, turned to leave, and slammed the door shut behind him.

CHAPTER TWELVE
BRITISH

A bitter rain lashed at the windows of the tall gray townhouses as they marched upwards to join the clouds that hung low above Great Russel Street, at the center of London. Oliver pulled the collar of his long grey jacket tight around his throat and wished, for the tenth time since leaving his hotel, that he had brought a wide brimmed hat with him. He tightened his grip on the slim brown valise that he held in his left hand, leaned forward into the wind, and hurried along the narrow flagstone sidewalk towards the inviting amber glow of the Royal Tavern, a corner pub located a stone's throw from the black wrought iron gate to the Royal Museum. He leapt over the narrow side street that ran beside the pub, now more a shallow stream than a street in the torrential rain, and pushed in through the black and bronze doors of the pub.

The air within the pub was thick with the complex aroma of beeswax and stale beer, riding on an undercurrent of ancient tobacco that still seeped out of the upholstery and floorboards, though smoking within the pub had been outlawed for a decade. Oliver paused just within the door to slick the water from his red hair, wipe his face, and shake off his woolen overcoat. The pub was packed with a late afternoon mix of residents of the surrounding townhouses and museum employees recently off their shift. A few patrons spared Oliver a glance as he dripped onto the thick black doormat, but the majority ignored his intrusion and continued their conversations. The bartender waved a cheery greeting to Oliver, who returned his wave and approached the bar.

"What can I do for you?" the bartender asked.

"Pint of whatever ale you prefer, so long as it's local," Oliver replied. "I like trying new brews."

The bartender eyed Oliver critically, as if the sight of an American ordering a local brew were suspicious, then said, "It'll be hoppy."

"The more the better."

"Right."

As the bartender set his attention to drawing a glass of a chocolate brown ale from a tap, Oliver turned to survey the bar. He quickly spotted the man he had come to meet, seated at a corner booth beside the front window of the pub, where he could watch the street and door with no more than a flick of his eyes up from the tablet on which was reading.

"Five," said the bartender, setting down a pint glass of thick ale brimming with an inch of heavy foam on the top. Oliver fished a crumpled note from his inner pocket and laid it on the bar, then lifted the glass, nodded to the bartender, and strode over to sit opposite the man he had come to meet.

"Mr. Lucas," the man said in his thick British school accent. "I had almost hoped that you would not show."

"That's not nice, Sam. Besides, I texted you that I was coming before I left my hotel."

"One can always hope for unfortunate accidents along the road, especially in such weather as this."

Oliver shook his head bemusedly and sipped at his ale. He savored the thick, tart flavor of it, it was indeed one of the most hoppy ales he had ever tasted, and took the moment to study the man opposite.

Samuel Gower had changed little since Oliver had studied under him fifteen years past, back before his academic career had imploded with a spectacular whimper. Back then Oliver had been an enthusiastic student of ancient literature and early European languages, studying at Oxford on a semester abroad from Old Dominion University, who showed little sign of the rough and tumble man he was to become. He had enrolled in Gower's lecture on the migration of Norse religion and blown through the course work before midterms, then begun pestering the professor for more resources to study. Then, as now, Gower had been painfully thin, dressing his gaunt frame in clothes so old fashioned that Oliver had initially thought them an ironic affectation, and possessed of an acerbic wit that that had been known to reduce pupils to tears.

"Is that the same jacket, or did you buy them in bulk twenty years ago?" Oliver said, nodding to Gower's brown corduroy jacket, the leather elbow patches of which appeared worn down identically to when Oliver had last seem him.

"Some of us take care of our property, Mr. Lucas. Speaking of which, pray tell, what have you stolen of late?"

Oliver smiled and raised his glass in silent salute, then took a deep drink. He set the glass back on the table, wiped his chin, and said, "I've got something I need you to translate for me."

"And you think I will do it because?"

"You met me here."

Gower scowled and lay his tablet down on the table. Oliver caught a glimpse of archaic writing scrawled across a yellowed sheet of parchment as the screen wiped to black.

"I've got a folio here," Oliver said, patting the leather valise beside him, "written in ancient German. It's one of a kind. Recently acquired from a private collection, where it remained hidden from academic study for over a hundred years. I've made a rough translation, but I want your opinion on its authenticity before I go any farther."

A sheet of lightning ripped across the sky, rattling the wide pane beside the booth. It was followed by a gust of wind that drove heavy drops of rain into the glass, briefly drowning out the noise of the crowded bar. Gower glared at Oliver through half shut eyes, as if the only reason he didn't walk away at that moment was that the weather was just too god-awful for even his overwrought English sensibilities. Oliver felt a brief flash of guilt at using this man, who had taught him so much, but he pushed that thought away and turned his mind to the goal. It was, after all, people like Samuel Gower who had driven Oliver to seek out disreputable means of income after they had driven him out of academia. He sipped from his beer and waited for Gower to make his decision.

"How do I know you didn't steal it?"

"You don't, but I can promise you that if I didn't have this it would have been stolen by someone far worse."

"Hard to imagine," Gower said, but his voice had taken on a distracted tone and Oliver recognized that his barbs were more automatic than heartfelt. "Let me see what you have."

"Here?"

"Obviously. I will not bring you into the museum unless it is absolutely necessary. Many an artifact has been examined in this pub, so I doubt that whatever you have brought with you will attract attention."

Oliver nodded and pulled the valise onto his lap, then unsnapped the worn brass buckle on the front and flipped the leather cover open. He reached inside and removed a thick bundle of yellowing vellum, sealed within a clear plastic bag, and a pair of white cotton gloves. He set the gloves atop the bag and pushed them towards Samuel.

"Take a look at the outermost page. If you still don't want to work with me, I'll put the folio back in my case and be gone, but something tells me you'll want to help."

Gower scowled at Oliver and leaned over the table to lift the plastic wrapped folio. His eyes scanned over it and Oliver knew that he was rapidly shifting into the mindset of a skilled historical translator, searching the faded text for clues that would reveal not only its language, but the general date at which it was written and the level of education of the author. It took only a minute for Gower to finish scanning the first page before he paused and set the folio down on the table.

"Is this genuine?"

"As far as I know. It was in a private collection for at least fifty years before the owner died and his heirs sold it to a museum."

"Which is, I presume, where you stole it?"

Oliver smiled and lifted his glass for another sip, savoring the bitter flavor of the hoppy beer, then set the glass on the tabletop and leaned back against the wall of the booth. "Like I said, someone far more dangerous than I was trying to steal it and I rescued it before they could get their bloody hands on it."

"This is the Wagner folio, isn't it?"

Oliver raised his eyebrows, but didn't blink. "I'm impressed, Sam. I didn't think you paid much attention to news more recent than the Norman conquest. Yes, this is the folio that once belonged to Richard Wagner, you can see his handwriting in the margins of each section."

"The reports I read stated that a deranged killer broke into the castle and stole this in the middle of a fundraising gala.

He is said to have wounded one of the trust managers and killed a guard."

"That's about how it happened," Oliver said, nodding gravely, "except that I took the folio, not the killer."

"How do I know you and the killer aren't one and the same?"

"You'll just have to take my word on that, I'm afraid. But Sam," Oliver paused and leaned across the table to fix Gower with a bitter glare, "I can't believe that your opinion of me has dropped quite that low. I didn't kill anyone. If I hadn't taken the folio it would have been stolen by that same killer."

Gower studied Oliver for a long while, his finger tapping at a corner of the plastic bag while his eyes searched for some lie in Oliver's face. Finally he said, in almost a whisper, "My contacts in Germany say that the killer was shot twice in the chest from less than three meters and the castle is still closed as restoration experts work to remove blood from the murals and floors."

"It's true, so far as I know. There was a lot of blood."

"You seem healthy enough."

Oliver laughed and sat back again with a wild grin on his face. "You want me to take my shirt off, Sam? Show you that I don't have any wounds? I'll do it."

Gower shook his head and pushed the folio back across the table. "Put that away. We need more space to work, and a proper environment where it won't be destroyed if someone spills their beer on the table."

"So I get to come in?"

"Yes, but only this once. I presume you won't leave the folio with me?"

"You are correct."

Gower nodded and slid out of the booth, then grabbed his

tablet and tucked it into an inner pocket of his long tan overcoat before saying, "We'll go to my lab and I will take a look at the folio. If this takes more than a couple hours you can return again tomorrow evening."

Oliver packed the folio away in his valise and quickly finished the last half of his beer, then rose and followed Samuel out of the pub and into the lashing rain outside. They strode down the sidewalk side by side, crossed Great Russel Street four doors down from the pub, where a raised brick crosswalk peaked above the surge of water flooding down the street, and paused before a locked wrought iron gate. A female guard in a black raincoat leaned out of the gatehouse and Gower waved his identity card at her. She waved a greeting and ducked back inside to press a button on the security panel. A rugged speaker box mounted to the corner of the guard house squawked a desultory alarm and Oliver heard a heavy click reverberate through the iron gate before Gower pushed it open. They both waved back to the guard and Oliver followed Gower across the flooded flagstone yard to the west wing of the museum.

"Still in the same office, are you?" Oliver called above the roar of the wind and rain.

"That's right. Some of us are quite content to stay where we belong and keep our noses clean, a lesson you'd do well to learn, Mr. Lucas."

"Bah. If we all did that your precious museum wouldn't have half the precious artifacts of the colonized world packed away in its guts and you'd have nothing to translate."

Oliver almost thought he saw Gower smile through the curtain of grey rain as they paused at a thick steel door set into the side of the west wing. "Perhaps there is a bit of room for the likes of you, Oliver, but I fear you might have taken more than you can chew this time."

"We'll see about that, won't we?"

Gower pressed his card to the reader beside the door. The reader chirped, a green light winking on above the touch surface, and Oliver heard the solid clank of locking bolts retracting into the frame. They pushed through the door and Oliver blinked as they stepped into a long hallway with white granite walls, broken in slits above their heads by windows of thick leaded glass, and a floor of polished black stone, illuminated by the brilliant glow of LED bulbs set into the old fixtures of brass and blown glass which hung from the high ceiling. Oliver recalled that the British Museum had been one of the first public buildings in Britain to install electrical lighting throughout, after decades of being lit only by the sunlight streaming in through the high windows. Now, with the production and import of incandescent bulbs banned throughout much of America and Europe in favor of more efficient solid state diode lighting, the museum was illuminated more brilliantly than ever. They strode down the hall, past another security checkpoint, and through a heavy door crafted from a single slab of polished walnut wood. Here the stone floors were carpeted with long, intricately braided runners, which Oliver recognized as expensive Persian handiwork, despite their obvious age and wear. All about them were the signs of an institution that had been established, and through much of its history maintained, by a mighty empire that had drawn riches into itself from across the globe. Little new had been added in the last forty years, but Oliver could sense the prideful care which was showered upon the remnants of that grand past.

Gower stopped at a door of polished wood, set with a window of frosted glass, and pressed his badge against the anachronistic black metal box set into the stone of the doorframe. The lock clicked and he pushed the door open, then stepped aside to allow Oliver to enter the room first.

"Here we are," he said, shutting the door firmly behind him. "I've got good lighting in here, and plenty of references." He gestured in turn to a broad light box table standing at the center of the space, the cluttered bookshelf set against the wall to the left of the door, and the modern workstation with a sleek flat panel computer and several racks of solid state drives to the right.

"Not bad," Oliver said. He shrugged out of his still damp overcoat and hung it on a coat tree beside the door, then stepped up to the work table and set his valise down.

"Our funding is not what it once was, but it suffices."

Oliver removed the plastic bag from the valise, put on the white gloves, and extracted the folio from the bag. He lay the folio out on the worktable and switched on the overhead light. He had completed a rough translation of the text in his hotel room earlier that day, but exactly why it was valuable to Loki was still a mystery to him. The folio was written in a precise hand, the sharp geometry of the letters apparently scribed into the vellum in a faded black ink, and the language was a variant of Old German which Oliver had studied at University. For someone fluent in German, as Oliver was, grasping the surface meaning of the text was no more difficult than reading Chaucer might be for the average speaker of English, but such a reading was unlikely to bring Oliver a true understanding of the text. It would take Oliver months of painstaking research to gather sufficient knowledge of the cultural context in which the text had been written that he could truly understand the import of the text. Gower, on the other hand, had devoted his life to the study of Norse and Germanic cultures and languages. Oliver suspected that his old professor would be capable of identifying clues to the rituals that Odin sought in mere hours, rather than weeks or months.

Gower set his tablet on the worktable, hung up his own coat, and returned to the table wearing his own pair of cotton work examination gloves. He pulled the overhead lamp closer to the table and bent down to examine the sharp lettering of the formal German script and creamy yellow of the aging vellum through the thick lens of a broad magnifying glass.

"This appears genuine. The vellum is worn precisely as I would expect from six, perhaps seven centuries of exposure to a mild preparation of iron gall ink. Can't tell whether it is oak or walnut, but spectrographic analysis would bear that out." Gower looked up from the folio, as if waiting for Oliver to reply. He was, perhaps, searching for a sign that Oliver had doubted the document's authenticity, but Oliver just nodded and waited for him to continue. He scowled, cleared his throat, and looked back to the folio, saying, "I'll need some time. I presume you still won't leave the document with me?"

"You would be correct in that."

"Then take a seat and stay out of my way."

Oliver grinned at that. He turned away from the work table and settled into an old leather wingback chair beside the bookcase. He pulled out his phone and began scrolling through the dozens of documents related to Wagner and his most famous work, the Ring Cycle, which Amber had finally forwarded from Hank that morning.

He began with the first opera, Das Rheingold. In Hank's succinct, and heavily commented summary, it comprised a tale of greed, magic, and lust for power, stretched out over nearly three hours of soaring orchestral music and bombastic German vocals. While the themes of the opera were familiar, and the tale of Odin's conniving felt oddly familiar, he found nothing in it that reminded him of what he had read in the folio.

He glanced up and saw that Gower was still bent over the work table, examining the folio through a magnifying lens. The old man's lips moved and he furrowed his brow in concentration as he worked through the ancient text.

Oliver looked down at his phone again, moving past Das Rheingold into Hank's summary of Die Walküre. Recalling what the attendant had said to the drunken patron at Neuschwanstein, Oliver paid careful attention for any mention of Siegfried. He found nothing particularly useful in the first act, but he did take note of the large ash tree, into which Odin had plunged a magic sword. That, he thought, might be a clue to the ritual that Odin and Loki had performed. It wasn't until he reached the third act of Die Walküre that Oliver came across the name of Siegfried, as the unborn son of Siegmund and Sieglinde.

"Oh my..." Gower breathed. His magnifying lens clattered to the tabletop and Oliver glanced up in time to see him step from the table as if leaping away from a coiled viper.

"What is it?" Oliver asked, locking his phone and slipping it into a pocket as he stood.

Gower looked to him, his face hardening into an indifferent mask, as if he had forgotten that Oliver was present in the room. He shook his head and said, blushing, "Oh, just a rather shocking passage about Norse sacrificial rites."

"I wouldn't think anything they did could surprise you anymore. I still remember when you made that poor girl nearly collapse with your descriptions of the sacrificial hangings, when warriors would dedicate prisoners of war to Odin by hanging them from an ash tree and impaling their still twitching bodies with a spear."

"Of course you would remember those aspects of my lectures."

Oliver strode over to the worktable and tried to determine what could have caused Gower such distress, but there was no way for him to tell where the old man had been reading when he cast his lens aside. Meanwhile, Gower grabbed his tablet and retreated to a padded chair at the computer desk and began tapping hurriedly at the screen. Oliver shook his head then pulled out his phone, set it down beside the folio, and started reading through the summary of the next opera in Wagner's cycle. As soon as he saw the title of the third work, Siegfried, Oliver smiled. If the attendant at Neuschwanstein had been correct, this opera was the obvious connection between the works of Wagner and the ancient ritual to gain access to Mímir's well among the roots of Yggdrasil.

"This truly is a magnificent piece of work, Oliver," Gower said, rising from his desk chair. "It's a shame you lost your way, or you might have been able to appreciate it yourself."

Oliver bit his tongue and forced a smile, suppressing the urge to bite back at him then looked up and said, "I'm glad you can appreciate it, Sam. Why don't you tell me what you have found, since there's clearly more to it than some grisly pagan ritual."

Gower grimaced and looked away from Oliver, glancing down at something on his tablet. He tapped a few times, then set the tablet on the table and said, "I'd say that this one document is worth any three in my collection for the details it provides about the use of Norse runes in rituals to worship the gods."

Oliver nodded and tapped at the phone in his pocket. "I've been reading about Richard Wagner's Ring Cycle, and from what I can tell Wagner drew upon the details in this to create some of the most dramatic scenes in his operas."

Samuel stepped up to Oliver, his short, round frame seemingly deflating as he did, and reached up to lay a hand on Oliver's shoulder. He looked up at Oliver with his round, brown eyes, and said, "You need to take a step back, Mr. Lucas. You already destroyed your career by publicly espousing your radical theories, and now you seem to have been pulled into a situation with some extremely violent persons. Can you please just take my advice and step away before you destroy yourself?"

"It's nothing I can't handle."

"Are you so sure of that? Oliver, you're treading a precarious path through a fetid morass, filled with snakes. You need to be more careful. You need to leave this with me and go home, now."

A sarcastic response died on Oliver's tongue as he looked down into Gower's ruddy face. The man he had come to know in his semester at Cambridge had been utterly fierce in his pursuit of knowledge, terrifying to undergraduates and colleagues alike as he doggedly plowed through even the most obscure texts, meticulously assembling one of the most comprehensive descriptions of the beliefs of ancient Europeans from the shattered fragments of the past. How could it be, Oliver wondered, that this man would quail in the face of uncomfortable truths? He opened his mouth to say as much, then paused, closed his mouth, and turned away from Gower to examine the folio again.

"So be it," Gower whispered behind him. Oliver heard him begin to tap purposefully at the screen of his tablet. After a moment he set the device down again and moved to stand beside Oliver.

Oliver didn't look up from the folio as he said, "Like I said in the pub, I've got an idea what this is about, but I'm rusty on my ancient Germanic languages, so pieces of it are too dense for me." Oliver pointed to the passage in the third section of the folio, annotated by Wagner so many years ago, which had been troubling him. "Here's one. Wagner's notation suggests that this passage would be useful for the opening scenes of the Götterdämmerung, which I think was his last Ring opera, but all I can make out from the folio is that it has something to do with fire."

Gower cleared his throat, lifted his magnifying lens, and leaned forward to study the passage that Oliver had indicated. "Yes, I had noticed that on my perusal. That particular passage appears to give precise instructions for carving a set of runes into a tree and painting them with the blood of a human sacrifice. Not an uncommon practice among ancient religions, blood sacrifice, whether done to appease an angry god, break through the veil between this world and the divine or, indeed, the western notion of blood sacrifice as substitutionary atonement derive more from the mono..."

"Sam," Oliver interjected. He tapped a gloved fingertip against the passage he had previously indicated.

"Oh, yes. As I was saying, this is a remarkably complete description of the ritual of the ash tree, which I had previously only seen referred to in the most oblique manner."

"Any particular reason for that?"

"It's difficult to say. Some have argued that the ritual was never written down because it was only taught to the most devoted followers of the Norse religion, individuals who would have rather died than betrayed the secrets of their faith. Others claim that they have reconstructed the steps of the ritual from a variety of old texts, but I give little credence to such claims as they generally come from individuals with a direct interest in reviving ancient religious practices."

Oliver squinted at the black lines of text, wishing that he could decipher their meaning purely by force of will and get to the heart of this mystery. Working with Gower was beginning to stretch his patience, as he had suspected it would, but he needed the man's greater depth of knowledge to unlock exactly why this folio had been of such great interest to both Odin and Loki. That was Oliver's weakness, he knew. His formal education had allowed him to learn over a dozen languages, both dead and living, across much of the world, and his efforts since leaving academia had provided him with a working knowledge of the often treacherous borderlands between long discounted myth and true, but forbidden, histories of ancient powers. Oliver believed that all of this allowed him to see patterns of influence and belief that wove throughout history, and it certainly helped him to remain logical and somewhat detached when faced with long forgotten magics, but the breadth and eccentricity of his knowledge often necessitated moments like this, when he was forced to call upon experts in a specific field to aid him in comprehending the nuances of a particular culture.

"Can you provide me with a precise translation of this passage, quickly?" Oliver asked.

"That depends what you mean by precise and quick. Given a day I could probably provide you with a workable translation of the text, which might aid you in your efforts, or leave you in the dark on some obscure point of culture. A more thorough translation, with cross referenced annotations and historical commentary, might take me a week. Honestly though, this is a piece of remarkable value. One could easily devote a year or more to accurately translating the text in a culturally relevant manner, drawing on comparisons to contemporary texts, taking in to account the potential for bias since this is, after all, a fourteenth century translation of an even older text, and in…"

"Sam, I don't need perfection. You're not completing a new translation of the Bible here. I need to know the essentials: what the rituals entail, where they should be carried out, any obvious warnings to intruders, stuff like that. And it I need it by the end of this week."

Samuel set down his magnifying lens and leaned his bulk against the worktable. He fixed Oliver with the same concerned gaze as before and said, "Please, just leave this be, Oliver."

"No."

"What if I refuse? You haven't said anything of payment and I do have other work to do."

"Then I'll go elsewhere. I can think of a few other historians who would give an eye for the chance to study this."

"You haven't shown this to anyone else, have you?" Gower said, his eyes bulging and his throat visibly constricting.

"You thought you were the only one?"

"Who? Dear god, Oliver, how could you be so stupid?"

"Don't worry, Sam. Nobody else is going to publish before you."

"Oliver, I don't think you thoroughly grasp the importance of this situation. Please, just leave the folio with me and go back to America. I'll find a way to settle matters with the German police and you'll be free to continue your exploitation of archeological sites."

"Enough Sam," Oliver snapped. He turned away from the man and began gently folding the folio back along its original crease lines to pack it away. "I don't need this. Mock me all you want, call my theories lunacy or lies, but do not try to get in my way. You do not know the full situation and, trust me, this is a mystery that needs to be uncovered." He slipped the folded folio back into the plastic bag and tucked the bag away in the leather valise, then rounded on Samuel. "I'm going back to my hotel. If you want further access to this text, which you have acknowledged as remarkable, send me a message. If not, then just forget about this whole incident and go back to remembering me as the student who failed you."

Without waiting for Gower to respond, Oliver stalked away from the table, grabbed his jacket, and stormed out the door. He barreled past the desk guard, brushing away her surprised inquiries with a curt, "Ask Gower." and stalked down the hallway by which he and Gower had entered the museum. He shrugged his jacket on as he walked, pulled it tight about him, and hit the panic bar of the heavy exterior door at full stride. The wind whipped in, spattering icy rain against his face as Oliver hurtled out into the cold London evening, face fixed on the ground before his feet as he muttered curses at Gower, the museum, and the whole damned institution of academia.

He was so preoccupied that he nearly blundered into the side of a large blue panel van parked about ten meters from the door, between the museum and the wrought iron gate that stretched across the driveway. He saw the vague shadow of it in the pooled water of the drive and glanced up just in time to see a large man in a black raincoat step towards him and level a gun a his face.

Oliver froze, his eyes fixed on the hooded face of the man with the gun. He heard the slap of a footstep on the wet stones behind him and felt a sharp prick at his neck. Then everything went dark.

CHAPTER THIRTEEN

THE SHAPE THINGS

"We need to know how close he has come."

"He blundered into it, that's all. Others have before. He can't know the significance."

"We have been aware of someone gathering them together for years now, and we know that mister Lucas here has an interest in both unusual artifacts and at least one of the shards. It must be him."

"Then we deal with him. It wouldn't be the first time."

Oliver resisted a deep, animalistic urge to groan in pain as the first vague semblance of consciousness returned to him, bringing with it the muddled impression of voices and the clear, achingly precise sensation of ropes cutting into the flesh of his wrists and ankles.

The first voice came again. Male, vague accent that could have been British, but was equally lilted with something that struck Oliver's ear as half way between a southern American drawl and something out of the middle east, but that could have just been the muddled state of his senses. "Have you searched him?"

"Yes. His name is Oliver Lucas. As you suspected, he is from America and I found a keycard to a London hotel, as well as ticket stubs from the Chunnel. His vest contained an assortment of what appears to be camera equipment, though given the concealed gun I would not be surprised if other weapons were hidden within the camera gear, and a smartphone. He had the gun concealed in the bag. Nine millimeter Glock, thirteen rounds in the magazine, a model seventeen variant only sold to private security firms in Germany."

"The missing one?"

"I presume, but no bullets were recovered from the scene and we have no contacts within the staff of that particular security contractor, so we'll need to get prints off the ammunition and run them against the dead man's license record. That could take a while." Female, that voice, and faintly Scandinavian beneath the British accent, Oliver thought.

"And the folio?"

"In the main compartment of the bag."

Oliver wanted sorely to open his eyes, but he feared that his captors would notice and begin their interrogation. He wasn't looking forward to that. He had been captured before, by mercenaries, tribesmen, cults, but something about this situation filled him with a cold dread, like the ache that set in when wearing wet clothing on a cold day. Perhaps, he mused, that was precisely the issue. He was still wet from the rain and, now that the thought had entered his mind, he realized that he was cold as well, as was the metal chair to which he was tied. But there was still something more in the voices of his captors, which seemed to shiver with a chill metallic ring.

"He'll be coming around soon. Search him more thoroughly before he does. We need be sure that mister Lucas has no more surprises in store for us. Anyone with the nerve to transport a stolen weapon across international borders is likely more dangerous than he appears."

Footsteps crossed a floor that echoed with the sound of, not concrete, perhaps stone or tile, and Oliver felt warm fingertips press against the back of his head for a moment, then pull away. The footsteps came again, circling Oliver, and then the fingers were at his throat, unbuttoning his shirt. They paused and Oliver heard a sharp, feminine intake of breath, then a sudden pain in the back of his neck as the leather cord around his neck was grasped and yanked forward. He cried out, eyes snapping open, and saw a short woman with straight blond hair crouching before him, the broken cord of his pendant dangling from her fingers. She raised her arm so the singed knot of leather cord, which Oliver had wrapped in an intricate braid about the smooth heartwood, dangled between them. Her eyes fixed on Oliver for a moment, then returned to the heartwood. She raised a hand as if to caress the gleaming surface, then hesitated, her eyes filling with uncertainty.

She thrust the pendant at Oliver and hissed, "How did you come to posses this?"

He remained silent, but his face must have revealed something of his puzzlement, because the woman grasped his hair and leaned closer to study his face. Oliver met her gaze and felt though his breath were ripped away from his lungs as he stared into the deep, nearly opalescent gray of her eyes. He felt in that moment as if the entirety of his soul was laid bare before her, every act, motivation, and desire spilled out to this strange woman through the irresistible connection of her gaze.

"What is it?" the man said from behind, his voice breaking into Oliver's mind like a piercing note shattering a glass.

The woman released Oliver's head and his chin dropped to his chest. He didn't know how, but for some reason he felt more drained than if she had spent hours interrogating him. She rose and walked around behind Oliver, still carrying the necklace, and said, "He was wearing this around his neck."

"No."

"It does seem unlikely."

How can they know what it is? Oliver wondered. His mind was starting to wind back up after the numbing assault of whatever drugs they had used to sedate him. There were only, he paused to count, four people in the world who knew the significance of the heartwood pendant he had worn about his neck since returning from Egypt with the shattered remnants of Moses's staff. Of those, only Diana had been present when he broke the staff to prevent its power from ever being used for ill and had witnessed the smooth, almost oily gleam of the heartwood fall from the staff to rest upon the sands.

Oliver pulled his head upright and risked a look about him.

He gasped and blinked, certain that his eyes were deceiving him, but the view remained the same. A wall of glass rose up from the black and white tiled floor before him, comprised of hundreds of triangular sections of glass, each separated by a narrow band of metal, studded with rivets and painted with a thick accretion of many layers of white paint. Beyond the glass Oliver could see a school of fish nibbling at the long, green, wavering fronds of an underwater plant. Shafts of sunlight cut down through the water in a continual dance of radiant spears, which sparkled across the curving dome of glass above his head whenever they struck it.

"Breathtaking, is it not, mister Lucas?" the man asked.

Oliver twisted his head to look behind him and see the speaker, but he could only catch a glimpse of a shadowy figure from the corners of his eyes as he strained. He twisted his body violently about, attempting to knock the metal folding chair around, but a heavy hand descended on the back of the chair and held it in place.

"I come to this place whenever I have the opportunity. It holds a particular fascination to me, like the ruins of Petra, or the crumbling remains of a Roman ludus. Do you know what all of these remind me of, mister Lucas?"

Oliver shook his head, almost afraid to ask.

A hand settled on his shoulder, the long fingers flexing slowly, purposefully, as if to display their strength, then coming to rest as the thumb of the hand caressed the nape of Oliver's neck. Oliver heard a hushed rustle and crack, like a large silk bed sheet being snapped out of its fold, then settling down to the bed through hushed air, then a breath of warm, dry air gusted across his left cheek as the voice whispered in his ear, "It reminds me of the corruption of mankind. Always you reach outward and upward, grasping, clawing, pushing yourselves beyond where you rightfully belong. Your kind was made to live in gentle harmony with the world, tending to creation as gardeners, not the brutal engineers you have become."

"Who the hell are you?" Oliver growled, jerking his head away from the hot breath of his captor. The fingers at his neck pressed more tightly and Oliver stopped moving. He held his breath for what felt like several minutes and found that his eyes had fixed upon the distorted reflection of his own face in the glass wall.

The silence was shattered by a raucous laugh, which echoed from the walls and crashed into Oliver's ears like the cry of an entire crowd. A dry heat blasted along the left side of his face. The pressure on his neck tightened for a brief moment, then disappeared entirely. Oliver again heard the strange rustling sound, then the familiar creak of old wooden joinery as a body settled into a chair behind him. Footsteps clicked across the tile floor and Oliver felt himself tilted backwards until, looking upward, he could see the woman who had stripped him of the heartwood standing above him, gripping the back of his chair. He could just see the glint of her eyes, which were squinted beneath the gold of her hair, which fell in a short sweep around her ears and perfectly framed a delicate face the shape and color of an almond. The hint of a frown creased the corners of her thin red lips and Oliver wondered, only for a moment, whether she might feel pity for his predicament.

Then she grimaced and turned his chair around to face the other man.

Oliver's eyes were torn from the woman and fixed upon her companion, as if by an irresistible magnetism. For a moment Oliver could not focus on the man, as if he were at once a man sitting ten feet away in a wingback chair of red velvet, and a giant, squeezed down to the size of a human by a trick of forced perspective as he sat upon a mighty red throne hundreds of feet distant. The flickering rays of sunlight, twisted and shaded green by their passage through the water above, cut through the air with shafts of color. His eyes, visible even from this distance under a heavy brow, were the same silvery gray as the woman, and they seemed to glimmer as rays of sunlight passed over him. He was dressed in a formal white shirt, open at the neck and secured at the wrists by sapphire cufflinks, under a finely cut vest of grey wool, with matching grey pleated slacks. His white hair slicked back with painful precision above a high, bronze forehead. He lounged in the wingback chair and studied Oliver with a contemptuous curiosity as he idly dangled the heartwood pendant from his left hand.

"Oliver Lucas. Treasure hunter and smalltime, but effective, smuggler of artifacts for unscrupulous museums and collectors throughout America. Masquerades as a travel photographer. Am I wrong about anything so far?"

Oliver glared back at the man and shook his head.

"Obviously, your old professor turned you in to us. Theft of a valuable, some might say priceless, historical document. Assault. Murder. Destruction of property throughout Germany. These are serious charges, mister Lucas."

"I haven't killed anyone," Oliver growled. Clearly not police of any sort, no matter what they might pretend, he thought. Police didn't drag you to an underwater lair for questioning and, come to think of it, Oliver doubted that even the British police had adopted drugging suspects at gunpoint as a standard procedure for arrests.

"I beg to differ. Just last month you killed a man in a cavern on one of the Cook Islands, did you not?"

How the hell does he know about that? A voice whispered in Oliver's head. He bit down on his tongue and focused on keeping his face under control, then tilted his head to one side, miming confusion.

The man shook his head and chuckled. "You are welcome to continue your charade, mister Lucas, but I would advise against it." He looked away from Oliver to the heartwood pendant dangling form his fingertips. He pulled it up to his hand with a deft flickering of fingers and examined it closely, saying, "This is a remarkable piece to be carrying around you neck so casually. In another age it would have been revered as a holy relic. Pilgrims would have traveled thousands of miles to gaze upon it, pray near it, purchase a vial of holy oil that had been blessed by a priest who held it." His fist closed about the heartwood and he glared at Oliver with undisguised hatred as he said, "It is not to be worn about the sweaty neck of a thief like some trinket you picked up while on vacation! Do you even know what this is?"

"It is a piece of the staff that Moses carried when he freed the Israelites," Oliver replied.

"Impressive. I had wondered at the specific origin of it, but you still have not told me what it is."

"It's..." Oliver faltered. He was unsure how to answer the question, and still trying to figure out how much this man knew about him. Clearly he didn't know all of the details of the Egyptian adventure, but he somehow knew about what had happened in the cavern with Loki.

"Precisely. You know the shape of the thing, Mister Lucas, but you fail to know what the thing itself is." The man tucked the heartwood away in the pocket of his vest and leaned forward, resting his elbows on his knees and steepling his fingers before his narrow lips. "Much like your obsession with certain shards of a particularly cold metal."

"I don't know what you're talking about."

"Please, save the lies. We've been watching you for years now."

"I've yet to hear anything that convinces me you're more than a rival. I do have a lot of enemies."

The man chuckled and his face contorted into a smile that turned Oliver's blood cold. Something in the casual twist of the lips, the calm poise of his posture, the utter stillness of his eyes as he laughed told Oliver that this was a man who was in utter control, both of himself, and the situation. He held Oliver's gaze for a long while, then glanced upwards and gave a barely perceptible wave of his right hand. "You're just like them, the builders of this place. You think that you are special, that the universe can be bent to your will, that the inevitable decay of time will not catch you in its net and pull you down into the maw of history. Trust me Oliver, I have seen more time than you can imagine, and the only constant for you mortals is your inevitable death."

"I'm quite aware of my own mortality," Oliver growled. He strained at the ropes binding his arms, trying to work a deep kink out of his left shoulder. "What about you?"

"Then there will be no need for me to compel you to tell me the truth."

"Truth?"

"Where are the shards that you stole?"

"Shards?"

"Oliver, don't make me hurt you to get the information I need. You're obviously talented and," he patted the pocket of his vest, "there must be something special about you to have gained access to this. It would be a shame for someone like you to die in agony, or for your beloved cousin to reveal what she knows about the shards in exchange for no longer receiving pieces of your body in the mail."

"You keep her out of this," Oliver shouted, surging up until his body bucked against the restraints and he fell back, wrists bloodied and strained ankles screaming.

"Ah, I thought that would be your heel. Sweet Amber, isn't it, with her husband who knows nothing of your shared adventures, and she has a child on the way now, doesn't she?"

"How the hell do you know any of that?" Oliver hissed.

"It is my business to know. Now, if you will excuse me, I think you could do with some time to think about matters." The man unfolded himself from the wingback chair and strode towards the narrow door set in the far wall of the dome, where the glass panes gave way to a wide sheet of metal, lined with empty brackets where shelves had once rested. He paused at the door and said, "Think carefully Oliver. We are going to know one another very well, one way or another, and it is up to you whether we work together, or I remove your extremities one joint at a time and mail them home to your precious cousin."

CHAPTER FOURTEEN

LIVING ELECTRICITY

"You aren't really going to torture him, are you?"

"Why not? He is a threat to everything we have fought so long to preserve. He has at least four shards, Remiel. Four! Not since Babylon have so many been gathered together in one place. We have killed men for less. If not for the recent troubles we would have captured Oliver Lucas long before now."

"You forget what else he possesses," Remiel said. Her grey eyes narrowed and she stepped closer to her companion. "You must not harm him, Zedekiah."

"Why, because he stole a holy relic?"

"Because he has been chosen to carry it."

Zedekiah shook his head and made to turn away, but Remiel placed a hand on his arm and said, "You must give it back to him. We can explain the truth to him and demand that he deliver the shards to us. If he is an honorable man..."

Zedekiah scoffed and pulled away from her grip. He extracted the heartwood from his vest pocket and held it up between them, dangling the leather cord between two fingers. "Do you think he came by this honorably? Please, Remiel, stop speaking before you convince me that you are a fool."

She made to snatch the cord away from him, but Zedekiah flipped it up out of her reach and held the smooth yellow wood between two fingers to admire it. "For thousands of years this rested undisturbed in the deserts of Egypt, lost to all of mankind, its location forgotten even by our brethren. Now, it has returned to us." He closed his fist around the wood and slipped it back into his pocket. "I will say this for mister Lucas, he has brought us a fine gift. If he cooperates and delivers the shards into our protection I will show him mercy. He may even leave this place whole, if he does not delay too long in sharing what he knows."

Remiel scowled at Zedekiah and swallowed a bilious unease that had been growing within her belly for longer than she cared to remember. Zedekiah had been a friend for many years, and a mentor before that, and she had traveled far and worked hard alongside him, but she now felt as though she were seeing him for the first time. She stepped up to him and placed a hand against his chest, looked into his eyes, and said, "Do you even remember what we are fighting for?"

Zedekiah blinked in surprise, and for just a moment she hoped that he would reconsider, then his eyes hardened and he looked down at her and said, "Go to America and find the man's cousin. We must be prepared to exert greater persuasion if he does not respond to physical pain."

With that, he turned away from her and ascended the spiral staircase to the pavilion on the surface of the lake. Remiel watched him go with a deepening sense of dread. When she finally heard the door above slam shut, and the echoes of it had died away, she turned back to look down the riveted metal walls and stained black and white tile. Just around a bend in the passage, Oliver Lucas sat tied to a chair, waiting for whatever tortures Zedekiah had in mind.

"What am I going to do with you?" she whispered.

Oliver glared at his distorted reflection in the glass and bit his lip to distract himself from the pain in his wrists. He had spent the last hour straining against the ropes that bound him and his wrists, already aching from the awkward position in which they were tied, were now rubbed raw.

The mahogany door swung open with a creak of rusting hinges and slammed against the metal wall, sending a slight vibration through the entire structure.

"You trying to drown us all?" Oliver shouted, heaving his body towards the door so the chair teetered on two legs, briefly threatening to keel over and slam Oliver to the floor, then spun beneath him.

He found himself facing the woman with the deep grey eyes.

She stood in the doorway aiming a black handgun at Oliver's head. Oddly, it was not the gun which captured Oliver's attention. Instead, he suddenly realized that he was looking past the weapon and into the woman's steel eyes, which didn't so much look back at him as swallow his gaze whole. Snap out of it! Oliver told himself. She's your enemy, so stop falling for her eyes. He tore his eyes from hers and fixed his gaze on the tip of her nose, but that only left him admiring the perfect curve of her olive skin, so he moved his gaze to the gun she held. It looked remarkably like the one which he had stolen from the dead guard at Neuschwanstein, but the Glock model 17 was a common enough weapon that he could not be certain.

He pasted a sarcastic smile onto his face and said, "I wouldn't shoot that in here, if I were you. If you miss me and hit the glass we're both dead."

"I wouldn't miss, mister Lucas."

"Oliver, please. I always maintain a first name basis with my captors. I find it keeps the relationship more, equal, you might say."

"Fine, Oliver. If I shoot at you, I promise that I won't miss."

"That's better. I'd hate for us both to drown when there's the much simpler alternative of just me dying by a gunshot. Now, I've got a couple questions for you, but I fear that I don't know your name."

The woman hesitated and for just a moment Oliver was able to look her in the eye and see something different, perhaps it was doubt. She stepped forward into the room and kicked the door shut behind her, then stepped forward and glared down at him.

"I am Remiel," she said.

"Well howdy-do, Remiel," Oliver drawled in an affected Texas accent. "I'm Oliver and I'm sure glad you're to be my first torturer of the day."

She crossed the room at a rapid stride and had the gun pressed beneath Oliver's jaw before he could even flinch. He felt a cold shiver run through him and was suddenly aware that his bladder was just about full. Those eyes, so beautiful, so captivating, were now inches from his own, boring into his soul, delivering a clear message that she would not hesitate to blow his head off if he did not can the sarcasm.

Oliver swallowed, his brain screaming in terror as his Adam's apple pressed against the warm plastic of the gun, and whispered, "What do you want from me?"

"A little respect to start."

"No disrespect, Remiel, but it's difficult for me to be polite to someone who plans to mail me home in pieces. So, why don't we cut through the intimidation and you tell me what you want. If I've got it, I'll tell you and probably hand it over. If I don't, I'll say that and you can be sure I'm not lying."

"How can I be sure?"

"Well, for starters I'd probably give you my bank login

credentials right now if you'd untie me so I could take a piss."

"You're not a fool, Oliver, I'll give you that." Remiel pulled the gun away from his throat and stepped behind him. Oliver heard the snick of a knife opening and nearly fell off the chair as his legs were released and turned to rubber beneath him.

"There's a toilet at the end of the hall. I'll take you to it now, but you must move quickly and quietly."

Oliver frowned at that. He wasn't going to question being taken away from this room, but he couldn't help wondering why she should be concerned about him making noise. Don't get your hopes up, he urged himself. This is probably some sort of good cop, bad cop routine. Not that he was going to complain. If this mysteriously captivating woman wanted to play the good cop, he was happy to play along, all the while keeping an eye out for an opportunity to escape.

It took several minutes for Oliver's legs to stop trembling so that he could walk from the room. With Remiel behind him, still holding the gun, Oliver walked unsteadily through the doorway into a short tunnel. The walls, which bowed out, then in again on either side in a shape vaguely reminiscent of an egg, joined together at a point barely two feet above his head. They appeared to be made of the same thick, riveted metal as the supporting structure of the glass dome. Their footsteps echoed from the metal walls and tiled floor, reverberating with a ghostly echo that made him feel like he was walking inside a tin can. They turned a sharp corner and Oliver saw that the black and white checkerboard pattern of the floor continued to another heavy mahogany door. Half way between Oliver and the door, the space opened up into a wider atrium, at the center of which a metal spiral staircase twisted upwards and out of sight.

Sunlight shone down into the space and the long passages leading away from it were illuminated by aging incandescent bulbs set into narrow white cages along the ceiling.

"Here," Remiel said, indicating a door set into the side of the passage, just a couple steps beyond the turn. "Be quick about it, we need to be on our way."

Oliver bit back a sarcastic retort, recalling the discomforting warmth of the gun beneath his jaw, and looked back over his shoulder at Remiel. "What about this?" he said, pulling at the ropes that bound his wrists.

"I trust you can manage to get your hands in front of you?"

Oliver scowled at her, bent into a tight crouch, and stepped backwards through his tied wrists. "This would be a lot easier if you'd just untie me."

"I'm sure you think so, but I need your cooperation. Now, please be quick about it."

Oliver pushed the door open and fumbled at the wall beside until he found the round button of an antique light switch. The bulb above his head winked on, bathing the tight space in yellowish light. He stepped into the bathroom and kicked the door shut behind him.

Remiel relaxed the tension in her shoulders, but maintained a tight grip on the pistol in her right hand. She tossed the leather satchel against the wall beside the bathroom door and strode to the corner of the atrium, where she paused, leaning against the wall and listening intently for any sound that might indicate Zedekiah returning. This is the right thing to do, she told herself. He must be a good man at heart or he would not have been chosen to carry the heartwood. She licked her lips and glanced back at the door to the bathroom, praying for Oliver to hurry.

***

Oliver spun the polished brass knob on the sink until water stopped flowing into the porcelain basin, then inspected his reflection in the heavy, silvered glass mirror above the porcelain sink. His face was bruised above the left eye and a streak of blood stained the collar of his shirt but, other than the damage to his wrists, he appeared to be mostly unharmed. He briefly considered shattering the mirror and using a shard of the broken glass to cut himself free, but he knew that would be a waste of time. Doubtless Remiel would kick the door open and shoot him before he could finish cutting the ropes.

"Keep it together," he told his reflection. "Just look for the opening and..."

A fist pounded on the thick wood of the bathroom door and Oliver heard Remiel hiss, "Oliver, get out here, now."

He took one last look in the mirror, winked at his reflection with bravado, and pulled the door open to face Remiel.

"So, what first? Are you going to just ask me questions or is it time for your cynical friend to start pulling out my fingernails?"

"We need to get out of here as quickly as possible, then we'll talk about what I need to know from you."

Oliver cocked his head to one side and raised his eyebrows. Before he could say anything, Remiel nodded to the satchel beside the door and said, "Grab that and follow me." She darted down the corridor without waiting for Oliver to respond, pausing at the foot of the spiral staircase and peering upwards.

Oliver shook his head and grasped the carry loop on top of the satchel, then followed Remiel to the stairs, the satchel banging awkwardly against his knees as walked. Remiel glanced back and nodded at him when he reached her, then darted up the steps. He followed and they climbed the staircase rapidly, ascending from the eerie echoing space of the submarine atrium into a sunlit gazebo in the center of a placid lake. The interior of the gazebo was paneled in rich cedar wood, a dark yellow streaked with cherry red, below tall windows of rippling leaded glass set in a pattern of alternating diamonds. Through the window Oliver could see across the rippling water to a wide, silvery green lawn, leading up to the rear of a grey stone manor house. A path of crushed stone ran down from the house to the edge of the water, where it gave way to the boards of the dock that ran out across the water to the gazebo.

Oliver took all of this in at a glance before Remiel threw herself backwards and slammed into him, bearing them both to the stained wooden floor as she hissed, "Stay down!"

She had seen them rounding the corner of the manor house just as Oliver reached the landing of the gazebo, Zedekiah and two of his acolytes. One of them carried a large black toolbox. They would all be armed, in one fashion or another, so a direct confrontation on the dock was out of the question. That left only one other option for escape.

"What's wrong?" Oliver whispered beneath her.

"Zedekiah has returned more quickly than I anticipated."

"Who's that?

"The man who wanted to cut you into little pieces. He's come back with the tools to do it."

Oliver looked puzzled, then his face shifted as he recognized that she was helping him escape. "Untie me and give me the gun, now."

Remiel shook her head. "No. We can't fight them. Quick, back down the steps."

"No way. I don't know what you're playing at, Remiel, but I'm above water now, there's no way I'm going back down there."

She turned the gun on him and hissed, "I'm not going to shoot at them unless absolutely necessary. Now get your ass back down those steps and I'll show you another way. Go!"

Oliver knew when to stop arguing, so he turned and hurried down the steps as fast as he dared. He couldn't believe that he was trusting this woman who, for some inexplicable reason, was now helping him escape from the dour man who had threatened to dismember him. The whole situation was beginning to remind him of a bad crime movie, with his enemy supposedly helping him just to gain his confidence, but he didn't see any other options at the moment. He reached the bottom of the steps at a run and skidded across the tiles to hit the curved metal wall opposite the staircase. Remiel leapt down the last three steps and pointed to the tunnel leading left, away from the room in which Oliver had been held captive.

"There, into the billiard room."

Oliver ran down the hallway and hit the solid mahogany door with his full weight, twisted the ornate cut glass knob, and spilled into another underwater dome. Here, the filtered blue and green light spilled over the rich red velvet and polished mahogany of a billiard table, which stood at the center of a room ringed with upholstered chairs, each accompanied by a silver ash tray on a tall stand, and low tables topped with white and black veined marble. He searched for any sign of another exit then, finding nothing, rounded on Remiel as she followed him through the door into the room.

* * *

"Quiet," she hissed, seeing the rage in Oliver's face and cutting him off before he could open his mouth. She pushed the door shut and crossed to Oliver in a rapid stride, then grabbed the front of his shirt, pushed her mouth up to his ear, and said, "You know nothing about where you are or who we are so, if you want to live, get under the table and keep your mouth shut."

Oliver dropped the satchel at her feet and dove under the table, muttering curses.

Remiel took the satchel and glared at Oliver as he slipped rolled under the table, then slipped the straps over her shoulders, walked to the door, and listened, straining for any sign that Zedekiah had entered the underwater complex. She hoped to wait until he was descending the staircase, so that the clatter of heavy feet reverberating through the metal walled atrium would cover the sound of the secret door beneath the billiard table opening, but she heard nothing from beyond the door. It was only when she heard the faint squeal of hundred year old gears from under her feat that she realized her mistake. She turned to warn Oliver, but even as she turned a warning whispered in her mind and she turned back toward the door, just as it exploded inward in a burst of splinters and flickering blue light.

Under the billiard table, Oliver felt the floor beneath his back shift. He rolled towards the curving glass and steel wall just as the air above the table was ripped apart by thousands of shards of splintered wood and the sound of a lightning bolt. He scrabbled around behind one of the large, rounded legs of the table, then risked a glance over the table edge.

The man who had threatened him, who Remiel had called Zedekiah, stood in the doorway, filling the space with his broad shoulders and bronze face, once again seeming larger than physically possible in the space he occupied. He was glaring at Remiel, who leaned against the billiards table, brushing splinters from her face with one hand while she pointed the gun directly at Zedekiah's imposing form.

"I should have know you would betray us!" Zedekiah whispered. His voice, though quiet, pulsed through the room and shook Oliver to the bone, knocking the breath out of him and sending him ducking down under the table again. "Hand him over now and you may yet be spared the fires of Gehenna."

Oliver's mind was racing, trying to piece together the events of the last few seconds, when he saw the man emerge from the passage that had opened under the billiards table. His gun hand came up first, followed immediately by his head as he climbed whatever hidden ladder or stair was beneath the floor. The back of the man's head was towards Oliver as he climbed, but Oliver knew it was only a matter of seconds before he swiveled his head around and spotted him. Oliver threw himself away from the table, landed awkwardly on his knees and bound wrists and let out an involuntary cry of pain, then grabbed the base of a tall silver ashtray stand with both hands. He heaved himself around, swinging the stand as he rolled, and sent the long rod of silver plated steel spinning away under the table. The man must have heard Oliver, because he had just begun to turn his face towards him when the twisting stand struck him squarely in the temple, knocking his head into the side of the passage. He cried out and fell back down the hole to land with a heavy thud, followed by the clatter of metal on brickwork as the ashtray followed him down the hole.

Remiel heard Oliver cry out in the same instant that Zedekiah spotted him tumbling towards the ashtray.

Zedekiah lunged forward into the room and Remiel reacted without thinking. She pulled the trigger once, twice, then two more times in rapid succession as a scream of dismay ripped out of her lungs. The first shot struck Zedekiah in the chest, arresting his charge and twisting him around with the impact of the shattering hollow point round, the second slashed across the right side of his face, and the final two winged off the metal ceiling above his head with a screech of colliding metal. He dropped to the floor and lay still at the center of a widening pool of blood.

Remiel froze, overwhelmed with the magnitude of what she had just done. It was one thing to defy Zedekiah and help Oliver escape, but this was far more. She slumped against the table and dropped the gun to the tile floor, limp with fear. How can I ever explain this? she thought, eyes fixed on Zedekiah's shattered body. It didn't matter whether Zedekiah had strayed from the true purpose of their ancient order, as she had long suspected, or she had fallen irredeemably from the true path. She was now committed to aiding Oliver Lucas and could never go back to the other watchers. She fell to her knees, then dropped the gun and began crawling towards Zedekiah's body, all thoughts of escape washed away by the horror of her deed.

Oliver saw it first: the vague hint of movement in the body, an unnatural stirring beneath the folds of the fallen man's clothing, then the flicker of an eye opening to just a slit as Remiel crawled closer. He shouted a warning, but it was too late.

Zedekiah's body exploded outward from the crumpled form on the floor, like the unfolding lines of a fractal shattering out from a hidden space between the molecules and atoms of his skin, shivering into the visible world in infinitely repeating folds of ivory, crimson, and sky blue. The air seemed to ripple around Zedekiah's expanding body and Oliver heard again the same whispering, featherlike sound he had heard when tied to the chair in the other dome, then Zedekiah exploded out of the corner in which he had lain and slammed into Remiel with a roar that reminded Oliver of a screeching owl. As he flew upwards, Oliver caught a glimpse of shimmering white and silver lightning trailing behind him, as if the outline of a hawk's wings had been sketched into the air by living electricity. Then Remiel cried out and both of Oliver's captors escaped from his view, ripped upwards by the force of Zedekiah's assault.

Oliver rolled under the billiards table, barely avoiding the trap door to the secret passage, and scrabbled for the gun that Remiel had dropped. It was hard to get a firm grip with his wrists tied tightly together, but he managed it and rolled face up just in time to see Zedekiah fling Remiel's limp body down at him. He shouted in surprise and scrabbled back under the table, but it was not necessary because, as she fell, the air around Remiel distorted, then filled with crackling red veins of living flame, which fanned outward like wings to arrest her fall. Zedekiah roared again and struck out at Remiel with a flurry of fierce blows that would have immediately cracked the ribs of any human victim. Remiel blocked the first three blows, then took the fourth directly to the center of her chest and was hurled backwards into the wall of the dome. The steel supporting structure moaned and Oliver heard the distinct crackle of glass spiderwebbing with stress fractures, like the sound of ice cubes being dropped into a glass filled with hot water.

Remiel dropped to the floor and braced herself, apparently preparing to launch a counter assault, then the first triangular panel of glass shattered under the tremendous load of the lake water above. A torrent of water gushed through the hole and fizzled against the burning network of light that extended from her body. Some of it simply vanished, caught up in invisible vortices and pulled away to some impossible place between the filaments of her wings, while the rest burst into billowing cloud of steam. Then the rest of the fractured glass gave way, unleashing a surge of water that hammered down on Remiel and knocked her to the floor.

Oliver cursed and raised the gun, hoping that his half formed plan would not see him drowned, then pulled the trigger. He pulled it again, and again, and again, each shot slamming a hot slug of lead into Zedekiah's body. Oliver lost count of how many times he fired. He kept the gun aimed steadily at the center of Zedekiah's chest and pulled the trigger until the slide of the gun locked open and the trigger no longer clicked. Zedekiah's chest was a tattered wreck of ripped flesh and fragmented bone, but his eyes still gleamed, seeming to glow from within with a deep ivory radiance as he fixed Oliver with a malevolent glare. Then the wall of glass behind him shattered and a gout of water flooded into the dome, striking Zedekiah in the back and knocking his tattered body to the floor in a wash of water, blood, and shattered bone.

Oliver tottered to his feet and was nearly swept back to the floor by the surging swirl of darkening water, which had risen half way to his knees, just in the last few seconds. He glanced around and saw Remiel pushing herself unsteadily to her feet as water surged around her legs through the rent in the dome behind her. She caught Oliver's eye and he jerked his head towards the door. They struggled through the rising rush of water towards the doorway, skirting Zedekiah's mangled body as it twitched and writhed in the foaming water, and reached the hallway just as the dome behind them gave a tremendous groan and collapsed in a cacophony of twisting metal, shattering glass, and roaring water.

"Go!" Oliver screamed, digging his toes into the floor and racing for the spiral staircase. He reached the steps and leapt up them two at a time, slamming into the railing and pushing off from it again with each step as he raced the rising flood. Remiel ran after him, pulling herself upwards with hands gripping the railing, each jarring step sending surges of agony through her battered chest. Below them, the water had filled the hallway and was spewing out into the atrium in a foaming stream, which disgorged shattered glass, twisted metal, and broken pieces of furniture into the open space below.

They reached the top of the staircase and tumbled out into the gazebo. then Remiel took the lead, guiding Oliver across the dock, down the gravel path, and around the corner of the stone manor house. A gunshot cracked the air and Oliver dove sideways, knocking Remiel off of the path and under a thick boxwood beside the trail as bullets cracked through the air over their heads. Oliver pressed his mouth to her ear and hissed, "For the last time, cut me free and I will help us both escape."

Remiel pushed him off and crawled forward, peering through the branches to see if she could locate the shooter. She spotted him, crouching low at the corner of the black sedan that she had foolishly neglected to move before returning to rescue Oliver from the dome. That had to have been what tipped Zedekiah to her betrayal. He had ordered her to leave for America a full twenty minutes before he returned, and the presence of her car in the curved drive before the house, while she was absent from the manor house, was a dead giveaway. Another shot cracked out and Remiel ducked as a shower of splintered wood burst from the tree above her head.

She crawled back to Oliver, pulled a knife from her pocket, and said, "Don't leave without me, Oliver. You need me more now than ever."

"Fine, just cut me free."

Remiel sliced through the rope binding Oliver's wrists, then put her knife away and turned back to the path. "We've got to take him down and get to my car." She glanced back and saw that Oliver was already crawling along the ground on the far side of the shrubbery, slithering closer to the front of the house.

Oliver crawled along the trimmed shrubbery until he reached the corner of the garden. He crouched, took two quick breaths to calm his nerves, and glanced around the corner of the shrub. A manicured lawn ran down from the side garden to the curved driveway at the front of the house, where the gunman still crouched behind the trunk of the car, about twenty feet away, peering around the rear of the car to look for Remiel and Oliver along the path from the rear of the house. He waited, tense, knowing that if he timed this wrong he would probably get shot, then his chance came. The gunman popped up over the back of the car and fired again. Oliver darted out from behind the shrubs, across the lawn, and leapt towards the car in a low tumble. He hit the gravel and tumbled, plowing into the gunman's left knee with the full weight of his shoulder. They went down together and Oliver slammed his fist into the wrist of the man's gun hand, which spasmed and dropped the gun to the gravel, then he rolled away, sprang to his feet, and delivered a brutal kick to the man's groin. The gunman screamed in pain and curled into a tight ball, hands clutched between his thighs.

Oliver scooped up the gun and called over his shoulder to Remiel as he ejected and checked the magazine, "I got him. Let's get out of here." Seven bullets remained in the magazine. Counting one in the chamber that wasn't a lot of ammunition, especially in Britain, where he lacked the license to buy more, but it was better than nothing.

Remiel appeared from beneath the shrubbery and walked towards Oliver across the gravel drive. He slammed the magazine back into a gun and turned to face her, keeping the gun pointed at Zedekiah's fallen acolyte, who lay curled on the ground, moaning in obvious pain.

"Should we bring him along?"

"No. He doesn't know anything that I don't."

"Then let's get the hell out of here," Oliver grunted. "I don't trust that your friend in the lake won't come flying out, shooting lasers from his eyes or something. I've seen far too much of people coming back to life this last week to trust that he'll stay down there."

"I'll drive," Remiel said, shrugging the satchel from her shoulders and pulling her keys out of a side pocket.

She stepped towards the fallen acolyte, but Oliver blocked her and said, "Let's go now. You already almost got us killed going soft on one of them back there."

Remiel's fist clenched around the key ring as she unconsciously channeled her pent up rage towards Oliver, but she caught it in time and, setting her mind to a meditative calm, turned away and strode to the driver's door of the sedan. The car recognized the radio key on her chain and emitted a cheerful chirp, then hummed to life as she settled into the driver's seat. Oliver jumped in the passenger side and she floored the accelerator, peeling out of the curved drive with a spray of gravel and the whine of electric motors adjusting to the shifting surface.

"Where are we going?"

"Far away. You were right about Zedekiah reviving. It will take a long time, maybe as much as two days, more if he sheds this shell and has to incarnate another, but when he wakes up we had both better be as far away as possible."

CHAPTER FIFTEEN
The Watchers

Remiel guided the sedan along the local roads in silence for about fifteen minutes, driving as quickly as she dared on the narrow, winding strip of pavement. She knew that she ought to take a few moments to heal herself and pray for guidance, but with Zedekiah laying at the bottom of a lake and Oliver beside her, she was finding it difficult to focus on anything other than the enormity of her decision. Oliver was, thankfully, quiet. When the A3 motorway came into sight she pulled onto the onramp and engaged the autodrive. A soft tone sounded and the car accelerated smoothly to slot into place among the midday traffic. She released the wheel and, for the first time since spotting Zedekiah and his acolytes approaching the dock, felt herself breathe easy.

"I don't know if I like this," Oliver muttered, glancing at the autodrive indicator on the dash. "Is there any way they can track the car through the navigation network?"

"Of course they can, but nobody at the safe house has the authority to access the national surveillance system."

"What about Zedekiah? He seemed to know a lot about me."

"Except him, yes. But it will be a long time before he is fit to use a phone."

Oliver shifted in his seat to look more directly at Remiel. Her blond hair was plastered to the side of her face, mostly covering a dark bruise that had begun to form above her left cheek. A dark line of blood ran from the bridge of her nose nearly to her mouth, streaked in places where she had wiped her face while driving. Altogether, Oliver thought, she looked remarkable healthy for a woman who had recently been thrown against a glass and steel wall.

"About that, are you going to tell me exactly what the hell is going on here?"

"We're escaping."

"I get that, and I get that I was betrayed by that bastard Gower, but what I don't understand is what exactly you want from me, or who you are. I'll tell you, I've had an insane week and I don't know how much more I can take of veiled swordsmen, magic robes, disappearing women, and mythological gods. I've spent the better part of my adult life dealing with things that most people don't believe are real, or if they believe them, they think that they only happen in old bible stories, but this is getting ridiculous. Next you're going to tell me that you and Zedekiah are some sort of angels or something and, you know what, I'll probably go right ahead and believe you." Oliver lifted the gun, cocked the hammer with a trembling thumb, and rested it on his knee, pointed directly at Remiel's belly. "Now, I'm not going to shoot you unless you attack me, but I do think it's about damn time that I got a few answers."

Remiel looked from Oliver's eyes, which glinted back at her between the slits of his scowling brow, to the gun, a 1911 style pistol which was clearly loaded and ready to fire, though Oliver's finger was resting along the barrel, rather than on the trigger. This man was clearly dangerous, and perhaps beginning to crack under the strain of recent events, but he was also under control of his actions.

"Angel is a poor choice of word, but it will do for now."

Oliver blinked, surprised more at the act of her confession than the substance. He said nothing and waited.

"I'm not sure that I can explain exactly what you are up against, or who we are, in a way that you can understand, Oliver."

"Try me. Why don't you start with who you and your friend back under the lake are?"

Remiel hesitated for a moment, the words catching in her throat as she recalled what she had done. It had all seemed so simple, at first: take Oliver away so Zedekiah wouldn't torture him, convince him to join her cause, then return to the other Watchers with both the missing shards that Oliver had recovered and, potentially, a new acolyte for their order. But now, now that she had taken direct action against her brother, had stood by as Oliver damaged, potentially even destroyed, his incarnation, now it was likely that she would never be accepted back into the communion of her brothers and sisters. She watched the countryside slide by out the window as the car continued to speed north along the highway and was grateful that Oliver didn't press her any further. After several minutes she heard a soft clicking and, looking away from the window towards Oliver, saw that he had uncocked the gun and engaged the safety, but was still glaring at her.

"You have to understand the magnitude of what I have done in helping you escape."

"I'm pretty sure I do."

"No. No, you don't. You probably never can. You're mortal, Oliver. You can't know the weight of guilt that piles up on someone over the course of centuries, of millennia."

"Spare it, Remiel. You're not the first immortal to moan to me about the weight of your gift, you're not even the first this week, so get on with it."

"I'm a watcher, Oliver."

"That's not especially descriptive, especially here in Britain. Practically the whole country is under surveillance."

Remiel sighed in exasperation and said, "That's not what I mean. You said that you wouldn't be surprised if we are angels, and I'm telling you that you are partly right. Angel is just too general a term. It is used in many religions and refers to everything from beings who carry messages for the gods, to celestial choirs, to supernatural warriors, to literal incarnations of god on earth. So, I need you to understand that I, and Zedekiah, and all the other leaders of our order are watchers."

"Fine, I can believe you. But you still haven't explained what any of this has to do with me."

Remiel took a deep breath and gripped the steering wheel. She closed her eyes and muttered a silent prayer, afraid to speak the truth to an outsider, even though she had already bound her fate to him. Finally she looked down at her lap and said, barely above a whisper, "We watch over the path of human progress and, occasionally, give it a nudge in one direction or another. We also..." she hesitated again, almost trembling at the thought of reveling one of her most closely guarded secrets. She bit her lip, looked at Oliver in silence for a long moment, then said, "We also watch over the shards of an ancient device, which the founder of our order destroyed at the dawn of human civilization."

Oliver gasped and felt as if his heart might burst within his chest. He clutched the gun, focusing on the hard physicality of it. Hold yourself together, he thought. You've suspected it for years. You knew it was ancient. Just keep breathing and... He let out an earsplitting whoop and pounded his left fist on the door of the car. After so many years, after being run out of academia, after scratching together a career on the edge of ethics and legality to support his continued search, to hear someone else confirm what he had suspected all along filled Oliver with an elation he had never before experienced. Then the doubt struck. What if she's lying? There was enough detail in my initial paper that she could be trying to entrap me in... but no, I saw what happened back there. Oliver looked back to Remiel, who was looking at him with an expression half way between amusement and exhaustion, and grinned. This had to be the real thing, at last.

"You're a part of the Creed, aren't you?"

"I'm sorry?"

"Oh, sorry, that's a name I've been using to describe your organization for the last seven years or so, ever since I started to suspect your existence. I got it from an old Latin manuscript that I found in my travels through eastern Europe. The monk who wrote it was the only survivor from a monastery that was supposedly sacked by the Mongol horde as part of their conquest, but when he made his way to Minsk to report to his bishop the monk claimed that the monastery had actually been attacked because they gave shelter to a man who had stolen a relic from the khan. He claimed that the monastery was attacked in the night by a band of robed travelers. They tortured the thief until he revealed where the relic had been hidden, then killed everyone else who heard the confession, including the abbot. I started calling the group the Creed because of what the abbot supposedly said before he died, that only those driven by an unshakable creed could commit such deeds for such a little thing."

Oliver paused, his enthusiasm waning at the sight of Remiel's face, which had grown suddenly dark.

She looked away from him, not willing to meet his eye, but said, "I had hoped that no account of that event still existed."

"You know what I'm talking about?" Oliver exclaimed.

She nodded. "The monastery at Orsha."

"Exactly! So you were involved in the attack?"

"Please, Oliver, I do not wish to speak of the events at Orsha. It was long ago and there is nothing that can be done to change the past."

"Fine, I'll give you that. I imagine that after several thousand years anyone would have a few memories they would rather not revisit. Anyway, that's where I got the name Creed from. But you said that you are actually called Watchers?"

Remiel shook her head. "No. That's what I am, not the name of my group. If you want to go on calling us the Creed, that's fine with me. It's as good a name as anything. We don't exactly have a formal name, at least not in any language you know. We are a brotherhood, a sacred order of beings tasked with protecting humanity from destroying itself."

Oliver grinned at that and shook his head in wonderment. "You know, the more you tell me the more you confirm that I was right all along. You can't imagine how justified I feel after so many years of being labeled a radical. That said, I still don't understand why you got me out of there. How do I know this isn't some elaborate plot?"

"You saw what happened under the lake."

"I saw you put one bullet into an immortal angel then collapse into a sobbing pile of guilt. Maybe you were just putting on an act."

"If you won't take it on faith, then I can't make you believe me, Oliver. All I can tell you is that I trust you are a good man, and that somehow you are destined to be involved in all of this."

"How do you figure that?"

"The piece of wood you wore around you neck. You said that it came from the staff Moses carried during the exodus?"

"That's right. I tracked it down about a year back and retrieved it from a temple lost in the deserts of south-western Egypt. That was quite the adventure, and had its share of weirdness, but I have to say it made a lot more sense than everything that has happened to me in the last few weeks."

"And the piece of wood?"

Oliver shifted uncomfortably in his seat, unsure if he wanted to share the memory of what had happened in that temple with Remiel. The fire. The bones. The clouds of blood, dried to a fine powder by centuries of exposure to heat and magic, bursting out from the animated corpses and hellhounds. The terrifying intimacy of that supreme consciousness, what he supposed to have been the mind of God, invading his consciousness and shining hot white light into the darkest corners of his being. He shivered at the memory, turned back to Remiel, and simply said, "Something I can't explain told me I should break the staff, to prevent its power from being used for evil, and when I did that piece of wood fell out, already perfectly polished. I kept it."

Remiel nodded and lapsed into quiet contemplation for several minutes. She had suspected as much, and Oliver's story confirmed in her mind that she had made the right decision to help him escape, but she wasn't sure where to go from here. Clearly, she had to help Oliver, but she still didn't know the truth of why he had come to Britain carrying a document that had been lost for the better part of a century.

"What is so special about the heartwood, Remiel?" Oliver said, after waiting what he deemed an inordinate time for

Remiel to react to his story.

"Hmm?"

"The piece of wood from the staff. Tell me what is so special about it."

"It's the reason I helped you."

"Oh, thanks for that, I guess I'll start carrying around bits of olive wood in my pocket wherever I go, just on the off chance I'll meet a woman who will save my life in exchange for a piece. Can you stop being so cryptic and just tell me how this all fits together?"

She sighed, wiped a hand down her bloodied face, and looked at Oliver with the same intense gaze that had captured his attention when he was tied to the chair in the underwater dome. "Oliver, that piece of wood is so much more than you can imagine. You're a relic hunter by trade, so you know that there are, how can I put this, objects here on Earth that transcend the normal boundaries of space, time, the mortal realm."

Oliver nodded.

"That piece of wood is one such object. Bound within it is a small part of the mind of an entity that is so far beyond your understanding that merely looking upon him would likely kill you with awe, though the sheer brightness of his form would possibly blind you before that could happen"

"You're talking about God."

Remiel hesitated for the briefest of moments, then nodded.

Oliver leaned back in his seat, puffed his cheeks, and blew slowly out through pursed lips, turning over that thought in his mind. It wasn't especially hard for him to believe, he had believed in God since childhood, when his mother had taken both him and his cousin to church services every week, and most of his adult life had been spent tracking down artifacts that were created by devotees of one religion or another. Much of what many people took on faith Oliver had personally witnessed as he explored ancient temples.

"Tell me Remiel," he said, turning his face towards her, "is this truly God, as in capital 'G', the actual singular creator of the universe, or are we talking about the sort of magic that I deal with when I'm tracking down relics? The sort that seems to power the shards of that mechanism that I've been collecting."

Remiel's face grew dark and she tilted her head in puzzlement. She knew that mortals were singularly gifted at missing the point, but Oliver had carried the divinely infused knot of wood around his neck for months. Something of its knowledge had to have seeped into him in that time, she expected. "You don't know?"

"No, Remiel, I don't. I'm not an immortal angel with thousands of years of knowledge and a direct link to the almighty to help me figure out the truth. I'm just a man who's been mucking around in the remnants of a hundred dead cultures, sorting out which bits of their mythology are true, which are based on misunderstandings of science, and which are outright lies told by charlatans. I have faith, sure, but all I know for certain is that when I first touched that piece of wood I heard a voice in my head, and when I touched it and a shard at the same time it just about set me on fire."

"You have touched a shard while carrying the heartwood?" Remiel said, leaning forward and studying Oliver's face intently.

"Of course I have. I've been carrying that bit of wood ever since Egypt, it felt like a bit of a good luck charm. Just last month I managed to track down another of the shards on the Cook Islands, but you already know about that, don't you."

Remiel nodded, still studying Oliver's face.

Oliver was growing uncomfortable and his frustration at the woman's obtuse answers was rising. If it weren't for the growing certainty that he was stuck at the center of a large web of intrigue, on which at least two different and equally venomous spiders eyed him from opposite sides, he would have given in to the urge to give up on the whole affair and catch the next plane back to the United States. See what Odin does then, what the Watchers, Creed, whatever they call themselves do if I just back out of it all, he thought. But Oliver knew that backing out wasn't an option. Whatever Samuel Gower had seen in the Wagner folio had been sufficient to trigger a rapid, and effective, kidnapping plot, and now he was apparently being rescued by one of those kidnappers solely on the virtue of wearing a piece of olive wood as a necklace.

Oliver shook his head and threw his hands up, then slammed them down on his knees. "What's the deal here, Remiel?"

She shook her head and blinked, as if dismissing the sight of a particularly gruesome roadkill, and said, "I'm just surprised you don't understand what you're protecting, what you're seeking."

"That's the point: I don't know. The shards are a mystery. They're more ancient than any nation, any society, any race, but virtually nobody even suspects that they exist."

"They're dangerous, Oliver, that's why we guard them."

"Clearly. And your whole group is doing such a great job guarding them that I've successfully acquired five before you even tried to stop me."

Remiel ignored the jab and carried on. "You don't know what you're dealing with."

"And you obviously don't know me." Oliver leaned closer, bracing against the dashboard above the center console and boring into Remiel's eyes with his own, "I am not going to give up hunting down those shards until I know the truth about what they actually are. Are you going to tell me?" He paused, steeling his nerve to not be pulled into the depths of Remiel's eyes.

Remiel, for her part, said nothing. Oliver's sudden aggressive posture startled her, but she did not draw back from him. She held his gaze, matching him blink for blink, breath for breath.

Oliver shook his head and said, "I didn't think so." He sat back and leaned into the seat, then twisted his head to watch her as he said, "I'm not going to give up my search, Remiel. If you're willing to help me, we can talk, but if not then I'll thank you for saving my skin back there and ask you to drop me off in the next town."

"What about your cousin?"

Oliver squinted and felt a tension ripple down his neck, shoulders, and through his arms into his fists. "What about her?" he growled.

"Zedekiah isn't going to stop, Oliver. If you disappear, he'll go after what's precious to you."

"Stop talking, now."

"I'm telling the truth. Before he went to get his acolytes Zedekiah told me to go to America and..."

The gun was in Remiel's face before she could blink, the hammer fully cocked, the safety down, Oliver's finger hovering beside the trigger. Looking past the harsh steel of the barrel with a cool born of ten thousand years, Remiel glared back at Oliver. Only when their eyes met did Remiel feel a chill run through her. Though she did not fear for her soul, the cold hatred in Oliver's eyes delivered an involuntary burst of adrenaline to her incarnate body, washing her with a fear she had not anticipated.

"You're not going to let that happen," Oliver whispered.

She said nothing. Did not move.

"I said, you're not going to let that happen."

She nodded.

"Is my cell phone in that bag?" Oliver said, inclining his head towards the leather satchel in the back seat.

"Yes."

"What else?"

"Your wallet, the folio, and a couple books that might help us interpret it."

"I'm going to get Amber to safety while you get us to London, without talking. When we get to London, you're going to take me to that bastard Samuel Gower, and he's going to tell me exactly what made him tip you off. Got it?"

She nodded.

"One last thing. Remiel, when this is all over, we are going to fix it so your bosses never touch Amber, or anyone else I care about."

"How do you expect to do that?"

"I've got a few ideas. Now, get the bag and set it in my lap, then face forward and leave me the hell alone for a while."

She did as he asked. Once Oliver had retrieved his phone from the satchel and verified that it had sufficient charge and was in working order, he safed the gun and set it on the floor at his feet, then unlocked his phone with a swipe across the fingerprint sensitive edge. He pulled up his e-mail, Twitter, and chat apps in rapid succession, using each to blast off a brief distress signal to Amber. It read, simply, "Danger! Call ASAP!"

Oliver balanced his phone on his thigh and faced forward, watching the landscape race towards them around the rear of a large van, which the highway navigation system maintained at a consistent three feet ahead of their bumper. It had been a mistake coming to Britain, he decided. If he had remained in Germany and accepted Odin's assistance in translating the folio, none of this would have happened. As soon as the decision took form in his mind, however, Oliver realized that it was a childish simplification of the situation. The Creed had clearly been watching him for a long while, just waiting until he crossed some crucial threshold or passed into their grasp. Perhaps they hadn't known his true identity until Gower tipped them off, they hadn't known about his recent adventure in Egypt or moved against Amber until he told them where the heartwood came from, but Zedekiah's knowledge of his actions in the Cook islands and rapid action against Oliver's family made it clear that, one way or another, they would have come for him eventually. Maybe this way is better, Oliver thought. At least now I have some idea what I'm up against and there is some chance that I can outwit them.

The phone vibrated and he snatched it to his ear.

"Oliver? What's wrong?" Amber said on the other end of the connection.

"You need to get to safety."

"How do I know this is real?"

Good girl, Oliver thought. After their first adventure together, when Amber had elected to remain home in Virginia and act as an emergency contact and research aid, rather than returning to the perils of field work, they had established several emergency codes. Amber had laughed at Oliver's instance that their codewords include an indication that she was in danger, all the way back in the United States, but she had relented at last. The agreed upon code for, "Get out of town, you're in danger" was determined to be the one food that Amber had been allergic to since childhood.

"Avocado. Serious guacamole, Amber."

"Oh, shit."

"Precisely."

"Are you sure?"

"Amber, they were about to go after you when one of them turned and helped me escape. I can't even be sure that she is genuinely helping me." Oliver shot a glance at Remiel, who remained stony faced, seemingly unaffected by his lack of confidence in her. "Please, Amber. You just told me you're pregnant a few days ago. You can't take risks for me. I couldn't live with myself if anything happened to you."

"What about you?"

"I'll survive this, trust me, and I'm working on a plan to keep us all safe in the long term. Go now, you and Tom both. You can still do your work, but don't tell anyone where you're going and shut down location services on your phones and laptops."

"Stay safe Oliver. And keep in touch like usual."

"You too. Love."

"Love."

Oliver dropped the phone to his lap and pressed his fingertips to his forehead, willing himself to remain calm. He had been careful to keep a wall between his work and his family, tried to protect those he loved from his illegal relic hunts and obsession with the shards, but that wall was clearly beginning to crumble.

"Avocado?" Remiel asked.

Oliver blinked away the stress and turned to her, his jaw set hard. "I thought I asked you to keep quiet until we reached London."

"I'm not yours to command, Oliver. We're in this together now."

Oliver didn't reply. He turned to watch the landscape of farms and small towns race by out the side window. Meanwhile, inside his head, the details of the situation shuffled, came together, and separated again like a jigsaw puzzle composed of living, shifting pieces.

CHAPTER SIXTEEN
ACOLYTE

Samuel Gower lived in an apartment over a set of storefronts, just off of Charring Cross road, south-west of the British Museum, with underground parking for those few residents who owned vehicles and convenient access to the Leicester Square tube station. For the purposes of an aging academic with a modest income from his research at the museum and frequent lectures at universities, a taste for live theater, and a budding addiction to casino poker, it was the perfect location for a bachelor flat. Unfortunately for Oliver, the situation of the apartment directly between two major cultural institutions and a prominent bank meant that every approach to Gower's apartment was thoroughly covered by the London closed circuit monitoring apparatus.

"Got a plan of how to get in?" Remiel asked him as they walked past the door to Gower's apartment, keeping their heads straight ahead as they both counted the white boxes mounted on building exteriors up and down the street.

"Not exactly. We're getting more of these surveillance setups in the States, but I'm not exactly experienced at the business of home invasion. Most of my work is done in places so remote I'm lucky to get a network connection."

Remiel nodded. She had suspect as much. "You are certain that you need Gower?"

"No, but I want him."

"I'm not going to help you get revenge for turning you in,

if that's what you're thinking."

Oliver's mouth twisted into a vicious smile, but he shook his head. "Don't worry about that, I'm not really the vengeful sort."

"Then what do you want with Gower?"

Oliver shook his head and paused beneath the wide blue awning of an Italian coffee shop, crammed into the tight street front beside a crowded Chinese noodle bar. He gestured to the signs and said, "Which do you want for lunch?"

"I'm not hungry."

"Well I am. It's been a hell of a day and the last thing I consumed was a beer almost eighteen hours ago. If we hadn't grabbed my things from the hotel before coming here I'd look like I'd been kidnapped and nearly drowned." He paused for a moment, still surveying the local dining options, as a wicked grin spread across his lips. "Oh, wait, that is what happened to me. Thanks for not raiding my room, by the way."

"Our resources aren't that extensive," Remiel commented.

"Could have fooled me. How about some pizza?" Oliver nodded up the street to a pizza shop which had a vacant seat in the window, from which they could watch the door to Gower's apartment.

"Fine."

An hour later Oliver had satiated the gnawing pain in his belly and said precisely ten words to Remiel. The anger that had surged through him when she had informed him that Amber had been targeted by Zedekiah had faded, leaving behind the almost pleasant glow of a large stockpile of bitter ammunition for sardonic remarks. Amber was safe, he had received a text confirming her departure for places unknown before he reached London, and the thrill of adventure was beginning to take hold of Oliver's spirit.

Meanwhile, Remiel had picked at her significantly smaller serving while watching Oliver intently from across the table. It did not surprise her that a man like Oliver, who was so obviously given to strong emotion and had an insatiable hunger for knowledge, might be accepted by the spirit that dwelled within the heartwood. Many corrupt men had come before him, serving the purposes of the greater good despite their innate flaws, and just as many truly good men had been duped into advancing the cause of evil. Still, there was something about his cavalier attitude that bothered her more than she might have anticipated.

Finally, she could take it no longer. "Why do you do it?"

"Do what?" Oliver asked, settling back into his seat and inspecting her face, while carefully avoiding eye contact.

"Look for the shards of the mechanism."

"Why should I tell you?"

"Maybe because I saved your life."

"You're not the first."

Remiel flushed, then felt her face color a deeper red as she grew angry at herself for letting Oliver get to her. "I'm just trying to understand you."

"Stick with me through this mess and you'll know me as well as anyone."

"If you won't tell me about yourself, then what about Gower, what do you want with him?"

Oliver crossed his arms on the table in front of him and leaned across the table, then whispered, "I will, but first I have a question of my own for you."

"Fine."

"Why did Gower sell me out to you?"

"How should I know?"

Oliver rolled his eyes and waved at the street outside the window. "Please. You knew where to find Gower."

"Gower is Zedekiah's acolyte, not mine. I'm not privy to their private communication."

Oliver believed that, but he decided to press a little harder, just to see what he could learn from Remiel while she was on the defensive. "And you don't have any acolytes of your own to call upon?"

"None that will help in this situation," Remiel said. Privately, she wondered if any of her acolytes would remain faithful to her when word of her betrayal spread through the ranks of the Watchers. Fortunately, the very same diffuse, highly isolated nature of their network, which had frequently frustrated their efforts, would now work in her favor by preventing Zedekiah from reaching out to the other watchers.

"So that's it? There's nothing you can tell me about why so many people are desperate to get their hands on the folio."

"Nothing in particular. It's certainly ancient, but I'm not any sort of expert in Norse religion, so I can't tell you if any of the content is revelatory."

"Then what good are you to me, Remiel? Seriously, I'm grateful to you for breaking me out of that place, but if you can't bring in any backup, if you don't have any insights to offer, then maybe we should just separate now."

Remiel shook her head. "No, I can help you Oliver."

"How?"

She shook hear head again. "No, not yet. It's your turn to answer a question."

Oliver raised an eyebrow. As far as he was concerned, asking questions was not the best way for Remiel to earn his trust, but there was a strange, cold magnetism to her that made him want to confide his deepest secrets. He hated that, thought of it as a failure of his will, to feel this sudden irrational connection to a woman he had just met, especially since she had initially been his captor. He pushed against it with all his might, endeavoring to bury the unwanted emotion beneath a sardonic detachment, but could still feel the warm fingers slipping through the barriers and wrapping bands of hot iron around his throat.

He cleared his throat, flashed a cocky grin that he knew came across as false, and waved for her to go ahead.

"Why do you need Gower to translate the folio for you? Don't you know enough of the old European languages to translate it yourself?"

"I could manage by myself, but I want an outside perspective."

"Why?"

"Because he's an expert in Norse religion and languages. He can tell at a glance details that would take me hours, even days of research to notice."

"Why are you in such a hurry?"

"I don't know, Remiel. Maybe it has something to do with being hunted by angry Norse gods and kidnapped by psychopathic guardian angels."

Remiel had to smile at that. She opened her mouth to bite back, but stopped when Oliver raised a hand between them.

"Here he comes."

Oliver and Remiel watched as Samuel Gower shuffled up the street from the tube station, carrying a small briefcase in one hand and a cheep plastic bag from a Chinese takeaway shop in the other. He passed by their table, not even glancing up to see them watching him through the plate glass window, and paused a dozen yards down the street, waiting to cross to his apartment door.

"Ready to share your plan yet?" Remiel asked.

"Just keep up and don't get in my way," Oliver said, rising from his seat and turning towards the door. "Oh, and try not to look suspicious for the cameras."

Remiel scrambled to follow after Oliver as he darted out the door, down the sidewalk, and crossed the street right behind Gower. They caught up with him just as he finished pressing his security card to the electronic sensor beside the door and bent to pick up his dinner bag, which he had set on the walkway while he fumbled with his wallet.

"I'll get that for you, buddy," Oliver chirped, stooping to grab the plastic bag of food.

Gower started and, when he saw Oliver's grinning face, nearly collapsed against the brown painted brickwork. "How... What..." he spluttered, glancing rapidly from Oliver to Remiel and back again. "Why is she..."

"Invite us up and I'll explain everything," Oliver said, maintaining a smile that told all passersby and the ubiquitous surveillance cameras that he was nothing more than a friend of the old man who hadn't visited for a long while. "It's been too long since we sat down for a chat. And of course you know my friend here, she's a friend of Zedekiah." Oliver gestured at Remiel as he twisted the handle with the hand holding the bag and nudged the door open with the toe of his boot.

"But Zedekiah..."

"Please, Mr. Gower, can we go inside to discuss this?" Remiel said, nodding to the open door.

Gower blinked uncertainly and glanced up and down the street, as if he expected someone to sweep in and rescue him, then shook his head and turned to the doorway. He preceded them up the narrow steps, between narrow walls papered in cheery blue and yellow flowers, to the second story landing, where he again pressed his security card against the sensor beside his apartment door. Oliver pushed him aside, gesturing for Remiel to remain in the hall, then entered the apartment ahead of the others and scanned the entranceway, cramped kitchen, and living room for any obvious weapons. Once he was reasonably certain that there were no guns, swords, or bottles of pepper spray within easy reach, Oliver waved for the others to enter.

"What right do you have to come barging into my home like this?" Gower blustered as soon as Remiel had pushed the door shut behind him.

Oliver slid the bag of takeaway onto the passthrough counter of the kitchenette with measured care, waited just a second until he heard the soft intake of break that heralded another outburst from Gower, then rounded on the old man and grabbed him by the collar. He propelled Gower back, through the cluttered living room, and shoved him back towards the tattered black couch. The back of Gower's legs hit the coffee table and he fell, arms wavering feebly, and landed on the couch at an awkward angle with his feet splayed out on the table.

Oliver leapt over the table and straddled Gower's legs, dropping down so his full weight rested on the man's thighs, pinning him down. He grabbed the lapels of Gower's jacket with both fists and bent until his face was mere inches from that of his old professor. "You sold me out, Sam."

"No..."

"Yes."

"You don't understand."

"Oh, I think I do. You're an acolyte of Zedekiah, right? What does that mean, Sam? Do you worship him or just hold him in reverence as your own personal conduit to god?"

"Oliver, I..."

"He's dead, Sam."

Gower's face twisted into a confused mask as his eyes darted from side to side, seeming to seek a place where they could see past Oliver's head, perhaps to see how Remiel took this news. Oliver moved his head to the side and let Gower get a look at Remiel, who stood behind them, watching impassively.

Oliver put one finger on Gower's chin and guided his face back to look at his own. "That's right, Sam. I killed him myself. You always looked down on me for putting my quest for the truth above the stuffy academic worship of long dead facts, but look where it's got you. I'm alive and your master is dead."

"Please, Oliver, you have to be lying. I'll do whatever you want, just stop lying and tell me the truth."

"He's dead. Look into my eyes when I say it and tell me if I am lying. I shot Zedekiah at least ten times in the chest and left his body at the bottom of a lake."

Gower began to tremble as the truth of Oliver's words began to seep into his mind. Oliver moved away from him and settled into a wide recliner that was set between two overflowing bookshelves across the room from the couch. Gower pulled himself up into a more comfortable position, then dropped his hands to his lap and sat with his chin on his chest, weeping quietly. Remiel took all of this in with stoic silence, then pulled a straight backed chair from the dining table, which was cluttered with papers and books, and sat down off to one side, where she could see both men at once. Oliver's sudden, violent outburst had surprised her, but she knew that she had to trust him and see where all of this was going.

Gower sniffed a few times, wiped his eyes with a trembling hand, and looked up at the other two. "So, you've come back to kill me for turning you over to Zedekiah, like you killed him?"

"No, Sam, I'm not going to kill you."

"What then?"

"Well," Oliver mused, savoring the word as he leaned forward and rested his elbows on his knees, his fingers twined and pointing towards Gower. "I could do to you what Zedekiah had planned for me. Any idea what that was?"

Gower shook his head, but Oliver caught a glint of fear return to his eyes.

"Zedekiah, the divine master who you turned me over to, planned to cut me into little bits and mail those pieces home to my family until one of us revealed the location of a relic that I tracked down last month. How about it, should I do that to you? I bet you could still translate the Wagner folio without your big toes."

"No! Please, Oliver, don't hurt me. I didn't know that Zedekiah would harm you, I really didn't."

Remiel cleared her throat and Gower flinched as if he had been struck, then darted his eyes towards her. He ran a trembling hand through his gray hair, then mopped tears from the corners of his eyes. Remiel lounged in her chair with her right foot propped on her left knee, idly tapping a finger on the side of her shoe as she said, "You know who, and what I am, do you not?"

He nodded and gave a soft whimper.

"Then you should believe me when I tell you that this man is not one to be trifled with. However you remember him as a student, just consider that when Zedekiah struck me down for my rebellion and I lay wounded and defenseless, Oliver Lucas stood unflinching before your master's power and shot him down. He is a dangerous man, yet I have seen the blessing of God upon him, so I have thrown in my lot with him and will not prevent him from doing whatever he deems necessary to complete his quest."

Oliver jumped back in to the conversation then, saying, "Which is her polite way of telling you to talk, now. I want to know why you handed me over to Zedekiah and what is so damn special about that folio."

Gower glanced back and forth between his two interrogators a few times, then wiped his nose on his jacket sleeve and nodded. "Can I have my tablet? It will make this easier."

Oliver strode over to where Gower's briefcase had fallen, tossed the battered leather case onto the table, and clicked it open. Inside he found a stack of papers and the same battered tablet computer that Gower had been using to read in the pub the night before. Has it really been only a day? Oliver shook his head, feeling the weight of the last twenty-four hours beginning to settle over him.

He carried the tablet back to the couch and set it on the coffee table, then stood beside Gower and said, "There you go. Start talking."

Gower unfolded himself from between the couch cushions and settled into a more comfortable position perched at the edge. He began tapping on the tablet, unlocking it, pulling up a research organizer that Oliver recognized from his own phone, and swiping through several nested layers of notes until he reached his objective.

"Here, look at this section of the translation that I started last night."

Oliver picked up the tablet and began to read. He immediately noted that Gower had sketched a rune, or in some cases two, above each stanza of the poem:

* * *

209

(ANSUZ)

In the days before his creation,

When the bones of earth were yet young,

Lord Odin dwelt in the land of Värmd.

A leader he was, and fine, strong of hand and deep of mind.

(BERKANO)

Maidens flocked to his bed,

Like crows settling upon fresh laid seed,

Mead they drank, sweet and strong, until

each left him, forever satiated of their hunger for men.

(URUZ)

The mightiest of warriors he,

Son of giants, fist of iron, spear like lightning.

The lord Odin ruled with strength.

The lord Odin commanded all that he saw.

* * *

(PERTH)

Across the ribs of the giant,

Over the giant's blood, clouds cowering in the ripple of his bow,

Not until he arrived at the shore did Odin perceive:

The Wanderer come to Värmd, wrapped in his night cloak.

(WUNJU PERTH)

He made his way to the hall of Odin

Wherein the mighty feasted, gorging themselves

Venison, fish, bread, and mead, heaped upon the tables.

The Wanderer entered Odin's hall and the winds howled around him.

(ALGIZ)

"Mighty Lord Odin!" cried he, standing tall

The cloak, black as night, danced in the winds around him

"None here can best you in strength, nor any in the world

Like a plow horse you are, in strength of arm, leg, breath, and loin."

(ANSUZ)
So hearing, the mighty Odin arose,
His breast, swelled with pride, heaving
His face, flushed with mead, glowing
His manly virtues, aroused at the truthful flattery, proud.

(WUNJU)
"What brings you to my joyful hall?"
Bellowed he, the strong one, the lord Odin.
"Such dour continence ill fits one so
Blessed by the gods to enter this place of feasting."

(PERTH)
The Wanderer opened his mouth,

A gaping hollow, redolent of decay. As flesh
Abuzz with flies, heaving with the maggots within
So did his tongue cleave black lips to speak:

(HAGALAZ)

"Strength of arm, virile might, respect of men, all
Pass away in the withering of time. So shall it be,
For you, mighty Odin.
The Worm awaits, his jaw agape, to consume all mortals."

(ANSUZ)

Within his breast Odin stirred,

Desire for life, for knowledge, for staying the hand of death.

He stepped from his throne and cried out,

"Do you bring nothing but ill words?"

(PERTH OTHILA)

Again the wanderer spoke, his words as gilt iron:

"To know the lay of all mankind, wherever they may stand

And stave off the maw of death, however grievous the wound,

I offer these to you, great lord Odin."

(ANSUZ)
Then did mighty Odin invite the stranger to sit.
Hospitality to the wandering man he did order.
A place prepared, mead poured, women to sing.
Together they supped and spoke of the secret ways.

Oliver looked up from the tablet and saw Remiel and Gower watching him expectantly. He handed the device over to Remiel and waited in silence, watching her as she read the translation. He thought he caught the slightest twitch in her expression, but it might have been nothing more than confusion at the imperfect meter of the translated rhymes.

When she had finished she shrugged and passed the tablet back to Oliver. "This is what pushed you to turn Oliver over to Zedekiah?" she said, leaning back in her chair and looking skeptically at Gower. "I'm glad that you don't have anything against me, if you turn people over to be tortured on such paltry evidence."

"But don't you see it?" Gower demanded. He lifted the tablet and pointed at a stanza. "This clearly depicts Odin as receiving his godhood, not through divine birth, but as a gift from a wandering stranger. I have not completed the translation yet, but later he is described trading his eye to Mímir in exchange for a nugget of gold, which he put in his head in place of the missing eye."

"Yes, it's typical mythological claptrap. Next you'll tell me that the Prose Edda is a truthful account of how the European continent was formed."

Oliver burst out with a sardonic laugh. He shook his head and said, "You're one to talk, Remiel. Living proof of divine intervention in the affairs of mankind, and you mock Sam for claiming to see evidence of magic in an ancient text. Hell, if I'm putting the pieces together correctly, this text describes the very same magical object that your order is sworn to protect."

"I'm not claiming that the shards do not exist, only that it is foolishness to presume that someone can gain immortality by shoving a shard into their head, let alone that such an action would become the basis for an entire religion."

Oliver contemplated Remiel's words for a long while, looking fixedly at her until she shifted uncomfortably beneath his gaze. It still struck him as odd that this woman could be so ignorant of the details of a mystery that she had helped to perpetrate for thousands of years. He wondered if the process of reincarnating, which she had mentioned as an option for Zedekiah if his body did not recover from being beaten, shot, and drowned, might possibly bring with it some memory loss. Perhaps that could explain why Remiel was so maddeningly obtuse at times. Of course, there was always the distinct possibility that she was lying to him.

"If I may interject," Gower whispered, his head resting in his hands as he stared forlornly at his feet. "I contacted my master because I knew that Oliver had dedicated his life to finding something remarkably similar to the secret device which the Watchers have long protected. I had considered calling him as soon as Oliver contacted me, but decided to wait, in hopes that Oliver would bring me word of some other quest that had distracted him. Only when I read this portion of the folio did I determine that, to all appearances, Oliver was once again in pursuit of one of the mysterious shards that so captivated him as a student." As he finished he looked up, did his best to straighten his shoulders, and looked to Oliver. "Please, Oliver, just leave well enough alone. You don't understand the powers with which you are meddling."

Oliver gave Gower a half smile and shook his head. "No, Sam, I'm not going to stop. The best you can do is help me interpret those runes so that I don't go blundering into a crevasse in a cave somewhere."

"Why do you need him to translate for you?" Remiel asked.

"Sam here wrote half the books worth reading on Norse culture. I could blunder my way through it, probably come up with the right answers in the end, but I don't have time for that."

Gower seemed to brighten some at that. He sat up and nodded along with Oliver's assertions, then added, "I taught this boy all he knows about Scandinavian culture and language, and he isn't even an especially good student. Always drifting off to some other culture or scrap of history, this lad. No true depth to his nature."

"Sam, don't make me reconsider not cutting off your toes," Oliver snapped, only half joking.

Gower flinched at that, but it seemed that he had gotten over the initial shock of Oliver's assault and the news that his master was dead, and was settling back into his accustomed role of Oliver's professional gadfly. He tottered upright and said, "If you'll excuse me, this ancient bladder needs relief and my dinner is growing cold. I cannot be expected to perform forced translation services under these circumstances."

Oliver rose as well and produced the gun he had taken from Zedekiah's acolyte and displayed it to Gower. "Don't try anything stupid, Sam."

The old man coughed a bitter laugh. "Please, mister Lucas, it would be quite foolish of you to fire that in the center of London. The surveillance network would pinpoint you to this building before my body hit the floor."

"I'm not sure I believe that, Sam, whatever your public service announcements say. Just don't go calling the police or digging an old 'collectable' weapon out of your bedroom. Give me what I want and I'll be out of your thinning hair before you know it."

Gower harrumphed and moved slowly across the room on popping knees, then disappeared into a doorway on the short hall to the side.

"Can you trust him?" Remiel whispered, rising and stepping close to Oliver.

He raised an eyebrow at her. "At least as much as I can trust you. Do you really think I buy that whole act you just put on?"

"What are you talking about?"

"Don't pretend with me. I don't know what you're hiding, but I can't believe that you don't think Sam is right about a shard being connected to the origins of Norse mythology."

Remiel's mouth tightened and she raised her eyes to meet Oliver's, but he turned away to pick up the tablet from the coffee table. He wouldn't allow himself to be put under her spell, whether it was genuinely a magical effect of her supernatural origin, or merely an incredibly strong chemical attraction that he had towards her. He brushed past her and began clearing off the dining table so that he and Gower could begin working out the meaning of the runes.

Remiel watched him for several minutes, wondering how much Oliver had intuited from what she had told him of the Watchers, and how much of their purpose he had gathered from his investigation of the organization he had called "the Creed." When Gower emerged from the bathroom and shuffled into the kitchen to unbox his Chinese takeaway, Remiel picked up the leather satchel from beside her chair and carried it over to the table where Oliver sat, engrossed in Gower's translation of the folio.

"Do you need this?" she said, pulling the folio out from the bag.

Oliver took the folio without comment and began unfolding it on the worn surface of the hardwood tabletop. He placed the tablet beside the folio, then pulled out his phone and swiped through the reference works Hank and Amber had uploaded to him until he found Hank's notes on the next opera in Wagner's Ring Cycle.

"What are those annotations?" Remiel asked, pointing to the darker, handwritten lines between the fading printed text of the folio.

"Wagner's notes," Oliver said.

"You mean he wrote on this?"

"Yes. It wasn't quite so valuable to him as it is to us. To him it was just one among many old texts that he consulted when researching German mythology in preparation to write the Ring Cycle. According to my sources, Wagner reached out to every connection he had while he was living in Zurich, using the influence of more successful composers and the influence of a few well-connected friends to track down a variety of sources for German folk literature."

"I never took you for an aficionado of continental opera," Gower muttered, settling himself in a chair to Oliver's left with plate of steaming rice and vegetables drenched in a thick brown sauce.

"I'm not."

"Fascinating then, that you know so much about Richard Wagner. One might even suspect that you had been planning this theft for a long time, preparing a little background research, perhaps."

Oliver jerked his head towards Remiel as she sat in the chair opposite Gower, "Like I told her, I have a source."

"And this source told you that Wagner used this manuscript as source material for das Rheingold?"

Oliver shook his head and leaned back in his chair, crossing his arms and looking critically at Gower. "No, my source doesn't even know about the folio. I put that together based on the fact that I stole the folio from an exhibit of German mythology that had just been completely reworked to display the folio as the centerpiece. Oh, and the handwritten notes that Wagner made on the folio." He raised his eyebrows and waited, a part of him hoping that Gower would press the argument.

The old man shook his head, shoved a forkful of rice and veggies into his mouth, and chuckled deep in his throat as he chewed. He swallowed and looked at Oliver and Remiel thoughtfully for a few long seconds, then waggled his fork at Oliver and said, "I think you're right, mister Lucas. I still don't like you, but you came to the same conclusion as I, and I can respect you for that."

"I can read the folio and notes, Gower, I just need your help getting this done fast."

"And you shall have that help, once I have eaten my dinner."

Oliver rolled his eyes and leaned forward to examine the folio again, eager for the translation to be complete. As he scrolled through the description he began to wonder if there might be a connection between the sequence of events described in the poem that Gower had translated and the plot of the opera. He grabbed a thick book from the corner of the table and flipped through the pages until he found a chapter on the rune known as Othila, the one which was drawn beside the first stanza of the poem Gower had begin translating. He skimmed over the pages to refresh his memory on the meanings of the rune, then returned to reading about the operas, searching for plot elements that might be related to the concept of inheritance, which the rune represented.

"You're taking the easy way, mister Lucas, even though you know it will only lead to disaster."

He shot an angry glare at Gower, who pushed another forkful of food into his mouth and chewed slowly, meeting Oliver's gaze with indifference. Oliver knew he was just toying with him, but he took the bait anyway. "What should I be doing, then?"

"Certainly not paying too much attention to the runes written at the beginning of each stanza."

"Then what would you suggest I pay attention to?"

"Those runes are little more than honorifics, intended to place the reader in the appropriate mood to read each stanza, based on the author's perception of the events described. At least whoever completed this middle translation had the good sense to leave those runes intact instead of translating them."

Oliver pinched the bridge of his nose and sighed deeply. He had already been awake far too long and endured far too much in the last few days, but he would have to simply let Gower's words pass over him, or he would never learn how to access the roots of Yggdrasil. "What should we do then?"

"I'd say that you need to pay attention to the actions of the characters in the poem. If you do that, then associate those actions with an appropriate rune, then you might find the answer you are looking for." Gower pushed aside his plate and pulled his chair closer to Oliver. "Get ready for a long night, mister Lucas. We have a lot of reading to do."

Over the next several hours Remiel watched in relative silence as the two men, one young and full of fire to track down a relic beyond his understanding, the other gray with age and clearly eager to be rid of his unwelcome visitor, worked through the night and well into the next morning to unlock the meaning of the ancient runes. Gower drank one cup after another of strong black tea and Oliver alternated between tea and cans of energy drinks delivered to the apartment with a large order of Chinese takeaway shortly before midnight. At first she did her best to appear interested in their work, interjecting questions into their discussions, peering over Oliver's shoulder at the books he flipped through on the tabletop or the glowing screen of his phone, and leaning to peer at the folio as they worked, but eventually she gave up and retreated to the couch.

She lay on the worn cushions, closed her eyes, and slipped into the meditative state of mind that came to her as naturally as falling asleep. In her mind's eye the disparate pieces of her situation hovered like elements of an especially intricate child's mobile, each twirling in empty space and moving according to her imagined prediction of where the future might carry them. This was her native realm, a place of spirit and thought, unhindered by the confines of mortal flesh, but which she could only access when she relaxed control of her physical body. She examined the situation, trying to determine just how much she should divulge to

Oliver, and how far she should allow him to go on this mad quest to capture more shards of the mechanism. She was especially concerned about the contents of the folio which, if accurate, could lead Oliver into places as dangerous as the shards themselves. If only Zedekiah had listened to reason, she whispered to herself, in that empty space. We could have worked together to bring Oliver into our fold, to harness his drive and find a way for him to help us protect humanity from the evil we have guarded for so long. But it was too late. Zedekiah had chosen to make an enemy of Oliver, despite his divine approval, and had fallen to him in battle. That, too, gave her pause. No matter how often she reminded herself that Oliver had clearly been chosen for some holy purpose, it was brutally obvious that he was a man of violence. Such had been used before, she knew, but rarely did their tales end in joy.

Distantly, she felt a hand fall on the shoulder of her incarnate body. Remiel reeled her consciousness back, wincing at the constriction of the carbonic mind as she wrapped herself in it, then opened her eyes of flesh and saw Oliver bending over her. A thick scruff of red stubble traced the line of his square jaw and dark shadows of exhaustion hung beneath his eyes. Despite the obvious signs of exhaustion, she saw a gleam in his eye as he stood upright and said, "We're going to Sweden."

CHAPTER SEVENTEEN
COFFEE SHOP

The man in black lounged in the shadows of his padded booth, watching a long blue and yellow train slip out of view under the structure of the central railway station across the canal. The air around him was thick with smoke and the scent of strong coffee. He glanced down at his own coffee cup, pondering the white lines of congealed cream twisting through the syrupy black brew, which had gone cold in the time he had waited. He wished that he could drink the coffee, but he did not yet trust his body to properly digest anything stronger than water and bland wheat crackers.

A waitress pushed through the haze and eyed the man's cup.

"Can I get you anything else?" the waiter asked in Danish.

He shook his head, no.

The waitress swallowed hard and, with visible effort, succeeded in looking at the man's face without fixating on the puckered skin stretched across the man's skull. "Perhaps a pastry?"

The man gave a long sigh that was almost a hiss and tilted his wretched face towards the waitress. Dim red light fell upon his misshapen nose and cast deep shadows into the hollows of his cheeks. He replied in flawless Dutch, his words punctuated with sharp pauses, "Do I look like I want a pastry?"

The waitress scurried back to the safety of the cigarette

counter by the front window, silently cursing her supervisor for prompting her to check on the man who had now occupied the booth at the rear of the coffee shop for over an hour.

The man in black curled his mouth into a cruel smile and returned to watching trains come and go across the canal through the forest of patrons, mostly tourists by their languages, who drifted in and out through the door.

Another hour passed before the woman he was waiting for arrived. Dressed in a sleek black dress that clung to her curves and a knee length jacket of wine red leather, she immediately captured the attention of half the customers when she swept through the door. She strode directly to the back table, shrugged out of her coat, and slid onto the bench opposite the man in black.

"Took you long enough," the man growled.

She ignored him and waved for a waiter. The timid waitress who had proffered baked goods returned and took the woman's order, then hurried away without even asking the man if he wanted anything.

"He's an old man, it took a while for him to say his goodbyes."

The man in black laughed bitterly and tapped at the side of his coffee cup with a single long finger. "Where is he going?"

The woman shook her blond head and wagged a finger in the air between them. "Not yet. First you pay, then I share your old friend's pillow talk."

"Haven't you already been paid?"

"Funny, but no. It might surprise you, but I actually like the old fool."

"And yet here we sit."

The woman nodded silently and chewed at her lower lip

for a moment, then caught herself and shrugged. "I'm a business woman. The old fool tells good stories and brews the best beer I've ever had, but in the end I'm just another one of his women."

"Indeed you are," the man said. "It may ease your guilt to know that if our mutual friend had not stopped in Amsterdam to visit you, then I would doubtless be having this conversation with one of his paramours in Berlin, or Copenhagen, or any number of other cities across Europe."

"You think I don't know that?" she spit back. "You don't have to rub it in my face."

"And we were just talking about how professional you are. You aren't developing an emotional attachment to him, are you? Those can be dangerous in your line of work."

She opened her mouth to curse him, but bit it back when the waitress approached their table with a small tray and set it in front of her. She paid, then inserted a long white cigarette between her lips, lit it with practiced ease, and inhaled deeply.

"A surprising choice," the man said, nodding at her cigarette.

She held the cigarette between finger and thumb to examine it, then shrugged and let out of stream of white smoke from between pursed lips. "You wouldn't understand. All you Americans can think of in Amsterdam is our sex and drugs, but if you truly understood European culture you'd realize that good tobacco is just as alluring when it is difficult to get."

"I'm not an American."

She raised an eyebrow and said nothing.

The man leaned forward and rested his elbows on the table, bringing his scarred face into the light, then intertwined his fingers and said, "We're getting off track.

Where is he going?"

"Payment."

"Of course."

"Now."

He sighed and pulled a large cell phone from his coat pocket. He tapped at it a few times as the woman studied the pattern of shadows the glowing screen cast across his wrecked features. Somehow, though she wouldn't have sworn to it, his face seemed marginally less damaged than it had when she sat down.

He set the phone on the tabletop and said, "Enter your account number here, then press send."

She took a long drag on the cigarette, watching his face carefully, then shook her head and picked up the phone. After a moment she said, "That was only half of what we agreed upon."

"That's right. Tell me what I want to know and you'll get the rest, keep delaying the issue while he gets away from me and the police will find you dead in a canal."

"It's not nice to make threats."

"I'm not threatening you," he said, his voice level.

She tried to look into his eyes, but quickly averted her gaze. The man's eyes glinted black like chips of obsidian in his head, cold and hard between the wrinkles of scarred flesh.

The woman tapped the icon to initiate the transfer to her Swiss account, then set the phone on the tabletop and took a long drag from her cigarette. She held the smoke for a moment, then let it out in a long stream from her nose. She lifted her leather coat from the seat beside her and shrugged it over her shoulders, more for the comforting weight than to ward off any chill, then reached into an inner pocket and produced a sheet of paper.

"I wrote it down so I wouldn't forget. He's going to Sweden to meet a man named Oliver."

"You're not telling me anything I didn't already know."

"I know where they are meeting."

"Better. And when?"

"That's all here."

"Hand it over," he said, holding a hand out to her. The skin of the hand was oddly patterned with a mottled scrawl of old scars and the nails were painfully short, as if they had all been ripped away and were only now beginning to regrow.

She hesitated, clutching the folded paper to her belly and chewing on her lower lip again. "You're not going to kill him, are you?"

"That's not your concern. I'm sure that you'll find another wealthy old man to lean on at all the parties and pay for whatever designer clothes he wants to take off of you."

She crumpled the paper in her fist and threw it at the man's chest, but it spiraled awkwardly through the air and he had to snatch it before it fell to the floor. He unfolded it read the words, which had been written across the paper in precise lines with an expensive pen, and smiled. He pulled his phone back and tapped at the screen a few times, then set the device on the table before her and read the paper again, even though he had already memorized it.

"Take your silver and go. If you can ever be of service again, you know how to contact me."

The woman completed the fund transfer and dropped the phone to the tabletop, then stood, slipped her arms into the sleeves of her coat, and glared down at the man. "I hope you burn in hell," she spat.

The man gave her a thin smile and tucked the paper into the folds of his dark woolen coat before saying, "Have no fears on that regard, my lady. I've known far worse."

She flicked the butt of her cigarette at him and stalked out of the coffee shop.

The man in black chuckled, deep in his throat, and gathered himself to rise and follow her out the door. He had a long journey ahead of him to catch up with Oliver and Odin at the gates of Värmd.

CHAPTER EIGHTEEN

Lake Vänern

The last rays of sunlight mingled with flickering candlelight across the rich red tablecloth as Oliver and Remiel sat, looking out over the darkening waters of Lake Vänern, at a window seat in the bistro that occupied the ground floor of their hotel. Remiel picked at the remnants of her slice of lingonberry cheesecake while Oliver nursed a tall glass of a pale beer, brewed only thirty kilometers to the south, which had come at the recommendation of their waiter. Across the water, barely visible through the thickening nighttime fog, the silhouette of an island loomed dark against the rapidly sinking sun.

"Why are we waiting here?" Remiel asked.

Oliver took a long sip from his glass and didn't say anything.

"Oliver, we've been here for two days. I'm about finished with touring churches and sampling Scandinavian cuisine. And you have spent the whole while pecking away at your phone looking up god knows what."

"Haven't you ever taken a vacation?"

"No, Oliver, I haven't."

"Sounds mighty stressful, living for thousands of years without ever taking a few days off to relax," Oliver said. He punctuated his opinion with another long drink and licked foam from his top lip.

"I was being sarcastic," Remiel snapped.

"Really? It's so hard to tell with you. Makes me glad that I managed to stop looking you in the eye back in London. I'd hate to fall for someone who doesn't know how to relax for a few days."

Remiel gritted her teeth to keep back another remark, then shook her head and ate the last bite of her cheesecake. The last three days, since they had departed from Gower's apartment in the early morning, had been maddening. Oliver continually pored over the notes stored in his phone, ignoring her as he cast himself into a tangled web of information ranging from Gower's translation of the folio, to summaries of the operas of Wagner, to scanned books that detailed the complexities of translating Norse runes. When she asked him questions he responded mostly with inarticulate grunts. It was clear to her that he resented her presence. More importantly, however, she was beginning to worry where his line of inquiry might end. Though the Watchers had lost track of several of the shards over the last few thousand years, Remiel was reasonably certain that there were none in Scandinavia, with the possible exception of one that she didn't especially want to think about.

"Oliver, please, at least tell me whether you actually have a lead on the shard, because if we're just hiding from Zedekiah or another of your enemies I can suggest a few places that are a bit warmer this time of year."

He shook his head and said, "Don't worry. The shard will be here soon, and I am almost certain that I know how to get it."

"Be here?" she said.

"That's right. I'm waiting for the shard to come to me, then I'm going to pluck it right out and bring it home to join the others."

"Don't be so hasty to pluck things, boy," a voice growled

from behind them, speaking in an English heavily accented with German.

Remiel turned her head towards the voice and felt the blood drain from her face.

"About time you got here," Oliver quipped, raising his beer in salute to Odin.

Odin swept his long gray coat off and dropped it onto a spare chair, then settled himself into the seat with an explosion of breath. Seeing him now, dressed in a gray tweed suit with a chocolate brown shirt open at the collar to reveal a scar that encircled his throat, Oliver was surprised at the muscular bulk of the old man. Thick cords of muscle ran down his neck, bulged beneath the fine wool of his dinner jacket, and braided across the backs of his hands. The black patch over his missing eye was supported by a narrow band of black elastic. His beard was trimmed close to the jaw and seemed to have streaks of yellow running through it. Only his gut, thickened by untold gallons of mead, remained the same. Overall, the impression was of a man who was younger than when Oliver had last seen him.

"You sounded confident enough on the phone, so I assumed that you had successfully evaded Loki since departing Germany and managed to learn what you needed of the folio, so I took the liberty of pausing in Amsterdam on my way here. One should never give up the opportunity to bed a good woman, Oliver, never forget that. Speaking of which, you haven't introduced me to your companion."

Oliver glanced at Remiel and saw a sour expression twisting the stately lines of her face. Not surprising, he thought. "This is Remiel. She helped me out of a tight spot in Britain, then insisted on accompanying me to make sure that I don't get in over my head again."

Remiel flinched, so slightly that Oliver might have missed it if he had not been surreptitiously inspecting her expressions for the last two days while she thought he was ignoring her. That had been the only way he could look at her without becoming lost in those eyes, a failing that he still could not put down to his inexplicable infatuation or some supernatural power.

Odin's brow wrinkled and he seemed to be trying to recall something, then he raised his eyebrows, shook his head, and leaned forward to proffer his hand. "Good evening to you, lady, I'm Odin. I suppose I ought to apologize if I have offended you with my womanizing, but when you get to my age you don't give a thought to voicing exactly what is on your mind."

Remiel nodded and her face shifted from sour to vaguely surprised, then rapidly dropped to a neutral expression as she regained control of her features. She did not take his hand.

"Silent type you have here, boy," Odin said, dropping his large hand to the tabletop with a bang that shook the cutlery. "Her voice as comely as her face, or has she never said a word to you?"

"Never mind her," Oliver replied, keeping his eyes fixed on Odin to avoid shooting a puzzled expression to Remiel, "I think I know how to do what you've asked of me."

"So you translated the folio?"

"Yes."

"And you're not just following in another's steps, are you? That is the whole reason I need someone like you, to find your own path through the fire, seeing as it's been so long since anyone worshiped the true gods like we did back then."

Remiel slammed her fist on the table and, turning to her, Oliver saw that her face had flushed a deep red.

"Something wrong, Remiel?"

She set her jaw, seemingly biting her tongue as she shook her head and turned her back on Odin to stare out the window.

"Sure about that? Because you've looked like you want to punch Odin since he sat down."

"It is a common enough reaction," Odin said, a smile cracking the corner of his mouth. "Women either love me or hate me, for the most part."

Oliver set his nearly empty glass on the table and pulled his phone from his pocket. He lay it on the table and pulled up a document that he had been working on since leaving Britain. He pushed the phone towards Odin and said, "This is what I've managed to work out from the folio. Tell me how it matches with your recollection."

Odin lifted the phone and began scrolling through the document as Oliver summarized it for the benefit of Remiel, who was still pointedly ignoring Odin. "I have to take your word for only a mortal being permitted to pass through the, I suppose we'll call it a barrier, or membrane, that separates the actual tree that exists in this world and the roots of Yggdrasil, wherever they might be. The folio mentions nothing about that, but I've worked out that the sequence of events that Wagner drew upon as the basis for the plot of Siegfried, the third opera in his Ring Cycle, are actually a sort of code. Each event in the original poem, many of which were adapted for the opera, can be mapped to the meaning of a Norse rune. If I have the location right, and understand the meaning of certain runes correctly, we should be able to perform the ritual tomorrow."

"And what exactly is this ritual you keep mentioning," Remiel said, turning to glare at Oliver. "Exactly how do you intend to defile your soul for the sake of a dangerous relic that I have repeatedly warned you about?"

Oliver looked back to her, trying to understand the cause of her sudden hostility. She was, of course, hostile to him tracking down the shards, but he thought that they had agreed to see this quest out to the end together. Now she was openly attacking him. He pulled the folio, still wrapped in a plastic bag, from an inner pocket of his jacket and laid it on the tabletop, then waved for Remiel to examine it. She hesitated, then turned away from the window and pulled her chair closer to the table to get a better look at the folio.

"Do you see these runes here, and here?" he said, pointing to several sharply angled lines placed between what appeared to be stanzas of a poem.

Remiel nodded, the mask of her rage slipping slightly. Odin set down Oliver's phone and leaned forward to examine the runes as well.

"I recognize those as well," Odin said. "It's been, damn, three hundred years or more since I tried to read these."

"Which is part of why you need me, and why I needed to go to Britain. It's only been a few years since I studied runes like this, and I was a bit rusty on their meanings. Anyway, the poem indicates that you, Odin, were a mere man when you stepped through."

"That's true enough, as well as I can remember."

"And the ritual?" Remiel said.

"I'm getting to that. First I have to reach the island where the tree is located, which shouldn't be terribly difficult as, if Sam's interpretation of the poem and my geographic extrapolations are correct, it is about twenty miles across that lake," Oliver said, pointing out the window to the dark waters, just visible in the glow of street lamps and dockside security lights. "There is a large ash tree in a valley at the center of Djurö National Park, and when I say large I mean it is one of the largest in Europe. Carved into the trunk of

234

that tree are the runes of the Norse writing system. Some historians believe that the tree was used for ritual sacrifice during the pagan era, but the location is so remote, and nobody has ever found evidence of a major settlement in the area, so nobody has made a serious effort at exploring it in over fifty years. The only people who visit the location are tourists and a small group of neopagans who come to the island twice a year."

"I think I do remember a long boat ride." Odin interjected. "Do you know what you are supposed to do when we get there?"

"Yes, Oliver, what are you going to do?" Remiel snapped. "You can't seriously believe that some lines carved into an old tree will let you step into a different world."

Oliver gave them both a puzzled look. He had a growing sense that his suspicions of Remiel knowing more than she admitted to were well grounded. All three of them were bent over the table now, examining the folio like pirates gathered around a blood stained treasure map, a vision that Oliver couldn't help admitting to himself might be fully appropriate. He shrugged, then smiled and tapped a finger on one of the runes, near the middle of the poem. "I won't tell you everything now, but I can say that it all begins with this, the rune for inheritance and knowledge."

He sat up and grinned at both of his glowering companions. "Just think, by this time tomorrow Odin will be human again, I will have another shard, and you, Remiel, will have tagged along on a grand adventure. Who knows, maybe you'll even tell me the truth about what you want once I have that next shard."

Remiel glowered at Oliver and said nothing. She risked a glance at Odin, but the old fool was already busy proposing a toast, then downing half his glass of beer in a single quaff. It looked like Oliver had indeed worked out the location, and possibly the ritual, to access the roots of Yggdrasil.

"Remiel, are you alright?" Oliver asked.

She shook her head, but managed to flash him a weak smile. "I am just concerned."

Oliver smiled. He didn't know what game Remiel was playing, and he still did not trust her, but something in him still wanted to draw her out of her funk. "Don't be worried for my sake. This is a great day, Remiel. Tomorrow I'll descend to the well of Mímir and capture my sixth shard, and then I will be that much closer to knowing what sort of device they all came from."

Remiel looked away from him. That's exactly what I am afraid of, she thought.

CHAPTER NINETEEN

NORSE PANTHEON

The next day dawned clear and cold, with a yellow sun arcing up through a cobalt blue sky over the shimmering water of the lake. They all ate a hearty breakfast, which Oliver thoroughly enjoyed despite Odin's hangover and Remiel's continued reticence, then assembled at the docks to board a rented motorboat. Oliver passed out packs of supplies for a day's hike, then climbed into the motorboat with Remiel and began preparing to cast off. Before leaving the dock, Odin raised his right arm to the sky and muttered something softly, then brought it down again with a large raven perched on his wrist. He bent his head, whispered something to the raven, then swept his arm out towards the lake. The raven gave a raucous "caw" and flew away towards the distant island at the center of the lake.

"Munin will scout ahead for us," Odin growled as he stepped into the boat.

Oliver nodded and took the wheel and they swept out from the dock and across the glassy surface, leaving a spreading wake of ripples behind the boat to glisten in the bright autumn sun.

As they sped across the lake, Odin repeatedly stood and scanned the horizon for any sign of his raven, Munin, but each time he sat down without spotting anything. The sun was high overhead by the time Oliver eased their rented motorboat up to the shore of the island at the center of the lake. Remiel jumped out of the boat and darted over the rounded, moss covered boulders to secure a line to a nearby tree, then Oliver followed her.

Odin clambered out of the boat, grasping at Oliver's hand and a convenient tree for support, then turned to survey the water. His eyes squinted, searching the horizon. Oliver stepped beside him and squinted as well, scanning the rippling surface of the lake for any sign of pursuit, or any inconvenient autumn vacationers, but saw nothing.

"He's not back yet," Odin muttered.

Oliver nodded, understanding now the concern on Odin's face. "Is that something we should worry about?"

The old man shrugged and turned from the water, not meeting Oliver's eye. He pulled a water bottle from his backpack, took a drink, and put the bottle away without speaking. After a time he said, "No, there's no cause for concern. Damned bird probably decided to hunt some wood mice along the coast."

Oliver nodded and pulled out his phone to send a quick message to Amber, then paused. She had gone to ground would not be checking their usual communication channels, and Oliver didn't want to use the emergency Twitter feed for a location update. Instead, he composed a brief message to Hank:

Think I've found another shard. Amber is offline, so giving you my coordinates in case I disappear. Don't come yourself, just raise hell if I don't contact you again within three days. - Oliver

They set off into the forest, following a GPS bearing on Oliver's phone. The location of the tree was well known, Oliver had found it with an internet search within minutes when Gower identified the likely region from geographical clues in the folio text, and he hoped that they would be alone when they reached it. He strode ahead of the others, occasionally checking his bearings and keeping one hand near the pocket where the 1911 rested. It had been more difficult storing its pieces in his modified camera body for the trip across the border, they were shaped somewhat differently from his usual Glock, but he felt safer with it, especially out in the wilderness with a mad god and a mysterious angel.

After nearly an hour of hiking they came to a steep incline, which Oliver's GPS app informed him was the descent into the valley of the ash tree. He motioned for the others to approach and showed them the route to the tree on his phone.

"It's not far. Stick close and stay quiet. There shouldn't be any traps, enough tourists come here every year, but I don't trust that Zedekiah, Loki, or someone working for them won't show up."

"How would they know where to go?" Odin asked.

"Loki brought you here originally. I have no idea why he is toying with us, but he has been pushing me towards this ever since we met in the South Pacific."

Oliver looked sharply at Remiel and Odin in turn, waiting until each of them gave him a nod, then he turned back toward the valley.

Down they went, stepping cautiously over slick, mossy stones, and being wary to test their footing before setting their full weight, lest a seeming patch of earth conceal a deep crevice between rocks, lightly covered over by decaying sticks and leaves. Oliver could hear Odin's strained breathing at the rear of the party and wondered that the old man had made this journey, drunk and blindfolded, without falling and breaking his neck. By the time the slope began to level out, Oliver estimated that they had descended over a hundred feet and were, according to the GPS on his phone, below the waterline of the lake that surrounded the island. Another fifteen minutes hike over weather worn boulders and through dense trees brought them to the edge of a clearing which, according to the poem and the canopy penetrating radar maps Oliver had examined, stood at the exact center of the circular valley.

Oliver felt his pulse quicken at the sight of a golden light streaming through the trunks of the pines, setting the broken ground at his feet aglow with its warmth. He hurried forward, forgetting his usual caution at approaching a new site, and stepped into the clearing.

Oliver froze, his mouth agape in wonderment at the sight before him. Remiel came to a halt before running into him, then stepped up beside Oliver and joined him in staring.

At the center of a clearing stood the largest ash tree that Oliver had ever seen. It towered over them, at least ninety feet tall from the top of its golden leaves to the base of its ghostly white trunk. The crown of it seemed to glow in the noonday light, as sunshine cut through autumn leaves, gathering a yellow radiance that was redoubled as it reflected from the crisp carpet of yellow and pale brown fallen leaves. Beneath that carpet, thrusting up through lush green moss, shoving cracked stone out of their way with implacable force, the roots of the ash tree spread out in twisting, heaving slashes of white, like a nest of snakes frozen in place as they writhed beneath the earth. The trunk of the ash tree was wide enough that Oliver and both of his companions could have circled it holding hands and still needed at least two more to fully circumscribe the wood. The bark of the tree gleamed a pale, mottled white in the sunlight, except for a ring of dark red scabs, which circled the tree at about head height.

"It's beautiful," Oliver whispered. He gulped in air, suddenly aware that he had not taken a breath in nearly a minute. He reached instinctively for the heartwood that he had worn around his neck for nearly a year, only to find it missing.

"Truly awesome," Remiel said. "It has been a long time since I saw such a thing."

Odin arrived at their side, panting, and draped a heavy arm on Oliver's shoulders, leaning on him for support as he caught his breath then said, "Never saw the like of it before that day, nor since. I'll tell you boy, I dreamed of returning here many a night these last thousand years, but never dared. After that first time..." he trailed off, not finishing the thought.

"You never returned here? After you received the shard, I mean."

Odin started and looked guiltily at Oliver, then shook his head and said, "No, I came back many a time. I mean, after the first time I brought a mortal back here to try and send him in after my eye."

"I knew I wasn't the first!" Oliver shouted, throwing off Odin's arm and stabbing a finger at his face. "You told me that you don't know the ritual, that I had to steal the folio and interpret it in order to learn the secrets of the world tree. I knew all along that it had to be a lie."

"Remarkable it took you this long to figure out, boy. Now get your finger out of my face and go perform the ritual."

"And if I don't? What will you do if I turn away right now and take the boat back to the mainland?"

"First, I'll kill you. Then I will find some way to go on living, forever." Odin leaned towards Oliver and whispered, "Remember, boy, that you've got the most to lose here. Sure, I want to regain my mortal soul, but I think I can learn to live with immortality again."

Oliver took a deep breath, preparing to bite back at Odin, then thought better of it. As much as he hated to admit it, the old god was right, so he stayed his rage, lowered his hand, and started to turn back towards the clearing. The moment he laid eyes on the bone white trunk of the world tree, however, the rage that had been building in Oliver since he was first pulled into this whole convoluted mess surged up again. There it was before him, a wondrous, living relic, and he could not honestly claim any part in discovering it. The rage at having been manipulated burst through the dam of his cool and, almost without noticing he was doing it, Oliver whirled back towards Odin and delivered a cracking blow to the old god's bearded face.

Odin took the blow and staggered back against a the trunk of a ragged old pine tree. He shook his head, dazed, then his eyes cleared and fixed upon Oliver. "You'll pay for that, boy," he growled. He gathered himself up and Oliver saw in the glint of his eyes and the square of his shoulders the sturdy warlord he had once been.

"Stop this!" Remiel shouted, stepping between them. She looked to Oliver and said, "You need to complete your quest, then we must decide what to do with the other shards. As for you," she said, wheeling to face Odin, "You are too old to play such foolish games. I swear, for all your knowledge you don't have the sense of an animal. Tell Oliver what you know now, everything you've been holding back, or God help me I will..."

"You'll what? Slap me, call me mean names? Please, woman, I'm more than a match for the both of you."

A harsh laugh stabbed into their debate, severing Remiel's reply like a sharpened blade slicing a string. It echoed through the clearing as the three companions darted their heads from side to side, up, down, searching for the source of the laughter. Oliver leapt to the side and crouched against a tree, then slipped a hand beneath his shirt and gripped the gun that he had concealed in a holster tucked at the small of his back. He thought that he recognized the laugh, though it echoed differently through the trees and across the steep walled valley than it had in a cavern, and he knew that they were all in trouble.

"Go ahead, Remiel, why don't you threaten him some more? Maybe if you revealed some of your true nature the old fool would recognize you."

"Who is that?" Remiel shouted. She turned about, searching for the origin of the voice, and as she turned her deep gray eyes began to take on a silvery radiance.

"Oliver..." the voice crooned in a mocking singsong, "Dear Oliver, why don't you just put that gun down now, we both know it won't save you any more than it did the guard you stole it from."

Oliver grimaced and pulled the gun, but instead of putting it down he held it out in front of him, muzzle pointing upwards, and continued scanning the edges of the clearing and occasionally glancing back behind him.

"And you, Odin! You old fool," the voice snapped, mockery replaced with bitter distain. "Why don't you come clean and tell your lackey why you could never dispense with your curse before now."

"Who the hell are you?" Odin roared. His fists clenched at his side and Oliver stopped scanning for the source of the voice to stare in amazement as the air around Odin seemed to twist in on itself, the very substance of reality apparently twisting like coils of smoke rising from a flame, and the long spear that Odin had held when Oliver first met him appeared in Odin's hand.

"Who else?" A tall, painfully thin figure emerged from behind the white trunk of the ash tree. It was dressed all in black and wrapped in a tattered black cloak with a deep cowl pulled up around its head. Its left hand rested on the pommel of a long sword, strapped about its waist with a belt of black leather, inlaid with geometric designs in silver. "It is me, Loki."

Oliver trained his gun on the figure and said, "I know you. Leo, right? I should have recognized you in Germany, but I thought you were dead."

"I'm not surprised you didn't. The bandages just came off my face last week," Loki shrugged and the hood fell over his shoulders, revealing a livid white face, still crinkled in places with wide patches of wrinkled, newly grown skin.

"It's not often I leave someone to die in a gas explosion and they show up again half a world away," Oliver quipped. He took a step towards Loki and said, "And what's with the pseudonym? Leo Cay? That's not especially different from your name."

Loki held his arms out and shrugged. "What can I say?"

"Start with what the hell is going on here."

"A fitting question indeed. Odin, why don't you listen to the lady and tell Oliver how you came to possess that remarkable bit of metal in your skull?"

Odin looked from Loki, to Oliver, to Remiel, and back to Loki again, his face growing a deeper red beneath his white beard. He flexed his large fingers into tight balls at his sides, then raised one and shook it at Loki, saying, "Damn you, Loki. I should have known that you would have a scheme to foil my plans."

"The story, old man."

"Odin, what is he talking about?" Oliver asked.

Odin turned to Oliver, his face flushed to a dark red, and

growled, "Don't trust a word from his mouth, Oliver. Even in your time Loki is known to be a liar, and the myths and folk tales passed down through the ages don't tell half the story. This damnable excuse for a man is deceit incarnate. You've seen him murder men yourself. He..."

"Tell me what is going on," Oliver screamed, turning his gun towards Odin, "Or I swear I will blow you to hell myself."

Loki laughed again and said, "Such a fascinating turn of phrase. So many say it, and yet so few know what it means. Do you not agree?"

Oliver squinted in confusion and glanced between the others, trying to work out what Loki meant. Of course he didn't literally mean he would send Odin to hell, he wasn't even sure if he could hurt the old god and, if he could, who knew what might become of his immortal soul. He was about to burst out that this was no time to debate idiomatic phrases when Loki stepped forward and said, "How about it, Remiel?"

"You know her?" Oliver said.

Remiel gave Loki a look of undisguised hatred, as if he had accused her of some unspeakable crime. She took three slow, deep breaths, and Oliver briefly wondered if he was about to see her transform, as she had in the parlor beneath the lake. Then she said, "Yes, Oliver, I know Loki. And I know Odin. As a matter of fact, the only stranger in this whole affair is you."

"I don't understand. How do you..." Oliver trailed off, lowering his gun as he worked to put it all together in his head. Somewhere in this whole puzzle he was missing a key piece.

"I don't remember her," Odin said, his brow furrowing in concentration. "I mean, she looks familiar, but when you've lived as I have most women remind you of someone you've bedded in the last few hundred years."

Loki strolled over to the trunk of the white tree and leaned against it as he said, "This is one woman you never touched, Odin. Not in your entire life. Go ahead, Remiel, refresh his memory, it has been so many years since he contemplated the vast depth of your eternal gaze."

Remiel opened her mouth to speak, but Odin grabbed her by the shoulder and spun her around, then grasped her chin in his callused fingers and gazed into her face. Remiel thrust a palm into his chest to shove him away and averted her gaze, but not before Odin cried out in recognition. He released her and said, "By the very blood of my body, you are Hel."

"Was."

"You must still be."

"She is."

Oliver felt whatever shade of control he had held over the situation slip from him, as if he had been grasping at a shadow. He aimed the gun at the nearest pine and pulled the trigger. The gunshot tore though the confused voices and sent a flock of gray and white birds screeching through the canopy into the bright sky. A deep silence settled upon the clearing.

"Enough!" he said, his icy voice loud in the sudden calm. "I don't give a damn who you all are. You each have ten seconds to tell me what you want, or we'll find out who can get back to the boat first. Remiel, you first."

"Oliver, I just..."

"No bullshit! Tell me what you want. Seven seconds."

"I'm a Watcher, Oliver. I've been known by many names, including Hel, over the centuries and I just want to help you make a wise choice about the shards. Please, just..."

"Time's up. Odin, talk to me."

The old god shrugged his wide shoulders and tilted his head to the side, squinting at Oliver. He paused for a moment, then raised a hand and tapped his eyepatch, saying, "I want to get rid of this damn shard of metal."

Oliver studied him for a long moment, then nodded and turned to Loki. "You've been playing this all along, haven't you? The book. The break-in. The attack at the castle."

Loki grinned and gave Oliver a theatrical bow, resting his hand on the pommel of his long gray sword. He took a step forward and said, "But of course. Though, I must admit, I had not planned on being caught in a gas explosion. I thought you would just leave me to die down under that island."

"And what's your game?"

"The same as you, Oliver. I want that shard in Odin's fool head. Get it for me, and I swear I will let you go home unharmed, despite the pain you caused me. I won't even keep up our little rivalry for relics."

Oliver frowned, considering how that fit in with the puzzle he had been constructing. If Loki had anticipated everything, well, everything except Remiel joining up with Oliver, then he truly had been played for the fool. Still, a question lingered in his mind. He glanced at the gun in his hand, knowing it was as useless as a stick against his three companions, and lowered his hand to tuck the gun back under the flap of his vest.

"Why don't you just take it for yourself? Or perform the ritual and go retrieve Odin's eye for him."

It was Remiel who laughed this time. She dropped to a crouch, then leaned back against the rough trunk of a pine tree, and said, "That's the whole reason Odin has the shard, Oliver. Didn't he tell you?"

Oliver shook his head.

"Go ahead, old man. Tell Oliver why you have that shard in your head in the first place. Tell him how you went from warlord who would have been forgotten in the depths of time to a god whose name would still be recognized and immortalized over a thousand years later, in virtually every country in the world."

Odin's chest puffed out and his chin rose at Remiel's words. Oliver couldn't help smiling at that. She might be mocking him, but it was true that Odin was still one of the best known of all the mythical gods. The old man took in a deep breath, exhaled it slowly, then turned to Oliver with a half smile twisting the corners of his mouth. "I fooled Loki," he said. Then his smile broke into a wide grin and he turned back towards Loki and shook his fist at him. "That's right. I fooled you." He stalked across the clearing, the light streaming through the leaves painting his white hair with patches of brilliant gold, and shouted, "You thought that I would climb down to the roots of the world, to the very bedrock of this earth and come back bearing that shard to you? Ha! You were wrong, Loki. I outfoxed you and emerged just as immortal as you, and infinitely wiser." Odin halted his charge mere inches from Loki and glared down his nose at the little man.

Loki held his ground, seemingly unperturbed by Odin's bluster. He looked up, a smile playing across his lips, and said, "Yet when you wearied of the weight of all that knowledge, and all those years, you could not go back, for only I knew the secret of the runes."

Oliver rolled his eyes and strode up the two men, shaking his head. Finally, it all fit together in his head.

"I've heard enough. Both of you get over to the tree line and leave me alone to look over these runes," he said, jerking his head towards the ring of scabs above their heads, which at this distance plainly formed the angular markings of nordic runes.

"And what of the shard" Loki asked. "Will you deliver it to me?"

"I'm not delivering a damn thing to anyone unless both of you back off and leave me to think. I've had about enough of gods, angels, and secret societies these last few weeks."

"Do what you will with it, boy," Odin growled. "So long as you get my eye back I don't care what you do with the shard."

"How noble of you. Now back off."

The two men exchanged glances. Odin shrugged and Loki gave a wicked smile in reply, stroking the pommel of his sword, then they both turned away from Oliver and shuffled through the carpet of leaves to take their seats against trees. Oliver watched until they had settled down, one on either side of Remiel, then shook his head and turned to examine the runes.

It all made sense now. Odin and Loki feuding over the shard. Remiel and the Creed watching all the shards and, somehow, being drawn into Norse mythology as the figure of Hel. Oliver searching for the shards for so long, and with such success, that all three of them had been drawn to him, each for their own purposes. It gave him a certain degree of pride to know that he, a mere mortal with a fixation on the same mystery that had destroyed his uncle, had been noticed by such important figures, despite his frustration at having been played as a pawn in Loki's scheme. Now he thought he could see the whole picture and, while it filled him with an impotent rage, he was relieved to finally understand the movements of the game that these three ancient beings had been playing.

He pulled out his phone and began swiping through the notes that Gower had helped him to translate. He found the appropriate page and scrutinized the series of angular symbols that they had determined would unlock the passage to the world tree.

As Oliver had found so many times in his years of searching for relics, the key to this particular puzzle lay in looking at the puzzle in context of a broad view of a culture's mythology, then carefully stripping away elements of myth that had been drawn from other cultures and layered on top of the original tale. Much as Oliver had worked out the location of the shard in the Cook Islands by carefully distilling the essence of Maori creation tales until he worked out the true origin of their religion, he and Gower had searched the folio for commonalities with both Wagner's Ring Cycle and the beliefs of the ancient Norse culture. They had found them in the structure of Siegfried's journey in the third part of the Ring Cycle.

Oliver looked up from the screen to examine the runes encircling the tree. The lines of each rune were cut cleanly into the wood, as if each had been hacked into the white bark of the tree with clean, decisive blows from a narrow bladed axe. He stepped up to the tree and stood on his toes to examine the marks, his forehead wrinkling in confusion at glistening red sap that dripped from runes. Oliver had been a Boy Scout as a child and, while he hadn't earned his Eagle rank, he still remembered the tree identification activities that the boys had gone through on several campouts. Ash trees were supposed to have pale yellow wood running with nearly clear sap beneath their white bark.

Oliver stepped back from the tree with a sudden feeling of dread icing up his spine and called out, "Odin, you said that you came back here before, but couldn't figure out how to open the pathway."

"That's right."

"When was the last time you did that?"

Odin stroked his beard and gazed up at the gleaming leaves for a long moment, then said, "Oh, it had to be over three hundred years ago. Before I settled in Germany and opened my brewery."

"How many?"

"Three hundred, boy. Or something close to that."

"No. How many others were there?"

"Oh," Odin said. He paused to think again, then shrugged. "At least ten or twenty. After that I stopped counting for a while, then I finally gave up hope."

Oliver looked around at the thick carpet of leaves and the knobs of root poking out from beneath, their white bark the color of bleached bones. He suppressed the frantic urge to begin kicking through the leaves, searching for the bones of his predecessors. Even if Odin had killed them, and left their bodies here, the bones would certainly have settled deep into the spongey earth of the forest floor by now.

"What about you, Loki. Why haven't you sent anyone before now?"

When there was no reply Oliver looked up and saw that Loki had pulled his hood down over his face and appeared to be sleeping, with his head bent and his sword resting on his knees. Beside him, Remiel watched Oliver unblinkingly with her strange gray eyes.

Oliver turned back to the tree and grimaced at the streaks of blood, still wet after three hundred years, glistening in the runes. Of course Odin would use blood sacrifice, Oliver thought. Loki probably did the same to him. That was one thing that he had not worked out, whether the ritual to unlock the path actually required blood, or if that had simply been a theatrical element. So many of the relics Oliver had uncovered had been bathed repeatedly in blood throughout the centuries, whether in ritual sacrifice, or by the adventurers who had preceded him, but he had found that few of them actually required blood to unlock their supernatural powers.

He walked slowly around the tree, examining each of the twenty four runes carefully. Every one of them glistened with a sticky wetness that bespoke the blood that had been spilled into the cut, which had somehow been preserved throughout the centuries of wind and rain. He continued searching until he came upon the rune that he and Gower had determined to be the first in the sequence.

"Othila," Oliver whispered, tracing the outline of the rune with his eyes. It looked like a diamond set atop a triangle with an open base and, in addition to serving as a soft vowel sound when used to transcribe spoken words, it represented the concept of a rightful inheritance. Appropriately, Oliver thought, the connotation of that inheritance was more often one of passing on knowledge than worldly possessions.

He looked around the side of the tree to where the others waited. Remiel had moved closer to Odin and was speaking to him in hushed tones, her hands gesticulating emphatically. For his part, Odin appeared to be ignoring her impassioned speech as he watched Oliver intently, his eyes narrowed in anticipation of the path he had so long sought being reopened. Loki still appeared to be sleeping, but Oliver noticed that his right hand was draped over the hilt of his sword.

There was no way for Oliver to perform the ritual without being noticed. He would have to move quickly and rely on the good fortune that three of the runes he needed were hidden from observation around the far side of the tree.

He stepped back around the tree and pulled a knife from his pocket and, before he could talk himself out of it, drew the blade across the thumb of his left hand.

CHAPTER TWENTY

RITUAL

Oliver raised his bloodied thumb to the first rune and whispered its name, "Othila." The rightful inheritance.

He waited, holding his breath, for something to happen, but nothing did.

Of course nothing happens, he thought. If there was any sort of feedback during the ritual Odin would have cracked it long ago. He grimaced and moved carefully around the trunk until he reached the next rune.

The dragon. "Perth," he muttered, pressing his thumb to the gnarled wound in the bark. In truth, neither he nor Gower knew the true meaning of this rune. After hours of arguing, searching through Gower's books and Oliver's files, and comparing the runes on the folio to the plot of Siegfried, Wagner's notes, and Gower's extensive knowledge of Norse history and culture, they had followed in Wagner's footsteps and settled on "dragon" as a likely meaning.

"Gebo." The blood. He didn't know if the blood actually necessary, though he suspected it was. The use of blood in rituals was well established in religions the world over, from the first blood sacrifices offered by Abel in the Hebrew scriptures to the Mesoamerican practice of offering grain blended with human blood to their gods, and while he did not understand the mechanics of the supernatural forces at work, Oliver was certain that there was a reason behind the independent worldwide emergence of the practice, just as he was certain the shards were related to the emergence of dominant cultures across the globe.

The next rune represented joyous singing, and it had been the key to Oliver and Gower unlocking the ritual. In his opera, Wagner had described the blood of the dragon giving Siegfried the power to understand the song of the bird, which was then able to tell him where to find the sleeping valkyrie Brünnhilde. That had been the most visible similarity between the narrative poem in the folio and the plot of Siegfried, and once they had decided to examine the poem and opera together, as different interpretations of the same basic plot, the remainder of the ritual had emerged quickly. "Wunjo," Oliver said, reaching up to smear a line of blood up the vertical line of the rune, then sharply downwards to complete the shape.

He heard the rustle of leaves and glanced back to see that both Odin and Remiel had risen and were watching him intently. Loki remained seated, but Oliver was certain that his head had tilted up a few degrees to watch him from beneath his dark hood.

He turned back to the tree, squeezing his thumb between the fingers of his right hand to coax more blood from the wound, and circled to the rune for fire. "Kenaz," he said, quickly swiping his finger across the rune. I've got to finish it before they come any closer. If I can just open the pathway and step through before they can stop me...

He reached the final rune, which represented a safe and profitable journey. He heard leaves shuffling as the others came closer to him and he reached under his vest for the grip of the gun as he pressed his thumb to the rune and called out its name, "Raido!"

He stepped away from the tree, drawing the gun and hoping that something would happen.

The white bark of the ash tree seemed to blur in Oliver's vision, even as the carpet of fallen leaves, and the surrounding trees, and the two forms hurrying towards him were drawn into a sharper focus. Then a bright red line of blood streaked down from each of the runes, etching itself into the vague, impressionist form of the trunk as it descended, as if the blood were a line of acid eating its way into the tree. The world around the tree appeared to slow, though Oliver could not be certain if that were true, or if it was merely an impression brought on by the rapidity of the ash tree's transformation, and then it was as if the tree itself were the at the center of a black hole, drawing all the golden light of the glade into itself. The smeared white lines of the trunk shimmered and suddenly grew translucent. Looking through them Oliver saw a stairway of black steps spiraling downwards around the twisting roots of the tree, illuminated by a vague glow that he could not rightly call light, more reminded him of darkness made visible by its juxtaposition against an even deeper darkness beyond.

He stepped forward, his legs moving as if through deep water, and looked down the spiraling steps into the darkness beyond. Deep below, so far away that it appeared no larger than a pinprick of light, Oliver saw a flickering in the darkness and somehow he knew that that was where he needed to go. He glanced up and saw Odin and Remiel running towards him, Remiel with her hand raised in mute entreaty, and behind them Loki gathering himself for a leap with his sword held ready at his side.

He looked away from them all, took one last breath, and stepped down into the darkness.

CHAPTER TWENTY-ONE
THE WORLD TREE

The black steps were solid beneath Oliver's feet. That was a relief. He had plunged through the filmy outline of the tree almost without thinking, moving quickly so as to escape from Remiel, Odin, and Loki, and he hadn't considered that the whole scene might be an illusion until he was already racing down the steps. He descended quickly, each step ringing loud in his ears, the fingers of his left hand brushing against the smooth white bark of the ash tree. The stairs descended around the wide trunk in a gentle spiral, never touching it, but seemingly hovering in mid air with all the solidity of a marble staircase. Oliver paused and crouched on a step, brushing his fingers across the matte black surface, the pulling them back in surprise. The step beneath his feet felt colder than ice, like he imagined it would feel to touch a block of dry ice with his fingers. He peered closely at his fingertips, expecting to find them blistered, but they were unharmed. He hesitated for a moment, then placed his hand against cold black surface. He cried out in pain at the sudden, intense cold, and pulled his hand back, but again found it unharmed. A ripple of movement stirred at the corner of his eye and Oliver twisted his head around, raising the gun to sight into the darkness. He saw nothing at first, but as he stood still, gazing into the black across the sights of his weapon, he saw the faint stirring of a deeper black against the distant black depths.

"What is this place?" he whispered.

Oliver half expected a response from the blackness, another supernatural being winging in across the void to tell him what it expected him to do. He was relieved when he heard nothing.

"Finally, a bit of peace," he muttered.

Oliver holstered his gun and continued descending the steps.

After what seemed a very, very long time, Oliver started to wonder how far down the steps went. Looking up he saw only the towering spire of the world tree, its white bark seeming to glow softly in the strange darkness, and the silhouettes of the steps above him.

He continued down the steps, counting now. Somewhere around the four-hundredth step Oliver began to notice a vague flickering light below him, like a warm fire crackling in the distance. After another thirty steps, and Oliver was able to pick out a web-like tangle of shadows silhouetted against the glow, which had begun to take on color, wavering between intense red and deepest blue at such a rapid pace that if he stared at it for too long the colors seemed to merge into a vague, wavering purple.

Oliver took another step, then froze.

Something was moving down there. A long, sinuous black form that wove through the web of shadows, disappeared into the crook of a branching shadow, then appeared again, slithering along the web of lines like a snake through the branches of a banyan tree.

Oliver realized that that he had been holding his breath and took a deep gulp of air. "You've come this far," he muttered, pulling the gun from its holster and checking that he had a bullet in the chamber.

He continued down the steps, laying each foot as quietly as

possible and pausing frequently to try and spot the cause of the slithering shadows below, but whatever it was remained as elusive as the origin of the continually shifting illumination. He reached the base of the steps with the tree standing between him and the light. Beneath his feet the ground was a wide plane of solid darkness. Above him, tendrils of solid blackness twisted away from the tree like choking vines, weaving together into a dark tangle that twisted downwards until it vanished into the distance. He leaned against the trunk of the tree, adjusted his grip on the gun, and crept around the curve of the tree until he could peek around the trunk and see the source of the shimmering light.

The black floor extended forward as far as Oliver could see, vanishing into a blinding core of pure white light, rimmed in a continually shifting edge of blue and red light. The glow shifted constantly before him, seeming to surge towards him with a burst of brilliant blue, which bled away to silver, then white, through pink, and into blood red as a portion of the colored border appeared to pull away from him. Oliver's eyes widened in awe and he felt a faint tremble begin in his fingertips as he tried to decide whether the light formed an unending tunnel for the black pathway, or if the walkway approached the light itself. Above his head the tangled black vines spiraled away from the trunk of the tree and meandered towards the light like random sketches of charcoal scrawled across a prismatic canvas. Though the light was blindingly bright, neither the vines nor the path reflected any light. Altogether, Oliver was left with the impression of standing inside a two dimensional sketch, looking through the thin veil of paper and charcoal to the terrible beauty of the fully formed world beyond.

Suddenly, Oliver realized that he had stepped out from

behind the tree and was gazing down the length of the black pathway, holding his breath and allowing his arms to hang limp at his sides. He glanced down at the gun in his hand and realized that it seemed strangely flat and unimposing. He blinked to clear his vision, glanced back at the swirling construct of light, then shook his head slowly as he slipped the gun back into its holster. Whatever this place was, Oliver was certain that human weapons would be no match for anything he might encounter. He had crossed over into a different realm, one in which everything he had ever known suddenly felt flat and insignificant.

Ahead of him, through a short tunnel of black vines and silhouetted by the distant radiance, Oliver saw a pedestal jutting upwards out of the black surface. He started to walk towards it, hoping that this was the well of Mimír where Odin had left his eye in exchange for the shard. He moved quickly, gaining speed with each step, until he was running across the black surface, his footsteps sounding solidly and without echo across the vast emptiness around him, hurtling towards the distant light.

Then a shadow detached itself from the snarl of vines above him, swung down, and slammed across his chest.

Oliver cried out and fell back, his feet skidding out from under him as his torso came to a sudden halt with a bone cracking jolt. His head slammed into the cold black of the pathway and his vision sparkled with yellow dots. He lay on the pathway, head lolling about, chest aching, the sound of his own labored breathing hissing in his ears.

A new sound broke upon his consciousness, slithering through his ringing ears and wrapping tight coils around his brain. It was not loud, but as the voice spoke, Oliver could hear nothing else, not even his own thoughts. It said, "Do not be so hasty, traveler, or you may rush to your doom. How came you to this place?"

Oliver raised one heavy hand and pinched at his eyelids, shook his head, then wiped his hand down across his sweat-slicked face and opened his eyes. A pair of obsidian slits cut into wide golden eyes stared back at him from an angular face composed of glistening black scales set at sharp angles. The scales parted to reveal a narrow mouth with a crimson forked tongue and long, white fangs.

Oliver opened his mouth to speak, but found his mouth dry and his lungs empty. He gasped for air and tasted only the bitter nothing of that empty realm. What was I breathing before? he wondered. There must be some atmosphere, right? I can't have just been holding my breath ever since I stepped through the tree.

The voice came again, sonorous and dark, soft, yet all-consuming. "Ah, I understand now. You have come from Midgard by the way of ash. It is long since we encountered anyone from that fell realm."

Oliver's eyes widened in panic as he desperately tried to breathe. He wondered if this thing, this mind-invading snake that had knocked him from his feet, had crushed his lungs. He tore his eyes from the black slits and glanced down across his body, to where the wide coils of scaly black hide lay across his chest.

"Do you need to breathe, traveler? Of course you do, but it is not I who am preventing you from breathing. You must only remember that you can breathe, that you are here in a place of infinite possibility, where one man can breathe deep the fresh air of his homeland while another suffocates directly beside him. It is merely a matter of your decision. Your will."

I can't believe I'm listening to… whatever this thing is, Oliver thought. His eyes darted about and he suddenly realized that his body appeared as flat as a sheet of paper in comparison to the incredible, he struggled to think of a word, dimensionality, of the snake and the light beyond. He closed his eyes and, with great effort, summoned a mental image of himself. He pictured his body as if from without, laying sprawled across a wide expanse of matte black stone with a huge black snake draped in loose coils across his torso. He felt his mind beginning to cloud and the panic rising up again, but Oliver fought back and pictured himself breathing, his chest rising and falling as precious oxygen flooded into his veins.

He gasped. Coughed. Nearly screamed with the pain of his diaphragm pressing against bruised ribs.

"Well done, traveler. Crude, but effective." The snake slithered off Oliver's chest and settled into a wide coil beside him.

Oliver pushed himself upright and slid back until he could rest against a tangle of low hanging vines. They seemed as hard as iron, yet as he rested against them Oliver thought he could detect a slow pulse pressing against his back, surging through the vines like blood pulsing through an artery.

He coughed and wiped a sleeve across his face, then swallowed hard and said, "What is this place? What are you?"

"Ah, the inevitable questions. It is always the same with you travelers, whether you stumble in from Midgard, Hiranyagarbha, or the planes of Oneiros, you all start off with the wrong question."

"How is it wrong to ask where you are?"

"Because, before you can begin to properly ask that question it is necessary to define what, exactly, you are."

"I don't understand," Oliver said, shaking his head and probing the edges of a painful knot that had begun to rise at the back of his skull. "I am me."

"And what is that?

"What am I?"

"An excellent question, traveler," the snake replied, flicking its red tongue out as if to scent Oliver and answer the question for him.

Oliver groaned and lay his head back against the vines, then cursed as he knocked the tender spot on the back of his skull. He leaned forward to rest his head between his knees. How the hell did it all come to this?

"Oh, if you are just going to sit there and mope I might as well be on my way," the snake said. It lowered its head and flexed the long coils of its body as if to slither away.

Oliver laughed then. It was a deep laugh, which burned through his aching ribs, resonated through his throat, and was twisted to a cynical bark as it left his lips. It felt good and he realized then that he had not laughed, not truly, in a very long while. After a moment he stopped laughing and pushed himself to his feet.

"My name is Oliver. I'm a thief and a seeker of knowledge. I have come to this place, whatever it is, to find the eye of a god and trade it to him for a fragment of an ancient device."

The snake turned back to Oliver and rose up on a long line of neck until its head was nearly level with Oliver's. "And now you begin to see the smallest part of the essential nature of the question you ask. Before you can begin to ask where you are, you must know what you are, for the nature of your being creates the structure of your environment."

Oliver thought about that for a moment, trying to decide if it was worth continuing to describe himself, or if he should try to pass by the snake and continue along the pathway. For all he knew, this creature was only toying with him. The snake looped itself around a nearby vine and slithered up into the shadows, then appeared again a moment later, dangling itself from the black lines above until its angular head hung only a few feet from Oliver's face.

"You have no reason to trust me, Oliver Lucas, but I assure you that I mean you no harm. I wish only to speak with you regarding your motivation for entering this most perilous of realms."

"And what realm is that?" Oliver asked. He wondered briefly how the snake knew his name, then remembered that it had been listening to his thoughts when they first met and was even now speaking directly into his mind.

"There is no way that you could understand the nature of this place, Oliver. The deepest philosophies of your realm have attempted to comprehend it for millennia. Your most advanced scientific minds, utilizing the most powerful machines devised by your species have only begun to scratch at the surface of the antechamber to this place. Try as you might, your feeble human mind will never truly understand the grandeur on display before you."

"Then explain it to me."

"I cannot. You said yourself that you seek knowledge. Unfortunately, knowledge is only half of the equation. Even complete knowledge of the nature of this place would show you only the consummate horror of its beauty."

Oliver stepped closer to the snake and said, "Tell me what you are. I told you what I am."

The creature stared back at him, its golden eyes unblinking.

"I have come for Odin's eye. Will you oppose me?"

"Odin? Truly, if you have come on a mission from that old fool you must be the most foolish of your kind. Allow me to give you a measure of counsel, completely free of charge:

Whatever you believe Odin has to offer you, it will be snatched away by another."

"You mean Loki."

The snake swung gently from side to side and Oliver had the irrepressible notion that it was laughing at him. "It appears that you are not as foolish as I had first considered, if you know of Loki and his machinations. Tell me though, do you know what Loki is?"

"Why should I tell you? You know my mind. You're speaking into it now. You probably knew everything that I am saying now before it reached my mouth."

The snake flicked its crimson tongue at Oliver and dropped a few inches, then curved its neck so that its head came up to his level again. "And there it is, the faintest spark of wisdom. There may be hope for you yet, Oliver, though your quest for knowledge drives you to meddle with powers far beyond your comprehension. Yes, I know both the breadth and depth of your knowledge better than a skilled seaman knows the currents that sweep along beneath the surface of the still waters, but as I said, it is not your knowledge that concerns me."

I've had enough of this, Oliver thought. He stepped past the snake and strode towards the pedestal. He half expected the creature to attack him, but it merely watched as he walked by, then retreated up into the vines above his head and followed along with languid sweeps of its long body. The question of what Loki might be had gnawed at Oliver's mind ever since Odin had explained that the man Oliver had known as Leo was more than a mere rival in the antiquities market. Then, after his encounter with Zedekiah, and Remiel's revelations about the Watchers, Oliver had been faced with the real prospect that he had dedicated his life to tracking down something truly dangerous.

He stopped a few feet away from the pedestal and turned back, searching the tangle of vines above his head for the snake as he said, "Alright, I'll tell you why I'm here, but I need you to tell me what you know about Loki so that I can defeat him."

The snake dropped from above, tongue flickering, scales glittering darkly in the reflected hues of the light, and said, "Loki cannot be defeated by one such as you."

"Why not?"

"The mere fact that you ask that question reveals that you are not prepared for the answer."

"Damn you and your riddles!" Oliver shouted. "I've been searching for the shards since I was twenty-three and finally, after fifteen years of work, I am making real headway in tracking them down, and you tell me that I am not ready to understand?"

The snake shook its head slowly from side to side, its tongue still flickering. "No, Oliver, you are not. Perhaps when you have returned to your world you will see the shape of it all, but I cannot explain it to you."

"Then what good are you?" Oliver shouted. Even as he said it, he knew the words were foolish. He was behaving like a petulant child, insisting that an adult tell him why he shouldn't play with fire and refusing to accept the answers given, and that was the generous interpretation of his actions. There was also the possibility, slight, but certainly there, that Oliver had begun to go mad. After all, how many rational people ended up in a shouting match with a psychic snake in a realm of darkness beneath a magical ash tree?

The snake studied him for a long moment, tongue flickering, eyes unblinking. After a time it said, "I will be here, gnawing at these black tendrils that link your reality to the superposition of the multiverse, drinking in the sweet sap of existence and contemplating the ineffable nature of deity long after your realm collapses into dust and ice. My brethren and I will bear witness as your feeble branch of the world tree rots from within, snaps under its own weight, and falls away into the abyss of the cosmos. That, Oliver Lucas, is what I am, for good or for ill. You, on the other hand, have been playing with death ever since you were a child and while your knowledge of it has grown ever more expansive, you still lack the wisdom to know when to stop."

The snake arched its sinuous body until its slitted black and golden eyes were mere inches from Oliver's face and said, "Go take your prize, traveler, and return through the gateway to Midgard. Pray that your wisdom outstrips your knowledge before you fall victim to your own pride."

Oliver watched in silence as the snake folded itself back up into the snarl of vines above his head, whipped its body into motion, and disappeared into the darkness. He waited for a moment, wondering if the snake would return, then he turned to face the shimmering light beyond the black pedestal.

Oliver approached the pedestal, willing himself to keep striding forward through a space that every sense told him ought not to exist, compelling his body to continue functioning as the universe around him screamed that he was too simple, too flat, to exist within this superdimensional realm. I am Oliver Lucas, he repeated, over and over in his mind, clinging to that knowledge as, with each step, he imagined that he could feel the very atoms of his being straining to break their orbits. I am here to retrieve the eye, so that I can get the shard, so that I can learn the purpose of the mechanism. I will keep breathing. I will continue to live. I am who I am. As he moved forward, the light seemed to recede away, as if no matter how far he traveled along that dark pathway he would never be able to approach the source of its pure radiance.

Suddenly, without any true sense of the distance he had traversed, Oliver realized that he had nearly reached the pedestal. It rose seamlessly from the flat black expanse of the walkway, like a spurt of oil that had been frozen in place just as it reached the apex of its ascent. At its tip, the otherworldly substance dipped downward to form a shallow depression, which appeared to be full of a silvery liquid that reflected the shifting colors of the light.

Oliver stepped forward and peered into the surface of that silver well.

Within the shifting surface of the liquid Oliver saw the valley in which the ash tree grew. He saw Remiel standing before a shimmering hole in the side of the trunk, seemingly guarding the entrance through which he had entered this place of darkness. Opposite her stood Loki, his sword drawn, his body pulled into a tight crouch, seemingly prepared to lunge forward and impale Remiel on the tip of his grey blade. To the side stood Odin, his arms waving in broad, angry gestures as he appeared to shout at the other two. There was a flash of yellow light, a spray of red, and then Oliver was standing in the dark light again, his hand in the middle of the silver pool and a scream on his lips. He pulled his hand back, expecting to find it wet, but was surprised to discover that none of the silver liquid had clung to his skin. He examined his left hand and found it completely unharmed, then looked down at the basin. The silver surface appeared unperturbed by his touch and Oliver began to feel himself slipping back into a vision of the glade, now tinged with flashes of azure light and a wide crimson spray. No! Stay here, he willed himself, pulling back from the vision.

He hesitated for a second, then reached out with his left

hand and plunged his fingers back into the invisible depths. He felt nothing as his hand passed through the glistening surface, until his fingertips brushed the burning cold of the black material that had extruded from the floor to create the basin. He gritted his teeth and continued to sweep his fingertips across the sides and bottom of the basin, blindly searching for anything hidden beneath the surface. After several seconds of excruciating cold, Oliver's fingers brushed against a round object that gave to his touch like a ball of gelatin. He fumbled with it for a moment, struggling to gain a grip on the slick surface, then grasped the object between his fingertips and pulled his hand from the basin.

It was an eye. The white orb shot through with thick red veins. The cornea thick with the milky rime of a cataract. A long tail of gore-covered optic nerve dangled from the back of the eye and the whole thing was coated in a film of smeared blood.

Oliver smiled.

"I've got it now, you old bastard," he muttered.

"Good for you, Oliver. You managed to lift a piece of dead flesh out of a pool. A truly stunning victory, if I may say so my self."

Oliver turned, reaching instinctively for his gun before he recognized the voice as that of the shadowy snake. The creature dangled from a vine above his head, the line of its body weaving gently back and forth like the curves of a sine wave as it glared at him through the black slits in its golden eyes.

Oliver held up the eye and grinned. "That's right. I don't know who you are, but unless you plan on trying to stop me from taking this out of here, why don't you get out of my way."

"Or else you will, what? Shoot me with that?"

Oliver glanced down and saw that the gun in his hand now appeared to be constructed from tightly folded origami papers. He gritted his teeth and concentrated on the weapon, recalling what he knew of a Glock's structure and composition, attempting to will it back into its original shape. The gun seemed to pulse in his hand, folding in on itself and twisting through several impossible shapes, before it returned to what appeared to be the proper form.

"Don't be to prideful about that, traveler. I simply ceased opposing your will. Remember, I am not your enemy here."

"Then who the hell is?" Oliver shouted.

The snake gazed at Oliver for a long while, its body continuing to undulate as it seemed to contemplate Oliver's question. Finally, it said, "You are."

"Excuse me?"

"In this place and moment you are the greatest enemy to yourself. You must break the bonds of your own pride and recognize that it is not external forces that hold you captive, but your own headless drive to possess that which you do not understand, and to understand that which is unwise for one such as you to consider."

"You sound like Remiel," Oliver growled, unconsciously tightening his grip on the gun. "How could you even know what I am trying to learn? You're trapped out here in this darkness, slithering along your vines and spitting doubt into the minds of whatever travelers come your way."

"Is it truly dark here, Oliver, or do you only perceive that because you do not have the eyes to see the glorious radiance of this place?"

Oliver thought about that for a moment, rolling the eyeball between his fingers and feeling a vague repulsion at the ease with which he handled the bloody object. He peered up through the tangle of vines above his head and into the distant glow of the ever shifting light. It really isn't dark here, he thought. Maybe it's just so bright that everything but the light is reduced to a shadow.

"A crude metaphor, to be sure, but it will suffice for your feeble mind," the snake said.

"You said that I am not prepared to understand this place, or the shards," Oliver said. "But can you at least tell me why Loki and Remiel didn't come here themselves?"

"You know that, if only you had the wisdom to understand it."

"I know! Alright, damn you, I know that I am a fool. Now can you stop running in circles and speak plainly to me?"

"Pause and think for a moment. Cast your mind back upon all that you know and examine through the lens of wisdom and experience, rather than blind knowledge."

Oliver sighed deeply, tucked his gun away, and fished in his vest for one of he plastic bags he used to keep his lens brush clean. He pushed the brush into his vest pocket, dropped the eyeball into the bag, and zipped it tight. That done, he put the bag in a vest pocket and stuffed his hands into the pockets of his pants.

He stared up at the intertwining vines above his head, trying to picture each of them as a strand of his experiences for the last month. Loki, masquerading as a rival relic hunter, intentionally letting his research journal fall into Oliver's hands. Samuel Gower, his old professor, turning Oliver in to the Watchers when it became clear that Oliver was on the edge of unlocking the path to yet another shard. Remiel, turning against millennia of silent, faithful service to the Watchers to help Oliver escape from their grip, all so that he could retrieve a shard that she knew about, but refused to explain to him. And Odin, a warlord from the depths of Nordic history, preserved for two-thousand years by the power of the shard embedded in his skull, now weary of life and willing to trade his immortality to rejoin the course of humanity. But Odin hadn't been able to retrieve his eye and return the shard from its resting place because Loki had not shown him the key to unlocking the pathway within the world tree, and so he had been forced to wait until Oliver came along and unlocked the secret hidden in Wagner's Ring Operas.

Oliver blinked. Of course! The Operas. The castle at Neuschwanstein. Oliver thought back to the mural in the third floor hall of the castle, which depicted Reginn reforging the sword Gram for Siegfried. In the background of the painting a face had captured his attention. The face, he now realized, of Loki.

"Loki has been behind this from the beginning," Oliver whispered. "He led Odin to Yggdrasil. He performed the ritual, then sent Odin through to retrieve the shard. When Odin traded his eye for the shard instead of simply stealing it, it became bound to him, and thats when Loki emerged as the trickster god, always opposing Odin and trying to get him killed."

Oliver turned back to the snake and said, "I understand it all, except why Loki didn't just come here in the first place."

"You know."

Oliver felt a gentle nudge, deep within his mind, and once again he was in the car with Remiel, speeding away from the disaster at the Watcher hideaway, and she was trying to explain to him the importance of the shards. A device that was destroyed by angels at the dawn of human civilization, the pieces scattered across the earth so that it could never be reassembled, and one of those pieces ended up central to the lore of ancient norse mythology. He looked around, searching his mind for the missing piece to the puzzle, and his eyes were drawn back to the pedestal, from which he had taken Odin's eye. How did it get here?

It was so obvious. Oliver cursed and slapped his forehead in wonderment at his own stupidity. Throughout it all he had never stopped barreling forward in pursuit of his goal to pause and ask himself how the shard had come to be hidden in this otherworldly place.

"The path to wisdom is often paved with self mortification," the snake said, its voice in Oliver's mind seeming to warble with amusement.

"How did the shard come to be here?"

"That is not my story to tell."

"Then whose it is?"

"Odin knew him as Mímir. It is from his grasp that you took the eye."

Oliver's mouth dropped open as he spun to look at the pedestal. It had not changed. He started to speak, but was interrupted as the snake said, "He cannot answer your questions, and I will not. He has chosen this path and it is not my place to question his will."

"Then why are you telling me all this?" Oliver demanded.

"I have told you nothing, only confirmed what you already knew. Until now, that is. I will tell you one thing, and that one thing only."

Oliver sighed, wondering if this meant that he would have to wisely choose a single question, like someone carefully selecting their last wish from a genie or leprechaun.

"No, Oliver, nothing like that. I will simply tell you this one thing, and it is up to you to have the wisdom to know what to do with the knowledge. Are you listening to me?"

Oliver nodded.

CHAPTER TWENTY-TWO

BLOOD

The matte grey metal of Loki's sword glinted dully in the golden light as it sliced a crimson arc, spraying blood across carpet of leaves, moss, and upthrust roots. Remiel saw the uncoiling of muscle and twitch of blade that heralded Loki's attack and reached into herself to unlock the hidden reserve of power that remained contained behind her human incarnation. The air around her rippled and a torrent of energy poured out of her, shredding frail fabric of her skin as winglike blossoms of power arced out from her shoulders.

She leapt forward on wings of pure energy and slammed into Loki, driving him to the ground and knocking the blade from his grasp, but not before the blow had been struck. Blood poured from Odin's throat, pouring out of his throat and spraying across both Loki and Remiel. Odin stumbled, tripped over a root, and sprawled out on his back, blood pumping out through clasping fingers.

Remiel felt a fist slam into her own throat, then Loki twisted beneath her and leapt to his feet. He reached out a scarred hand and the sword leapt from the ground to return to his grasp.

"I should have hunted you all down ages past," he growled.

Loki leapt towards Remiel, driving his sword towards her chest with a vicious double handed thrust. She drew on her powers, formed a vision of her will within her mind, then manifested it. She breathed a silent prayer of thanks as the blade slammed against a shimmering wall of azure light that had appeared just in front of her, turning aside in a cascade of blue and white sparks. She reached deep into a well of talents that she had long sought to avoid, then slashed her closed fist downwards as a flaming red sword materialized in her hand. The tip of the blade sliced through Loki's cloak as he twirled and danced away from her, raising his own blade into a defensive stance.

"You know he will rise again," Remiel said. "Why now?"

"I merely wanted him out of the way while I dealt with you," Loki hissed in reply.

He charged her again, moving with preternatural speed as he feigned low, then twirled to slash down from high above. Remiel parried his blow and expended some of her power to launch upward, then come down behind Loki from an improbable angle. She rammed the tip of her fiery blade toward Loki's back, only to cry out in pain as his blade met her own in a shuddering blow that knocked her aim aside.

She backed away from Loki, retreating towards Odin's fallen body while keeping one eye on the ghostly trunk of the ash tree. Remiel had no way of knowing how long it would take Oliver to reach Mímir, nor whether he would be successful in retrieving Odin's eye, but she had to be prepared to defend him when he reappeared. The translucent bark of the enchanted tree shimmered and Remiel thought she saw the vague outline of a man deep within the shadows of the world beyond.

"We should have hunted you down long ago," Remiel said, turning her full attention back towards Loki. "You are a disease, a blight on this world."

Loki cackled and flourished his blade, then started edging towards the tree. Has he seen Oliver? she thought, moving to intercept him.

"You will all fall in the end, Remiel. Nothing can stop the ascent of humanity. Not you, or Oliver, or your precious order of Watchers." Loki gripped his sword and smiled cruelly, shaking his head as he said, "I will assemble the machine and with it I will push humanity to its limits, rebuild the tower, and ascend to the very throne of God."

Remiel lowered the tip of her blade, gathered herself to charge at Loki, then felt a sudden burst of agony in her left leg. The sound of a gunshot echoed through the glade and Remiel toppled to the ground, thrown off balance by a second shot striking her in the shoulder. She squinted, reached deep within herself, driving her soul to heal the frail structure of her incarnation, then heard another shot and opened her eyes to see a dark spray erupt from Loki's back.

"You want to the eye?" Oliver shouted from somewhere behind Remiel. "Come and get it."

Loki screamed and charged towards Remiel, his sword raised to strike down Oliver with a single vicious blow. Three more fountains of black blood burst out from Loki's back, then Remiel heard an ominous click as Oliver's gun locked open, the magazine expended.

I can't let him get the eye, she thought. Abandoning the urge to heal her body, Remiel put all her energy into a single powerful swing, slicing her fiery blade upwards through Loki's legs as he charged past her. The blade of her conjured sword sliced through Loki's thighs and sent him toppling head first over her as she fell, exhausted.

Remiel managed to roll over and watched in fascination as Oliver walked up to Loki's screaming body and kicked the sword from his grip. He picked it up, looked down at his fallen foe, and smiled.

"You you want this back?" he asked.

A cruel smile started to creep across Loki's face, then halted before it got past his lips. His eyes darted from the sword, to Oliver, then to Remiel, then grew wide as he looked back to Oliver.

"That's right, Loki. I learned a trick or two myself down there. Now, if you want this sword, you're going to have to go get it yourself." Oliver turned and hurled the blade through the ash tree into the darkness beyond.

"I will destroy you!" Loki snarled. "Your body and soul are mine! When I am finished with you not even dust will remain."

"You'll have to catch me first," Oliver replied, turning to Remiel. He stepped closer and knelt beside her. "Will you heal?"

She looked up at him, hesitated for a brief moment, then nodded. Her eyes met his and she saw a depth within them that she had never imagined existing in a mortal man. "I will recover."

"Good. So, get up and help me throw this trash away."

Oliver helped Remiel to her feet and together they grasped the screeching Loki at the shoulders and dragged him close to the portal in the ash tree. Loki screamed, cursing them in a dozen mortal languages and more that Remiel knew she alone understood. Just as they reached the tree she hesitated, looking through the smokey veil with trepidation. Does he deserve this? she wondered, glancing down at Loki. By now his torrent of vulgarity was accompanied by rivers of tears streaming from his eyes. She had known only one of her kind to step beyond that veil, and after all those thousands of years the only word she had ever had of Mímir came in the form of Odin's drunken boasts.

"Are you okay with this?" Oliver asked.

She looked to him and, once more, found his eyes.

Strangely, she felt as if she were drawing strength from him. She nodded her head and replied, "Absolutely."

She stepped away from the deathly portal and watched without a shred of regret as Oliver shoved Loki, still screaming, through into the shadows.

CHAPTER TWENTY-THREE

MORTAL

Oliver tossed the last of Loki's severed limbs through the portal after his body, then reached up and stroked the rune for raido, the journey, ending the ritual that had opened the portal to Yggdrasil. The air around the mighty ash tree shimmered and a sudden gust of wind shook loose a downpour of golden leaves.

"Let's hope that is the last I see of you," he muttered.

He turned away from the tree and saw Remiel crouching between the roots of the tree, cradling Odin's head in her lap. His gray beard was caked with blood and the leaves all about him were spattered with it. Despite the grisly scene, Oliver couldn't help smiling when Odin groaned, turned his head to the side, and coughed up a large wad of bloody sputum. The old god put a hand to his throat and winced as his fingers traced the line of the wound that Loki had inflicted upon him.

"What happened to the seasoned veteran of a thousand bloody fields of glory?" Oliver quipped, settling into a crouch beside the other two.

Odin chuckled, then winced and spat again. Remiel helped him sit up then passed him a water bottle. He nodded to her and drank, his scarred throat throbbing with each swallow. After a moment Odin lowered the bottle, wiped blood and spittle from his beard, and said, "I guess I've spent a few too many centuries brewing beers and bedding women.

My reflexes are not what they once were."

"Lucky for you Loki attacked before I came back. If you didn't have that shard in your skull you'd be dead right now."

Odin nodded and took another swig from the water bottle, then said, "Yes, that thought had occurred to me."

"Do we still have a deal?"

Odin said nothing and for a long while sat quietly, apparently pondering Oliver's question. Oliver looked to Remiel and said, "Sorry about that, by the way. The first shot was through the portal and I could only see a shadow holding a sword. After that, well, I figured if I knocked you down I'd have a clean shot at Loki." That, and I didn't know if I could trust you until you cut him down, he added in his head.

Remiel shrugged and glanced at the ragged hole in the front of her right shoulder, then back to Oliver. "I can't say that I'm glad you shot me, but I have already healed the worst of it."

"I can't believe you people," Oliver said, shaking his head in wonder. "Is there anything that can kill you?"

Remiel's face fell and she looked away from him. Oliver followed her gaze and saw that she was staring pointedly at the ash tree behind him. He thought about what he had seen at the roots of Yggdrasil, the fate of Mímir, and what might happen to Loki in that strange place.

"Can he ever return?"

Remiel shook her head. "Mímir never did. No others would dare pass through." She looked to Oliver and gave him a crooked smile. "That's one thing you have on us, Oliver. We might live forever, but there are places in this universe that will irrevocably alter us. You mortals are more frail, but there is something in your makeup that is more... intense. Like magnesium, once you actually catch fire you can never be stopped until you are all burned up."

Oliver nodded. Their eyes met and he again felt the pull of her gray gaze, drawing him into her mind as they knelt beneath the branches of the world tree, but this time he managed to pull back, to keep his sense of self without turning away. Something had changed within him, he knew, though it might be a long while before he understood all that he had learned.

"I am ready," Odin interjected.

"Are you sure?" Oliver replied, turning from Remiel's captivating face to the battered visage of the old god.

"Damn right I am. I know exactly what the lady is talking about. I've still got a few good years left in me, if I can keep away from people who want me dead, and I certainly have the means to enjoy what time I have remaining."

Oliver smiled and pulled the plastic bag from his vest pocket. He held the bag up to the light and examined the eye within it. "Here it is. I hope you know what to do with it."

Odin snatched the bag from him and examined it, then pulled the top open and extracted the eye. He rolled the orb between his fingertips, his hand trembling with sudden emotion, then reached up with his free hand and pulled the black patch from his face. He closed his remaining eye and muttered something that Oliver could not hear. Then, without a word of warning or the slightest flinch of anticipated pain, Odin raised his empty hand, dug his fingers deep into his eye socket, and with the sickening wet slurp of a blade being drawn through flesh, extracted the shard of metal from his head.

"It is yours, boy," Odin said, holding out the shard in a trembling, gore-slicked hand.

Oliver grinned and accepted the shard. He pulled out a handkerchief and used it to wipe the blood and mucus from the shard, already feeling the distinctive chill that always emanated from a true fragment of the mechanism. He held the shard up and turned it around in his fingers, trying to picture how it might fit with those which he had already collected, imagining what the assembled mechanism might look like.

Odin set his recovered eye down on the ground beside him, pulled a travel first aid kit from the pockets of his greatcoat, and began packing sterile gauze into the bloody wound of his empty eye socket.

"Somehow I imagined that you would get your eye back," Oliver said as he wrapped the shard in his handkerchief and tucked it away in a pocket.

"No, those days are long past." Odin picked up his eye, which had already begun to shrivel, and put it back in the plastic bag. "You know, boy, I thought that I would feel different, knowing that I was mortal again, but it feels mostly the same."

"You'll begin to notice in a few years," Remiel said. She pushed herself to her feet and continued, "Sooner if you don't see a doctor and get some antibiotics for that eye."

Odin nodded and tucked his eye into a pocket of his coat. As it disappeared, Oliver noticed that it had flattened and shriveled into a clump of dried flesh, like the mummified organ of a long dead pharaoh being tucked away into a canopic jar.

"True enough. I suggest we all get out of here and make our way back to the mainland. We still have a long march ahead of us before we reach the boat."

Oliver and Remiel nodded their agreement and they both helped Odin to his feet. Once he was standing, Odin snapped his old eyepatch back in place and flashed Oliver a wicked grin. "What about you, boy? Any plans now that our deal is complete?"

Oliver slipped a hand into his pocket and ran his fingers across the chill metal of the shard. He pondered what he had learned amid the roots of the world tree, considering how much of what the snake had told him could be trusted, holding it up for comparison with what he had learned from Odin, Remiel, the folio, and his own experiences. Altogether, there was no particularly good angle on the situation. As he saw it, the best that Oliver could hope for was an uneasy alliance with Remiel against her fellow Watchers.

"I'll have to think about that," he said. He shot a glance at Remiel, who was watching him intently, and added, "And we'll need to talk."

Remiel made a show of stretching her wounded shoulder and flexing the leg that Oliver had shot, both now apparently healed, though her clothes were spattered all over with blood and bits of dry leaves. She stepped forward and put a hand on Oliver's shoulder, saying, "I am certain we can come to an agreement."

Oliver turned to her and their eyes met. For a long moment they stood in silence, and while Oliver could not tell what Remiel was thinking, he was fairly certain she could read his intentions. Then Odin cleared his throat, spat, and began clumping across the glade in the direction from which they had all come less than two hours before.

"You won't give up your quest, will you?" Remiel asked.

Oliver shook his head. "You know that."

"You must know I can't let you assemble the shards."

"But you know there is something in me, something that makes this mission important. And besides that, you won't allow Zedekiah to kill innocents. At least, you won't allow that any more."

Remiel sighed and glanced down at the ground, then

283

turned from Oliver and started after Odin. Oliver strode along beside her, waiting for a response. They reached the tree line and began picking their way up the steep hillside. Upon reaching the top they paused to allow Odin to catch his breath and sip from a water bottle.

"I still don't know if I can trust you."

"The heartwood did."

"So I thought, but what if I was wrong? You did just shoot me."

"I thought we were past that," Oliver replied. Then he smiled, hoping that she would catch that he meant it as a joke.

She returned his smile. "I did what I said I would. I helped you escape, I followed you to the end of this quest so I could witness what happened, and now I need to decide what to do with you."

"I have an idea. I don't know if you will like it, but it will at least give you more time to consider."

They started walking again, allowing Odin to set the pace even as they dropped behind him and began speaking in low voices. Oliver explained his plan, hoping the while that it would be acceptable to Remiel. It was far from perfect, and would serve more to keep everyone unhappy than to solve the problems he, Remiel, and the Watchers faced, but if everyone would agree to it, then he might have time to learn what the mechanism was.

They argued, compromised, and worked out improvements to Oliver's original scheme. Finally, just as the blue waters of the lake came into view through the trees, Remiel nodded and said, "It might just work."

Oliver held out his hand to shake on the deal and replied, "It will have to."

CHAPTER TWENTY-FOUR
THE DEAL

The autumn wind battered against the windows of the manor house, ripping the last of the leaves from the trees and pushing tiny waves across the lake to splash against the neatly manicured lawn. Beneath the rippling waters, Remiel could just make out the twisted remains of the underwater billiards room that had been destroyed in the fight between her, Oliver, and Zedekiah. Three weeks had passed since then and she idly wondered if Zedekiah had any intention of repairing the structures under the lake, or if they would be left to decay beneath the water, a mute reminder of his failure.

She heard the paneled door open behind her and turned. Zedekiah stooped in the doorway, leaning on silver-tipped ebony cane, dressed as immaculately as always.

"You have a lot of nerve showing up here after all you have done," he said in a voice as smooth and cold as dry ice.

"And yet you agreed to meet me."

"Perhaps I invited you here to entrap you. There are some among our kind who would willingly give their own souls to see a traitor such as you destroyed."

"Are you one of them?"

Zedekiah curled his mouth into a cruel imitation of a smile and strode across the worn carpet of the room to settle in a wide chair upholstered in rich, black leather. Remiel noted that, though he still carried the cane, he moved with the same ease as before their confrontation beneath the lake. She wondered if he had succeeded in regenerating this incarnation after being shot repeatedly in the chest and drowned, or if he had merely chosen to take the same form upon creating a new body for himself.

"I had considered it, but I prefer to take the long view of matters. Oliver Lucas is a threat today and, if we do not contain him, will quite possibly prove to be the greatest danger to our order since the Illuminati, but he is a mortal and will no doubt die one day. How soon that day will come, well..." he shrugged his narrow shoulders and lay the cane across his lap. "...That would depend on how much of a nuisance he makes of himself. You, on the other hand, are one of the Watchers. We are far more rare and valuable than the humans we guard."

Remiel nodded and, keeping an eye on the open doorway and the cane on Zedekiah's lap, stepped to the writing desk beside the window and perched on the edge. She kept her face carefully composed to hide her distaste at the implications of Zedekiah's words.

"Containment is exactly what I am here to discuss."

Zedekiah nodded, but said nothing.

"You may know that Oliver retrieved the shard that Mímir hid beneath the roots of Yggdrasil."

"That is not a surprise, considering what I learned from mister Gower."

Remiel nodded. Upon returning to Britain she had sought out Gower and learned that he had disappeared. He returned to his flat and his position at the British Museum several days later, but had refused to speak with her.

"Did you aid him in that effort?"

"It would be better to say that I did not hinder him. Oliver Lucas is a remarkable man, Zedekiah."

"And yet he is just a man. He is expendable, Remiel, if it serves the greater good of God's will for humanity."

"He has six shards now, Zedekiah. That is as many as the entire Illuminati organization managed to gather in half a century, and he has captured them all himself, some from the original locations, some from the remote locations where we hid them. He is half way to reassembling the mechanism, and he still doesn't even know what it really is."

"I was under the impression that you did not want me to have him killed."

"Oliver has spent the last week scattering the shards across America. I do not know where they all are, but I did instruct him in how to reduce their effect. They are hidden in small towns, far away from one another and from large cities. In fact, they are less of a threat now than when Oliver had them all locked away in a couple banks in Virginia. So, now Oliver wants to return home, as does his cousin, who went into hiding after Oliver escaped from you. He is concerned for both her and the rest of his family, not to mention his own life, so he has asked me to offer you a deal."

Zedekiah tapped a finger on the head of his cane and narrowed his eyes, but said nothing.

"If you swear to leave Oliver and his family untouched, he will leave the shards scattered and make no attempt to reassemble them. In effect, he claims, they are merely being moved from one hiding place to another, possibly more secure location."

She stopped speaking and waited for Zedekiah to respond, but he remained impassive. Only the slow tap of a finger on the tip of his cane and an occasional blink of his eyes betrayed him as more than a wax figure.

Eventually, Remiel said, "He won't promise to stop looking for the shards, but he says that he will not attempt to assemble them without my assistance and permission."

"Preposterous. All you have told me of this so called deal is that Oliver Lucas gets exactly what he wants and we get nothing but an unpredictable mortal stumbling across the playing field, ready to unleash chaos without warning. I believe this meeting is at an end."

He swung the cane down and prepared to leaver himself out of the chair with it.

"No, Zedekiah, it isn't," Remiel said in a soft tone. She slipped from the desk and took a step towards him. "Oliver is no fool. He has connections in both the relic underground and the American government. If anything happens to him, or to his family, two of the shards will be removed from their vaults and delivered to his contacts, along with copies of all his research notes and a list of the locations of the other shards." She took another step forward and glared down at Zedekiah. "If you kill Oliver, or harm his family, the shards will be at greater risk than they have been at any time in the last thousand years."

"You are aiding this mortal in overthrowing millennia of work!" Zedekiah snarled, leaping to his feet and slamming the tip of his cane into the floorboards. "If we do not regulate their development, if we do not contain the influence of the shards, humanity will destroy itself."

"I am no longer convinced that you are the wisest judge of that," Remiel whispered. "Now, do we have a deal?"

She looked up into Zedekiah's burning eyes, silently calling on the power within her, preparing to defend herself in the event that he attacked. But she could see defeat written in his face. His lips contorted into a cruel, bloodless smile and he said, "Oliver will be safe from us. You have my word."

"Swear it on the heartwood."

"That what?"

"The olive wood pendant that we took from Oliver when he was your guest. Do you still have it?"

Zedekiah hesitated for the briefest moment, then nodded.

"Place your hand upon it and swear that Oliver and his family will be safe."

"I don't have it with me. Do you think I carry confiscated relics around in my pockets? Oh, yes, right here I have a genuine ark of the covenant, and there in my left pocket is one of the Dead Sea scrolls."

Remiel shook her head, just enough that he could see. She had expected as much, but hoped that she was wrong. Zedekiah must have truly been corrupted, else he would have seen the pendant as a holy relic and carried it for himself at all times. At least, she knew that was what she would have done.

She turned away from Zedekiah and strode to the door with measured steps, her footsteps echoing in the silence. Just as she lay her had on the doorknob, Zedekiah called out to her, "Do not bother to return, Remiel. The next time I see you, I will kill you."

She pulled the door open and slipped out without a word.

Oliver Lucas sat alone at the counter of a roadside diner along Interstate 55, a hundred and fifty miles south of Saint Louis, Missouri, reading an e-mail from Remiel about her meeting with Zedekiah. The booths by the windows were occupied by a mix of locals, who seemed occupied in gossiping about one of the managers at the nearby metalworks, and travelers like himself. Half way between Memphis and Saint Louis, this place was the perfect watering hole for weary drivers.

Oliver finished reading a message from Remiel and smiled. They had been in contact by encrypted e-mail over the last week, but he had cautiously avoided telling her where he was. Now, with the six shards he possessed tucked away in the vaults of small banks across America, a detailed log of his research stored on multiple servers across the internet, and a dead man's switch e-mail prepared to blast messages to all of his contacts in both the relic trade and the government, Oliver was relieved to learn that he could let his guard down, if only a little.

He replied to Remiel with a simple, "Thanks, I'll be in touch."

Oliver set his phone down on the countertop, and turned his attention to the half finished plate of waffles in front of him. It had been too long, he reflected, since he had last driven the winding roadways of the American west. Maybe I'll take some time off from this business and do some traveling, take a few photos of American life, he thought. The idea brought a sad smile to his face, because Oliver knew that it was impossible. He had started in on this quest when he was only nineteen and first found his uncle's journals hidden in the attic. Now, after so many years, and so much work, he was just starting to understand what he was facing.

A pretty waitress stepped up to the counter and flashed Oliver a smile as sweet as the syrup on his pancakes. "You need anything else, darling?" she asked.

Oliver shook is head and turned his mouth up in a weary half grin. "No thanks. I'm just trying to decide where to go next."

"Sure a slice of apple pie wouldn't help you decide?"

Oliver laughed and pushed his empty plate towards her. He shook his head, smiled, and said, "You know, it might just."

She swept away with his plate and Oliver picked up his

phone to send a message to Amber, letting her know it was safe to return home. When the waitress returned with a large, steaming slice of pie, Oliver returned her warm smile and thanked her.

"No problem that can't be worked out over some good pie," she said. "Except maybe those what need a scoop of ice cream on top. At least, that's what my daddy always told me."

"He was a wise man," Oliver replied, speaking around a mouthful of hot apple and buttery, flaky crust.

The waitress moved off to another customer and Oliver continued eating his pie. There was time enough to decide what to do next, he determined. If there was one thing he had learned beneath the roots of Yggdrasil, it was the importance of acting with wisdom, rather than blindly chasing after the next fact, or relic, or clue.

Oliver finished his pie, left a generous tip, and strode out to his car. The sun was bright overhead. Empty fields stretched away as far as he could see to the west, and the Mississippi river flowed along its meandering course to the east. With the possible exception of some long lost relics of Native American lore, and the shard locked away in the vault of a bank nearby, there was nothing within five hundred miles that could draw him back into the game. He was free to pause, breathe deep of the autumn air, and reflect on what to do next.

He climbed into his car and headed south with no particular destination in mind.

THE DIAMOND OF SOULS PREVIEW

Continue reading for the first chapter of Oliver Lucas Adventures Book Three: *The Diamond of Souls*.

UNDERTAKEN

The UnderTaken was an underground club in every sense of the word. The club, which catered to an exclusive clientele of relic hunters, professional thieves, and confidence artists was so difficult to gain access to that the hottest metropolitan nightspot was a cover-free roadside dive by comparison. It operated on a strict referral basis, with members drawn from an equally secretive internet forum that was accessible only through a TOR-encrypted virtual network, and never operated in a single location for more than a week. It was, in essence, a pop-up restaurant that catered only to a self-policing cartel of gentlemen criminals, rather than wealthy hipsters. In its current incarnation, the UnderTaken club was actually located underground in the basement of a defunct brewery several blocks south of the French Quarter in New Orleans.

Oliver Lucas leaned against the bar of the UnderTaken and sipped his beer, a dark lambic heavy with the flavor of coffee and cherries, and listened patiently as his companion continued to mount a defense of his own personal career path.

"...is hurt, who cares? They're all insured, and half the time the bastards have slipped some insurance adjuster a few Benjamins to overvalue the art anyway, so they're making more from the insurance claim than they would from a sale."

Oliver put his glass down and tapped the bar beside his companion's elbow, shaking his head. "That's only half the story, Gregory. If the art is legal they are insured, but you must have stolen art that was already of," he raised a bushy red eyebrow and lowered his voice a fraction, "questionable origin. Maybe even something that I found for them. No way that was insured, and now your victim is out a lovely piece of art that they can't even report to the police."

Gregory laughed and waved for the bartender. "Right you are, buddy. Does that get to you? Knowing that some of your ill-gotten artifacts might get stolen again?"

Oliver shrugged and took another sip of his beer. "Just making an observation." He enjoyed visiting the UnderTaken whenever he could manage to be in the same town as the club, but even here he refused to let his guard down entirely. That lack of trust wasn't just because he was surrounded by other confidence artists, thieves, and smugglers. Oliver knew that at any given moment, in any moderately populated city around the world, he was likely to be within spitting distance of a thief of some variety, even if many of those thieves technically operated within the confines of federal financial regulations. Here, at least, he could be certain that everyone had something to hide. And everyone else knew the same of him. That mutual distrust kindled a sort of ironic, yet appropriate, mutual respect.

And it didn't hurt that the entire establishment was funded with password-locked cryptocurrency, so there was no point in stealing someone's phone or wallet unless you also intended to kidnap them and torture a passphrase out of them. In that respect, the UnderTaken club was actually safer than an average nightclub run on cash.

TheStill, it was just bad tradecraft to speak plainly in front of a bartender. Far better to keep up good habits than to risk a drunken indiscretion out in the public world.

When the bartender had departed, leaving a fresh glass of pale ale for Gregory, Oliver said, "Once I've delivered a piece to a client I don't especially care what they do with it. Don't get me wrong, I don't want some millionaire to use a pre-Columbian totem as firewood, but then I have a cover job that affords me the luxury of picking and choosing my clients." *Most of the time*, he added to himself.

"Yeah, I've seen some of your work on the Ars

Geographica photo spreads. You're not bad with a camera."

"Thanks," Oliver said. He glanced past Gregory and scanned the room. He enjoyed the easy camaraderie of the club, but every visit to the UnderTaken brought with it the niggling suspicion that someone in the crowd might be an undercover Fed. His eyes lingered on a dark-haired woman sitting with two men at a table some dozen feet away. She was dressed in a loose maroon blouse that hung from her shoulders in folds of sheer fabric over a black camisole, tight denim jeans so blue they were nearly black, and black combat boots that looked like they had seen heavy wear.

If she had been alone, Oliver might have broken off his conversation with the increasingly unsteady Gregory and gone over to introduce himself.

"But I hear you sometimes deal with, um..." Gregory hesitated.

"With?" Oliver prompted, turning his attention back to his companion.

"Don't laugh at me man, but I'm not too proud to admit that I'm a bit superstitious. See this?" He pulled a black cord from beneath his shirt and leaned forward, pushing the side of his head uncomfortably close to Oliver's face as he displayed a distorted slug of lead that dangled from the cord.

"I see it," Oliver said. He pushed a finger against Gregory's chest and the man swayed backwards, seemed about to fall, then steadied himself and leaned against the bar.

"That's the bullet that I took in Iraq, back before I got my foot into this game. Medic who pulled it out of my leg gave it to me, said I was lucky it just shattered my leg and didn't deflect off the bone and slice the femoral artery or take out my balls. I've carried it ever since and, you know what man, I haven't had a stroke of bad luck since."

"What do you call getting into this trade?" Oliver asked with a crooked smile.

"Best damn thing that ever happened to me. You know how much work there was for vet when I got out back at the tail end of that little dustbowl?"

Oliver took a long pull of beer and grimaced to see his glass was nearly empty. "I've got a feeling you're going to tell me."

"Not much, that's how much. Whole economy was still in the tank, at least for folks without a trade license. I could've gone private, but I never got on with those mercenary types all that well when we were running patrols out of the Green Zone. So when my uncle offered to let me in on a bit heist he was pulling, I figured it was worth a shot. Never looked back since, man."

Oliver glanced past Gregory to the dark-haired woman again. One of the men at the table laid a smartphone on the tabletop and Oliver caught a glimpse of a square arrangement of smaller black and white squares displayed on the screen. The woman held her own phone over the image for a second, then pulled it back and tapped on the screen a few times.

Oliver recognized the procedure. It was the same method that he had used to gain entry into the club and pay for his drink. The image displayed on the phone was a QR code, essentially an advanced barcode capable of holding a vast quantity of data in an easy to display format. Membership credentials for the UnderTaken club were secured with public-key encryption then encoded into a similar QR code, generated by the shadowy management of the UnderTaken, which the bouncers would scan before permitting anyone entry into the club. Any attempt to enter the club with a false membership card would result in a failed code read and swift ejection by security.

"So what about it?" Gregory asked.

Oliver started and realized that he had been so fixated on watching the woman at the table that he had lost the thread of Gregory's meandering story. How long had it been since he had spent time with a woman who might actually understand his trade? Diana was still in Paris. Remiel had disappeared back into the shadows of Europe and only occasionally messaged him.

"What about what?" Oliver asked, realign that he had ignored Gregory's question.

"What about those special items that I hear you sometimes track down for the clients you really like. As I recall there was some idol you found a few months back that gave wisdom and wealth to the owner."

"Ancient superstitions. Nothing more."

"Yeah? Ars-G was pretty damn impressed by the architecture and traps in that cavern that you photographed for them. Like nothing their scientists had ever seen in the Pacific Rim, if I remember the article right."

Oliver lifted his glass and drained the last of his beer to hide the moment of hesitation in his response, then said, "I was just a photographer on that expedition. Didn't acquire anything for a client."

"Right, Oliver, and I had nothing to do with that Caillebotte that vanished from the Elke collection two years back. The article I read said that it was one of the most intact finds in recent history, I'll give you that, but it went on at length about the supposed magical properties of the idols they found. That sounds a lot like the sort of stuff you comment on in the forums."

"Market hype. Link bait. That was just a preliminary survey to scare up funding for the serious scholars."

"But if the idol really did have powers," Gregory insisted, slapping his hand against the bar top with the uncoordinated force of a drunk, "would you have stolen it and given it to a client?"

"If they paid me enough, I suppose."

"But what if the relic could cause harm? Like, if it was a skull that gave you power to kill your enemies, like some sort of voodoo doll skull thing."

"You're drunk, Gregory," Oliver said, his lips twisting into a sardonic grin. "I was willing to conjecture on the what-ifs of a known relic, but now you've taken at least two steps farther from reality and resorted to calling your proposed relic a 'voodoo doll skull thing.' Maybe we should end it here and go sleep this off?'"

Oliver raised his hand to call over the bar tender and glanced past Gregory, who was spluttering and wagging his head, to the dark-haired woman. Maybe if he saw Gregory safe to a taxi he could make it back into the club in time to catch the woman when her business had concluded. He didn't anticipate anything coming of such a meeting, one night stands were the farthest thing from Oliver's style, but it had been such a long time since he had experienced any female companionship that didn't involve kidnapping and a gunfights.

Things did not look promising on that count, however.

Just as Oliver glanced over at her, the woman slammed her fist on the table and leaned forward, her narrow shoulders drawing up with tension as she hissed something at the men across the table. One of them, short and dressed in a slick black on black business suit, held up his phone and gestured to it as if blaming it for the woman's discomfort. The other man, who was nearly six feet tall, bald, and dressed in a cheep looking suit that barely concealed his muscles, leaned forward to meet the woman's gaze and shook his head tersely.

"Another round?" the barkeeper asked, pulling Oliver's attention away from the disturbance at the table.

"Oh, no. My friend here is finished for the night. Let me pay for our drinks and I'll get him into a taxi."

"Not done," Gregory insisted, his tongue thick.

Oliver gave the barkeeper a significant glance and pulled out his phone. He thumbed the fingerprint reader to unlock it, then pulled up his BitCoin payment app. "How much is the total?"

The barkeeper held up a tablet that indicated a price in BitCoins, the digital currency on which the UnderTaken operated, above the black and white grid of a QR code. Using a crypto-currency like BitCoin was a hassle, but it did afford the members an additional level of security, both in the club and in their general business. No cash meant that club members had one less thing to worry about losing while they were in a room filled with thieves. No credit cards meant that the club and its membership could not be tracked through billing records. Oliver also suspected that the club mandated the use of a crypto-currency because the technical and legal complexities of the BitCoin network made it easy for the club owners, and their clients, to hide their ill-gotten income in a monstrously tangled web of virtual accounts that even government supercomputers had difficulty correlating down into identifiable data on a single person. Oliver scanned the grid with his phone, waited for his payment app to interpret the data into a virtual BitCoin account address, and tapped the icon to send the requested payment to the indicated account.

"Oh, don't leave now Oliver. I'll buy the next round. Let's just…"

Gregory's protestation was interrupted by a howl of rage and Oliver turned just in time to see the woman he had been watching fall backwards in her chair as the short man leapt across the table at her. Glasses clattered across the table and crashed to the floor as the short man scrabbled to get off the table.

"I'll kill you!" he screamed.

Oliver darted forward and stepped between the woman and the furious man. "Hey, man. Just calm down and…"

The short man rolled, nearly lost his balance, then jumped upright and hurled an empty tumbler at Oliver's head.

Oliver dodged to his left and felt the edge of the heavy glass graze the side of his head, just above his right ear as it flew past his head and crashed to the floor behind the bar.

Oh, that's just not cool, Oliver thought.

He darted forward and clapped his left hand down on the short man's shoulder, then sank his right fist deep into his gut. The man doubled over and Oliver pushed his face beside his ear to whisper, "Let's just end it here. No need for any more violence."

Then he heard the crack of breaking wood.

Oliver glanced to his right and saw that the dark haired woman had just smashed her chair into the face of the burly man in the cheep black suit. The man grunted, grabbed the cracked based of the chair, and wrenched it out of the woman's grasp.

"Get her phone," the short man wheezed.

Oliver pushed the man backwards through the slush of broken glass and spilled liquor until he was leaning against the table. "What the hell is going on here?" he said.

"None of your business," the short man growled.

"Bastards double crossed me," the woman snapped. Even angry, her accent was recognizable as that soft blend of southern American and French that Oliver had only ever heard in Louisiana.

"Give it up now and I won't break you neck," said the muscled man in a calm, low voice. He spared Oliver a glance and added, "Back out of this now, man, or you'll get hurt too."

"Bit late for that," Oliver replied, touching a finger to his ear and feeling a trickle of blood starting to slip down behind his ear. "Listen, why don't I buy you all a drink and we can talk about... Nope, not going to happen," Oliver said, interrupting himself to grab a bottle from the table and throw it at the muscled man.

The bottle missed the large man and smashed to the floor several yards away, but he must have caught a glimpse of it flying past his head because he dodged to the side, giving the woman the opportunity to slip around him and grab something from the mess on the table.

The small man squirmed out of Oliver's grasp and swung a wild punch that Oliver blocked easily with his forearms. Oliver grabbed the front of the man's shirt with both hands, lifted his from his feet, and heaved him towards the bar. The man stumbled against the bar, knocking over more drinks as he spluttered incoherently.

"Take it outside!" one of the other diners shouted.

Oliver saw the bartender approaching the short man just as he started to shout, "You're both dead! I'll personally... argh!" An electric crackle broke the air and the man began to twitch, then slumped to the floor.

"Break it up now!" the bartender shouted, brandishing a stunning prod in one hand and a phone in the other. He snapped pictures of Oliver, the woman, and both of the suited men then shouted for them to leave.

Oliver stepped backwards and glanced around for the woman. He spotted her standing across another table from the burly man, brandishing a glowing cell phone and shouting, "You get me what you promised or I'll report everything I know." The diners who had occupied the table stood to the side, one still holding his drink, and Oliver felt a smile pull at the side of his mouth at the thought that they seemed more concerned about the fate of their meal than the outcome of the fight.

The burly man launched himself forward, knocking the table aside and catching up a chair to hurl at the woman. "You're not telling anyone nothing," he said.

The woman ducked and the chair spun away into the shadows above the low-hanging strips of ancient fluorescent lights, then crashed down somewhere amid the mess of defunct brewery equipment that had been piled at the edges of the room before the club opened. She darted forward, slipped around the burly man, and ran past Oliver.

"Come with me," she hissed, grabbing his arm.

Oliver followed her instinctively, drawn to her by an instinctive raw attraction, the likes of which he had not felt in many years, even as a more logical part of his brain screamed for him to stay away. They ran past the bar, through another cluster of tables, then out into the dark expanse of cracked concrete floor that separated the dining area and bar from the sturdy iron stairway leading up from the dining area and bar to the abandoned offices above.

"What is going on?" Oliver asked as they climbed the steps.

"You're Oliver Lucas?" the woman asked, not looking back as she continued to climb.

"Yeah," he said, glancing back over his shoulder as they climbed. He couldn't see the burly man in the cheap suit, but he could see the wake of his passing in overturned tables and angry customers standing and shouting towards the shadows below the steps.

They reached the top of the stairs and burst out into the area that had once been the offices for a modest southern brewery. Now the plaster walls were cracked, the wooden moulding dust covered, and the only sign of habitation was a wiry young man sitting at an old linoleum-topped desk, his scraggly beard and gaunt features illuminated by the glow of a laptop screen.

"Trouble downstairs?" the man asked.

Oliver nodded and threw a thumb over his shoulder as they continued to stride towards the exit. "Heavy coming behind us. Attacked the lady and tried to take her phone."

The young man tapped a few keys on his laptop. "I see here that your membership has already been suspended, pending adjudication of this incident by other members. Please leave. Now." Two figures dressed in black tactical gear emerged from the shadows of the room, each sighting on the door with a long-barreled Taser.

"Thanks," Oliver called back over his shoulder as they rushed towards the exit. Being kicked from the club roster was the last of his concerns at the moment.

They pushed out into the warm air of a New Orleans winter. Behind them Oliver heard the distinct thump and crackle of a Taser discharge, followed by a grunt and thud as the heavily muscled man fell to the floor. Ahead, the cracked pavement of South Peters Street stretched away in either direction, leading towards a dark expressway underpass in the south and the bustling nightlife of Canal Street to the north. Here, nearly a mile from the areas heavily trafficked by tourists, the air was calm and thick with the rancid, fishy scent of the nearby river and industrial port.

"Where are you staying?" the woman asked, turning back towards Oliver.

"Up on Bourbon," Oliver said.

"Let's go," she replied, turning and striding north along the street.

Oliver hurried to keep up with her, fighting a growing concern that he should have kept out of this woman's business. He didn't especially mind abandoning Gregory at the UnderTaken, he would find his way home safe enough, but he was beginning to suspect that there was more to the story.

OTHER BOOKS

Other Books by Andrew Linke

Oliver Lucas Adventures
The Staff of Moses
The Eye of Odin
The Diamond of Souls
Words of Binding
Words of Power

Science Fiction
Burning in the Void
Dyson's Angel
A Cold Day to Drown

AFTERWARDS

Oliver Lucas will return in *The Diamond of Souls*.

If you enjoyed this story, please consider leaving a review on Amazon, Goodreads, or wherever else you like to review books. Mentions on your favorite social media site are also welcome and, of course, I would love for you to share this book with your friends and family.

-Andrew Linke

CORRECTIONS

Thanks to the following people for hunting down errors in The Eye of Odin. All of the mistakes that they found have been corrected in version 1.4 If you find any additional errors, please use the Typo Bounty form located at www.alinke.com to report them. Readers who report errors are thanked in future editions, offered free books, and given the opportunity to join my beta reader program.

Amanda
Anna Dobritt
Ian Bowron
Pat Griffiths
Linda Linke
Mike
Mark Smith

Printed in Great Britain
by Amazon